SPACE MOVIES

with contributions from

Ray Bradbury
Werner von Braun
Clive Barker
James Blish
Arthur C. Clarke
Philip K. Dick
Robert A. Heinlein
Ward Moore
William F. Nolan
Stephen King

SPACE MOVIES
Classic Science Fiction Films

Collected and edited by
PETER HAINING

with contributions from

Ray Bradbury
Werner von Braun
Clive Barker
James Blish
Arthur C. Clarke
Philip K. Dick
Robert A. Heinlein
Ward Moore
William F. Nolan
Stephen King

SEVERN SH HOUSE

This first world edition published in Great Britain 1995 by
SEVERN HOUSE PUBLISHERS LTD of
9–15 High Street, Sutton, Surrey SM1 1DF.
First published in the USA 1995 by
SEVERN HOUSE PUBLISHERS INC of
595 Madison Avenue, New York, NY 10022.

British Library Cataloguing in Publication Data
King, Stephen
  Space Movies
  I. TitleII. Haining, Peter
  808.830108762 [FS]

  ISBN 0-7278-4790-2

Typeset by Hewer Text Composition Services, Edinburgh.
Printed and bound in Great Britain by
Hartnolls Ltd, Bodmin, Cornwall.

PROGRAMME

Note: This is a list of film titles. The original works on which these films
were based may have had different titles from those listed above.

CREDITS

The Editor and publishers are grateful to the following authors, their agents and publishers for permission to include copyright stories in this collection: International Scripts for the extract from Rocketship Galileo by Robert A. Heinlein; Fleetway Publications and MGN Newspapers Group for "It Came From Outer Space", based on an outline by Ray Bradbury, and "The Conquest of Space" by Werner von Braun; Fantasy House Inc. for "Lot" by Ward Moore; Scott Meredith Literary Agency for "Sentinel of Eternity" by Arthur C. Clarke and "We Can Remember It For You Wholesale" by Philip K. Dick; William Nolan for the extract from Logan's World; Bantam Books Inc. and Desilu Productions for "The Unreal McCoy" by James Blish; New English Library for "The Lawnmower Man" by Stephen King; and Little Brown for "The Forbidden" by Clive Barker. While every care has been taken in seeking permission for the use of stories in this anthology, in the case of any accidental infringement interested parties are asked to write to the Editor in care of the publishers.

PROLOGUE
The Cinema of Possibilities

There still exists in the vaults of the American Film Institutes in New York a faded print of a short, black and white movie with the intriguing title, *Dream of a Rarebit Fiend*. Shot in a single day during the Spring of 1906, this five-minute silent would probably have long since been forgotten but for the fact that its maker employed a technique so revolutionary that it would be used again – though few people are aware of the fact – over sixty years later in one of the most famous of all Science Fiction movies, *2001: A Space Odyssey*.

Dream of a Rarebit Fiend concerns a man who has dined rather too well on the famous cheese snack and afterwards falls into a restless sleep. Suddenly, he sits up in bed to find his room full of a nightmare assembly of huge pieces of food. These objects – all quite clearly actors dressed in rudimentary costumes – then proceed to chase the hapless, pyjama-clad fellow around the bedroom.

What startled audiences who watched the film back in the first decade of the Twentieth Century – and can still amaze any viewer lucky enough to be given a screening today – is the way the man and his weird pursuers run across the room, up a wall, over the ceiling and then back down the far wall to the floor again. There is no pause in the action, no suggestion that the sequence had been filmed in anything other than one continuous take. And so, indeed, it had. For subsequent research has established that what the unknown director did was to have all his actors run on the spot while

1

the entire set of the room turned through a complete circle in front of his camera!

Whether Stanley Kubrick the producer-director of *2001* ever saw this little piece of film history is not known. Certainly he has never admitted to the fact. But it was precisely this same technique he employed while filming an equally impressive scene in his 1968 spectacular when a stewardess on the lunar space station, unhampered by gravity, walks from the floor to the ceiling and through a doorway in the ceiling, as if it were the most natural thing to do. In order to film this effect, Kubrick duplicated the idea of the revolving set just as his unheralded forerunner had done in 1906.

Such are the facts of what surely deserves to be at least a footnote in cinema history. Yet I am using the evidence here for no other purpose than to underline the longevity of special effects in the making of pictures – in particular in the creation of Space Movies: those pictures in which man either travels beyond his natural confines on Earth or else confronts the possibility that there might be other life forms in the universe of which our world is only a tiny fragment.

In actual fact, film makers have been creating pictures about space travel almost since the advent of the cinema. One of the earliest pioneers was the French magician-turned-cinematographer, George Melies, who shot his 16-minute production, *A Trip To The Moon*, in his tiny Paris studio as early as 1902. He was followed by the German expressionist, Fritz Lang, with his dystopian masterpiece, *Metropolis* (1926), and *The Girl in the Moon* (1929) which is generally credited with inaugurating the space travelling tradition in Science Fiction cinema.

In the following pages I have assembled a selection of short stories which represent several of the landmark pictures in the genre, together spanning half a century of film history and technological development. Through them it is possible to note how the special effects that began as mere trick photography have progressed and now reached a kind of apogee in Virtual Reality. Of the stories themselves, each I believe lives up to the definition that "the father of modern Science Fiction", H.G.Wells himself, once offered to describe his books – and which, equally, might be used to define Space Movies themselves. For all are, surely, "Fantasias of possibility".

PETER HAINING,
London, 1995.

DESTINATION MOON

(Eagle-Lion Pictures, 1950)
Starring: John Archer, Warner Anderson & Tom Powers
Directed by Irvin Pichel
Screenplay based on *Rocket Ship Galileo*
by Robert A. Heinlein

Destination Moon, the American film which effectively initiated the boom in Space Movies, owed its production and subsequent success to the vision of one man, George Pal. A Hungarian-born, former film animator, Pal had fled from Nazi Germany at the outset of World War Two and moved to America where he became one of the most inventive and influential makers of fantasy pictures. Indeed, it was thanks to his pioneer work that the SF film became one of the hottest commercial properties in Hollywood in the Fifties – in turn encouraging the publication of many more science fiction novels and the belated entry of SF onto the television screen. Determined to make *Destination Moon* as authentic as possible, Pal enlisted a team of experts: the former German rocket scientist, Hermann Oberth, who now lived in the US; astronomical expert Chesley Bonestell who painted the backdrops for the space ship's journey through space; and the rising star of SF, Robert A. Heinlein (1907–1988). Heinlein, today regarded as one of the major figures in twentieth-century science fiction, based the screenplay on one of his own novels, *Rocket Ship Galileo* (1947). In this, a scientist Donald Cargraves and three young assistants, Ross Jenkins, Art Mueller and Maurice Abrams, make an eventful journey to the moon only to find they have been beaten to it by a group of renegade Nazis who have escaped from Earth! Although this element of the book was omitted from the movie, Heinlein's description of the flight to the moon which he wrote years before it actually occurred proved remarkably accurate, as did the starkly authentic reconstruction of the moon's surface devised by the art director, Ernst Fegte, also way ahead of the real thing being seen in close-up. The sum total of all this was a picture with an almost documentary feel that enthralled large audiences and opened a new era in cinema history. In the following episode, Cargraves and his companions make their "cinematic" touchdown in the year 1950 in a manner that would be almost exactly duplicated by Neil Armstrong and the crew of Eagle twenty years later on July 21, 1969 . . .

The *Galileo* continued her climb up from earth, toward that invisible boundary where the earth ceased to claim title and the lesser mass of the moon took charge. Up and up, out and farther out, rising in free flight, slowing from the still effective tug of the earth but still carried on by the speed she had attained under the drive of the jet, until at last the *Galileo* slipped quietly over the border and was in the moon's back yard. From there on she accelerated slowly as she fell toward the silvery satellite.

They ate and slept and ate again. They stared at the receding earth. And they slept again.

While they slept, Joe the Robot stirred, consulted his cam, decided that he had had enough of this weightlessness, and started the jet. But first he straightened out the ship so that the jet faced toward the moon, breaking their fall, while the port stared back at earth.

The noise of the jet woke them up. Cargraves had had them strap themselves down in anticipation of weight. They unstrapped and climbed up to the control station. "Where's the moon?" demanded Art.

"Under us, of course," Morrie informed him.

"Better try for it with radar, Morrie," Cargraves directed.

"Check!" Morrie switched on the juice, waited for it to warm, then adjusted it. The moon showed as a large vague mass on one side of the scope. "About fifteen thousand miles," he declared. "We'd better do some checking, Skipper."

They were busy for more than an hour, taking sights, taking readings, and computing. The bearing and distance of the moon, in relation to the ship, were available by radar. Direct star sights out the port established the direction of drive of the ship. Successive radar readings established the course and speed of the ship for comparison with the courses and speeds as given by the automatic instruments showing on the board. All these factors had to be taken into consideration in computing a check on the management of Joe the Robot.

Minor errors were found and the corrections were fed to the automatic pilot. Joe accepted the changes in his orders without comment.

While Morrie and Cargraves did this, Art and Ross were preparing the best meal they could throw together. It was a relief to have weight under their feet and it was a decided relief to their stomachs. Those organs had become adjusted to free fall, but hardly reconciled. Back on firm footing they hollered for solid food.

The meal was over and Cargraves was thinking sadly of his ruined pipe, when the control alarm sounded. Joe the Robot had completed his orders, his cam had run out, he called for relief.

They all scrambled up to the control station. The moon, blindingly white and incredibly huge was shouldering its way into one side of the port. They were so close to it now that their progress was visible, if one looked closely, by sighting across the frame of the port at some fixed object, a crater or a mountain range.

"Wheel!" Art yelled.

"Kinda knocks your eyes out, doesn't it?" Ross said, gazing in open wonder.

"It does," agreed Cargraves. "But we've got work to do. Get back and strap yourself down and stand by for maneuvering."

While he complied, he strapped himself into his chair and then flipped a switch which ordered Joe to go to sleep; he was in direct, manual command of the rocket. With Morrie to coach him by instrument, he put the ship through a jockeying series of changes, gentle on the whole and involving only minor changes in course at any one time, but all intended to bring the ship from the flat conoid trajectory it had been following into a circular orbit around the moon.

"How'm I doin'?" he demanded a long time later.

"Right in the groove," Morrie assured him, after a short delay.

"Sure enough of it for me to go automatic and swing ship?"

"Let me track her a few more minutes." Presently Morrie assured him as requested. They had already gone into free flight just before Cargraves asked for a check. He now called out to Art and Ross that they could unstrap. He then started the ship to swinging so that the port faced toward the moon and switched on a combination which told Joe that he must get back to work; it was now his business to watch the altitude by radar and to see to it that altitude and speed remained constant.

Art was up at the port, with his camera, by the time he and Morrie had unstrapped.

"Goshawmighty," exclaimed Art, "this is something!" He unlimbered his equipment and began snapping frantically, until Ross pointed out that his lens cover was still on. Then he steadied down.

Ross floated face down and stared out at the desolation. They were speeding silently along, only two hundred miles above the ground, and they were approaching the sunrise line of light and darkness. The shadows were long on the barren wastes below them, the mountain peaks and the great gaping craters more horrendous on that account. "It's scary," Ross decided. "I'm not sure I like it."

"Want off at the next corner?" Cargraves inquired.

"No, but I'm not dead certain I'm glad I came."

Morrie grasped his arm, to steady himself apparently, but quite as much for the comfort of solid human companionship. "You know what I think, Ross," he began, as he stared out at the endless miles of craters. "I think I know how it got that way. Those aren't volcanic craters, that's certain – and it wasn't done by meteors. *They did it themselves!*"

"Huh? Who?"

"The moon people. They did it. They wrecked themselves. They ruined themselves. *They had one atomic war too many.*"

"Huh? What the – " Ross stared, then looked back at the surface as if to read the grim mystery there. Art stopped taking pictures.

"How about it, Doc?"

Cargraves wrinkled his brow. "Could be," he admitted. "None of the other theories for natural causes hold water for one reason or another. It would account for the relatively smooth parts we call 'seas', They really were seas; that's why they weren't hit very hard."

"And that's why they aren't seas any more," Morrie went on. "They blew their atmosphere off and the seas boiled away. Look at Tycho. That's where they set off the biggest ammunition dump on the planet. It cracked the whole planet. I'll bet somebody worked out a counter-weapon that worked too well. It set off every atom bomb on the moon all at once and it ruined them! I'm sure of it."

"Well," said Cargraves, "I'm not sure of it, but I admit the theory is attractive. Perhaps we'll find out when we land. The notion of setting off all the bombs at once – there are strong theoretical objections to that. Nobody has any idea how to do it.''

''Nobody knew how to make an atom bomb a few years ago,'' Morrie pointed out.

''That's true.'' Cargraves wanted to change the subject; it was unpleasantly close to horrors that had haunted his dreams since the beginning of World War II. ''Ross, how do you feel about the other side of the moon now?''

''We'll know pretty soon,'' Ross chuckled. ''Say – this is the Other Side!''

And so it was. They had leveled off in their circular orbit near the left limb of the moon as seen from the earth and were coasting over the mysterious other face. Ross scanned it closely. ''Looks about the same.''

''Did you expect anything different?''

''No, I guess not. But I had hoped.'' Even as he spoke they crossed the sunrise line and the ground below them was dark, not invisible, for it was still illuminated by faint starlight – starlight only, for the earthshine never reached this face. The suncapped peaks receded rapidly in the distance. At the rate they were traveling, a speed of nearly 4000 miles per hour necessary to maintain them in a low-level circular orbit, the complete circuit of the planet would take a little over an hour and a half.

''No more pictures, I guess,'' Art said sadly. ''I wish it was a different time of the month''

''Yes,'' agreed Ross, still peering out, ''it's a dirty shame to be this close and not see anything.''

''Don't be impatient,'' Cargraves told him; ''when we start back in eight or nine days, we swing around again and you can stare and take pictures till you're cross-eyed.''

''Why only eight or nine days? We've got more food than that.''

''Two reasons. The first is, if we take off at new moon we won't have to stare into the sun on the way back. The second is, I'm homesick and I haven't even landed yet.'' He grinned. In utter seriousness he felt that it was not wise to stretch their luck by sticking around too long.

The trip across the lighted and familiar face of the moon was delightful, but so short that it was like window shopping in a speeding car. The craters and the "seas" were old familiar friends, yet strange and new. It reminded them of the always strange experience of seeing a famous television star on a personal appearance tour – recognition with an odd feeling of unreality.

Art shifted over to the motion-picture camera once used to record the progress of the *Starstruck* series, and got a complete sequence from *Mare Fecunditatis* to the crater Kepler, at which point Cargraves ordered him emphatically to stop at once and strap himself down.

They were coming into their landing trajectory. Cargraves and Morrie had selected a flat, unnamed area beyond *Oceanus Procellarum* for the landing because it was just on the border between the earth side and the unknown side, and thereby fitted two plans: to attempt to establish radio contact with earth, for which direct line-of-sight would be necessary, and to permit them to explore at least a portion of the unknown side.

Joe the Robot was called again and told to consult a second cam concealed in his dark insides, a cam which provided for the necessary braking drive and the final ticklish contact on maneuvering jets and radar. Cargraves carefully leveled the ship at the exact altitude and speed Joe would need for the approach and slipped over to automatic when Morrie signaled that they were at the exact, precalculated distance necessary for the landing.

Joe took over. He flipped the ship over, using the maneuvering rockets, then started backing in to a landing, using the jet in the tail to kill their still tremendous speed. The moon was below them now and Cargraves could see nothing but the stars, the stars and the crescent of the earth – a quarter of a million miles away and no help to him now.

He wondered if he would ever set foot on it again.

Morrie was studying the approach in the radar scope. "Checking out to nine zeros, Captain," he announced proudly and with considerable exaggeration. "It's in the bag."

The ground came up rapidly in the scope. When they were close and no longer, for the moment, dropping at all, Joe cut the main jet and flipped them over.

When he had collected himself from the wild gyration of the somersault, Cargraves saw the nose jets reach out and splash in front of them and realized that the belly jets were in play, too, as the surge of power pushed the seat of the chair up against him. He felt almost as if he could land it himself, it seemed so much like his first wild landing on the New Mexico desert.

Then for one frantic second he saw the smooth, flat ground ahead of the splash of the plowing nose jets give way to a desolation of rocky ridges, sharp crevasses, loose and dangerous cosmic rubble . . . soil from which, if they landed without crashing, they could not hope to take off.

The sunlight had fooled them. With the sun behind them the badlands had cast no shadows they could see; the flat plain had appeared to stretch to the mountains ahead. These were no mountains, but they were quite sufficient to wreck the *Galileo*.

The horrible second it took him to size up the situation was followed by frantic action. With one hand he cut the automatic pilot; with the other he twisted violently on the knob controlling the tail jet. He slapped the belly jets on full.

Her nose lifted.

She hung there, ready to fall, kept steady on her jets only by her gyros. Then slowly, slowly, slowly, the mighty tail jet reached out – so slowly that he knew at that moment that the logy response of the atomic pile would never serve him for what he had to do next, which was to land her himself.

The *Galileo* pulled away from the surface of the moon. "That was close," Morrie said mildly.

Cargraves wiped the sweat from his eyes and shivered.

He knew what was called for now, in all reason. He knew that he should turn the ship away from the moon, head her in the general direction of the earth and work out a return path, a path to a planet with an atmosphere to help a pilot put down his savage ship. He knew right then that he was not the stuff of heroes, that he was getting old and knew it.

But he hated to tell Morrie.

"Going to put her down on manual?" the boy inquired.

"Huh?"

"That's the only way we'll get her down on a strange field. I can see that now – you've got to be able to see your spot at the last half minute – nose jets and no radar."

"I can't do it, Morrie."

The younger man said nothing. He simply sat and stared ahead without expression.

"I'm going to head her back to earth, Morrie."

The boy gave absolutely no sign of having heard him. There was neither approval nor disapproval on his face, nor any faint suggestion.

Cargraves thought of the scene when Ross, blind and bandaged, had told him off. Of Art, quelling his space sickness to get his pictures. He thought, too, of the hot and tiring days when he and Morrie had qualified for piloting together.

The boy said nothing, neither did he look at him.

These kids, these damn kids! How had he gotten up here, with a rocket under his hand and a cargo of minors to be responsible for? He was a laboratory scientist, not a superman. If it had been Ross, if Ross were a pilot – even where he now was, he shivered at the recollection of Ross's hairraising driving. Art was about as bad. Morrie was worse.

He knew he would never be a hot pilot – not by twenty years. These kids, with their casual ignorance, with their hot rod rigs, it was for them; piloting was their kind of a job. They were too young and too ignorant to care and their reflexes were not hobbled by second thoughts. He remembered Ross's words: "I'll go to the moon if I have to walk!"

"Land her, Morrie."

"Aye, aye, sir!"

The boy never looked at him. He flipped her up on her tail, then let her drop slowly by easing off on the tail jet. Purely by the seat of his pants, by some inner calculation – for Cargraves could see nothing through the port but stars, and neither could the boy – he flipped her over again, cutting the tail jet as he did so.

The ground was close to them and coming up fast.

He kicked her once with the belly jets, placing them thereby over a smooth stretch of land, and started taking her down with quick blasts of the nose jets, while sneaking a look between blasts.

When he had her down so close that Cargraves was sure that he was going to land her on her nose, crushing in the port and killing them, he gave her one more blast which made her rise a trifle, kicked her level and brought her down on the belly jets, almost horizontal, and so close to the ground that Cargraves could see it ahead of them, out the port.

Glancing casually out the port, Morrie gave one last squirt with the belly jets and let her settle. They grated heavily and were stopped. The *Galileo* sat on the face of the moon.

"Landed, sir. Time: Oh-eight-three-four."

Cargraves drew in a breath. "A beautiful, beautiful landing, Morrie."

"Thanks, Captain."

IT CAME FROM OUTER SPACE

(Universal, 1953)
Starring: Richard Carlson, Barbara Rush
& Charles Drake
Directed by Jack Arnold
Based on a screen treatment,
"The Meteor" by Ray Bradbury

Another of the film-makers who helped to establish the Space Movie in cinema history was Jack Arnold – a man whom critic John Baxter has gone so far as to call "the great genius of American fantasy film". Writing in 1970, Baxter said: "From 1953 to 1958 reaching across the boom years, Arnold directed for Universal a series of films which, for sheer virtuosity of style and clarity of vision, have few equals in the cinema." Arnold, who began as an actor but learned his trade as a film-maker during the Second World War making training films for the Army Signal Corps, was specifically signed by Universal to get them into the SF boom. His first choice of subject was a treatment by Ray Bradbury (1920–), then one of the fastest rising young stars in American fantasy fiction. Ray's story of an alien space craft which crash lands in the desert and releases its occupants into a nearby town where they "borrow" human forms, had originally been entitled, *Ground Zero (The Atomic Monster)* but was changed to *The Meteor* before finally appearing on the screen as *It Came From Outer Space*. Arnold and his team took full advantage of the handy Arizona desert for much of their location shooting, and the picture was further enhanced by some outstanding special effects featuring the shape-changing aliens created by Clifford Stine and David S. Horsley. Another unique element of *It Came From Outer*

Space was the fact it was filmed in 3-D, thereby enabling it to be released as "the world's first 3-D science fiction film" – with special glasses handed to each member of the audience as they entered the cinema. Jack Arnold's brilliant camerawork and the sense of hostility the film generated from being set in a real environment that all viewers could relate to, made the picture unlike anything that had been seen on the screen before and once more suggested whole new areas of possibilities for the makers of Space Movies. The director himself went on to film several more SF classics including *Creature From The Black Lagoon* (1954), *Revenge of the Creature* (1955) and *The Incredible Shrinking Man* (1957). The reputation of author Ray Bradbury was also assured, and among his later works to be filmed have been *The Beast From 20,000 Fathoms* (1953), *Fahrenheit 451* (1966), *The Illustrated Man* (1969) and *The Martian Chronicles* (1980). The following adaptation of Ray's treatment is taken directly from the film.

A ship hurtled through airless space. It was a strange speck of alien geometry, moving almost at the speed of light. Behind it streaked the glow of ions – the atomic particles that flung it with world-splitting force across the gulf between the stars.

It was a survey ship from the planet Ool in the system of Sirius.

In the control room a puddle was talking to a cloud. Somewhere between the pair two eyes floated, egg-sized, luminous, yellow. Now and then a swirl of vapour passed across the delicate quartz of the instrument panel; a liver-coloured tentacle would appear as if from nowhere, make an adjustment and dissolve, leaving on the surface a trail like the slime of snails.

No words passed; but the thoughts went back and forth.

"We are about to pass a small star with nine planets."

"It's on the chart. Only one planet with life-forms – the third from the star."

16

The Meteor

"Intelligent life?"

"Our people have never mixed, but the planet has been surveyed from missiles. There are many forms of life. The leading type has developed language and tools. It stands on two legs, and it has only one body from birth to death . . ."

"That," said the cloud with a vibrating eye, "must be inconvenient."

"Yes. To be unable to change form is . . . unimaginable. Those beings are very strange."

"How much science have they?"

"Not much. They've only just discovered atomic energy."

The eye grew; the cloud spiralled and became a column. "Astrogator!"

A thing that looked like a spilled jelly stirred. "Sir?"

"We'll reduce speed to one light-unit and find a path between the second and third planets. I will take a look at them with the visorscope."

"You'll see their cities," said the puddle confidently.

*

Sand Rock, Arizona. A small town, now almost invisible from above in its blue-black blanket of evening. A spot of winking lights on the cold floor of the night-time desert, from which came a tiny sound of humanity as someone crossed Main Street, lurching from bar to bar.

There, under a spangle of stars, a mile out of town along the desert highway, Putnam's shack showed two rectangles of homely lamplight. The light spent itself in the emptiness of the surrounding desert, but just managed in its passing to gild the tube of a big telescope which stood near the door.

A tiny house and a tiny telescope, stuck drunkenly on the surface of the turning globe that is the planet Earth. Far away beyond the atmosphere – beyond, even, the far-flung orbit of the moon – something was happening that would soon bring terror to this patch of Arizona.

17

But this moment was one of peace; the coyotes cried in the outer ring of dark as they had always done; the stars whee'ed overhead. And John Putnam, struggling science-journalist, was talking about marriage.

"Maybe it's my money you're after?"

The girl looked startled.

"Money?"

"Well, I got a cheque to-day . . ."

"Johnny, you've sold another article!"

"That's right. Now I've got enough to finish building the house."

He grinned at her. She smiled back; spread her arms to include the room, the desk, the photographs of moonscape and nebulae on the wall.

"All this and heaven, too!"

"Let's go outside and take a peep at heaven," he said.

Ellen Fields followed him outside to the telescope. She was the local schoolteacher, and young for her job. John was young as well – amazingly so for one whose articles on astronomy were already piling up a reputation with the leading scientific journals. It was natural that the two best brains in Sand Rock should be engaged to be married.

"What are you working on?" Ellen said.

"Perturbations in the orbit of Jupiter Twelve."

"Oh, John, wouldn't it be wonderful if you found another Jovian moon."

"I'd call it *Ellen* after you."

"I'd never be able to live up to that," she laughed.

"Everyone would think you were a Greek goddess. But, after all, they wouldn't be far – "

He broke off.

"Look!"

She clutched him. They stood swaying, gazing upward, following the long arc of the metor-like object that was blazing across the sky.

At one moment the glittering stars had been hanging in

their old positions against the blue-black night; in the next they had been blotted out in the sudden flare of the visitor. It was as if some cosmic giant had drawn a careless line of fire across the firmament with a huge and terrible pencil; but before the first shock of surprise had faded the pair saw the meteor itself like a glowing fruit vanish behind the top of a nearby range. There followed a ground tremor which rattled the casements of the shack and moved sickeningly into their stomachs like the impact of a bomb.

In a flash John was at the telescope.

"What was it?"

"Meteor!" he snapped. "One of the biggest . . ."

"Can you see anything?"

He had the telescope at horizontal.

"Yep . . . plenty. Look."

She peered through the eyepiece; saw fiery, billowing smoke which obscured the view.

"That," he said, "is about four miles away. Somewhere by the old Excelsior Mine. Get your wrap!"

*

Diamond-hard, the alien metal had buried itself deeply in the crumbly rock. Clouds of heated dust swirled upwards. Rocks ran bouncingly down the steep sides of the crater, piling up against the red-hot thing at the bottom.

The thing was six-sided and the size of a large house. The odd second or so of passage through the atmosphere had heated its surface by friction to a dull glow.

Minutes passed. The smoke cleared slightly; the fall of rock paused as if the shaken ground had reached an uneasy balance. For a moment there was almost silence. Then in the hot hull a six-sided panel moved inwards; there was suddenly a hole of precise and accurate geometry in the side of the visitor. A black hole.

Slowly the blackness moved, as if touched by the mist of

dawn. A white, damp vapour gathered at the entrance, and in the midst an eye.

An eye yellow as saffron, with a cold, questing pupil like the yolk of an egg!

And then the creature poured slowly after its eye. It was at once liquid, solid and gaseous; it half-walked, half-floated. It was never still; at one instant it spread itself like the sensitive, oozy passage of a sea-squid; at another it would be a mere wraith that left a glittering wake of slime on the piled rocks; yet when a fall of earth in its path spelled manual work it seemed with some queer chemistry of its own to grow actual tentacles, whipcord-like and brown, which sucked and lifted, and then, the task done, withered into gas as if their owner had forgotten them.

Slowly the creature oozed up towards the crater rim.

Near the top a rabbit, petrified, lay under flat ears, quivering.

*

The car hummed along the desert road, John at the wheel, Ellen beside him.

The Excelsior was an old gold mine, a relic of the nineteenth century, but was still worked by casual prospectors who sometimes found there a streak of poor but marketable dirt. The entrance lay against the side of the shallow hill, the top of which had now been transformed into the still smoking crater that glowed faintly in the darkness.

They left the car near the shaft and toiled up to the crater rim. Breathlessly they peered over . . .

Mist and smoke and tumbled rock.

"It's really something," Ellen said.

"Honey . . . the biggest thing that's happened around here. I'm going to take a look."

"Be careful, John."

The Meteor

He picked his way down the slope. On a ledge below the level of her feet he turned to wave, but the rising smoke had already hidden her from view. It was a smoke that, strangely, did not attack the throat; nothing seemed to be burning, and he got the impression that rock and metal – the world itself – had been scorched beyond endurance, and that the smoke was the pure and angry energy of the wound that had been death. He touched a rock; it stung his fingers, and he followed the ridge downwards gingerly, his heart beating fast . . .

On the lower slope it was a craziness of boulders. He paused, blinded, not knowing for a moment the direction of up or down. Then the smoke cleared a little and the starlight began to gain over the blackness and chaos around him.

Or had the chaos been followed by something worse? Were his eyes playing tricks?

The bottom of the crater opened out into a wide and nearly horizontal shaft that must have been part of the old workings, now opened to the starlight. And half blocking the shaft was something huge and regular in shape, lathe-smooth and . . .

Yes, by heck! A door!

John Putnam knew no fear at that moment – only an immense interest. He started forward, stumbling slightly; it was only when the corner of his eye caught the strange glitter of slime on the rocks that he paused again, and the first quake and shudder went through him. He knelt and touched the slime with his finger.

Cold, cold . . .

He stood up; looked again at the smooth, half-buried object below. Then the fear took shape and leaped.

What he had mistaken for a door was no door. There was only a smooth surface.

Or . . .

A well-fitting door that had been open and was now shut? The thought brought out prickles all over him.

21

How long he stood there still and silent he never knew.

Suddenly he felt that he must regain the top at any cost. He turned, his boots scrabbling furiously at the rocks – and in the same instant there came a deep baritone rumble and a trickle of stones – a rumble that grew to a roar . . .

Landslide!

Above him the ridge . . . somehow he managed to wade upwards against the accelerating fall and press himself against its overhang. Soon boulders bigger than his head were pouring past; his shoulder went numb as a blow sent him sideways, he had a vision of chunks like automobiles plunging past him into the shaft as the dust took his throat, spots danced in front of his eyes and he lost consciousness.

*

"John! Oh, John!"

There was immediate gladness as he opened his eyes. He was lying on the gravel of the crater rim, and Ellen was rubbing his forehead and his eyes were full of stars – real ones.

"I'm okay." He got up, staggered, and an arm caught him.

"Guess you was almost a gonner."

He recognised Pete Davis, a truck driver from the town.

"Walloped over here soon as I saw that thing falling. Started down myself when the landslip took on. Just in time to yank you over the top of that overhang. How yuh feelin'?"

"Guess I wasn't really hurt."

"But your arm . . ." Ellen said, watching him as he rubbed it tenderly.

"Forget it. There was something down there . . ."

"Sure," Pete said. "A million tons of rock that nearly hit you."

"No, that's not what I . . . I mean something else. Some kind of ship."

"A what?"

"What kind of a ship?" Ellen asked.

"Like a huge ball, rammed into the old shaft at the bottom. And . . . and I saw an open portway."

"And inside," Pete went on triumphantly, "there was a bug-eyed monster!"

"Well . . . something. Next thing I knew the door was shut; and then the landslide started."

"Well, here come folks," Pete grunted, as headlamps appeared and car doors were slammed at the foot of the hill. "You're not gonna tell those people you saw Martians runnin' around down there?"

"Ellen! You don't believe me either."

"I . . . I don't know," she whispered.

The three were squatting on their heels. They did not get up as two tall figures strode slowly up the slope and stood over them.

"Resting?"

It was big Matt Warren, the Sheriff, bulky, self-confident, like the personification of a world in which nothing ever happened that had not taken place a billion times before. With him was a lanky reporter from the local newspaper, one Kenn Loring.

"Just washed up," Pete said. "We been down there, and there was a landslide."

"Tell us what happened," Loring asked.

"Meteor. Johnny here says it's the biggest ever."

"It was no meteor," John Putnam said; and he felt the girl's hand suddenly tighten in his as if restraining him. "There's some kind of ship down there. I don't know what kind."

"Sure, *I* know," Loring said. "A spaceship! Straight out of one of those stars you write about!"

"Listen," John told him. "It's really there – it's buried right down there. We'll have to get this whole area sealed off until we know what we're up against."

Ray Bradbury

The Sheriff lighted a cigarette with a calculated slowness, as if he had all the time in the world. He ignored Putnam.

"Did you see it, Ellen?"

"No . . . but if John says he saw it . . ."

"C'mon," he said. "I'll take you home, Ellen."

"No, thanks. Johnny'll take me home."

Once more Putnam felt the pressure of her hand.

"Let's get out of here," she pleaded.

*

The convertible sped toward Sand Rock.

"You're driving too fast," she told him.

"Sorry, honey – it's the way it gets me."

"You can't really blame them."

"Tell you I saw it! I even saw some kind of slimy tracks . . . Listen, I'm going to phone Doctor Snell at the Wayne Observatory. Ask him to get over first thing in the morning. Not to mention the army – it'd be awful wrong not to tell the army . . ."

"Aren't you taking on a lot, Johnny? All that's really Matt's job – he's sheriff. Why, I've known him all my life, and I just wouldn't like Matt to get angry at you, Johnny . . ."

"We're not exactly like brothers as it is," he said grimly.

"What's that?"

His foot came off the accelerator. He stopped at the side of the road.

"Some sort of bird, I think, front of the windscreen. I sure am jumpy."

"It wasn't a bird," she said. "I don't know what it was. It looked like an egg or something . . . an egg that glowed, up in the air. And a kind of mist around it. Oh, Johnny – I'm scared! What do you mean, thinking up all this stuff about Martians . . ."

But Putnam was out of the car, staring back along the dim road. Like the tail-end of a dream captured on waking,

24

he had almost fancied a thin, diaphanous stuff vanishing into the almost-tangible background of the night . . .

He felt the girl beside him as he took two or three paces along the road.

"Johnny, let's go . . ."

He stopped. Something was beside the road. It was a Joshua tree. Just an ordinary . . .

The tree froze his eyeballs. His whole body was held in an agony of tension; on the one hand the grip of curiosity, of manhood, and the presence of the girl told him to stay; on the other, the whole weight of ancestral terror, kept deep down in human kind since caveman days, pressed him to be gone. For there was something unutterably creepy about the tree – something impossible to define – a fleshiness, a sense of horrific intelligence.

He jumped as Ellen screamed.

"It's just a Joshua tree!" he mouthed as he half carried her to the car.

"Let's get away . . . quickly . . ." she sobbed.

*

The convertible faded away – became a faint pencil of headlamps on the desert road and a hum. And then nothing. The desert spoke to itself with a coyote's howl, and the stars seemed to drip from the sky.

The Joshua tree started to ooze away into the night.

*

Luckily John Putnam had the good sense to avoid a clash with the Sheriff by leaving that official to contract the military. He contented himself with a late call to Wayne Observatory and a brief account of his adventure. Doctor Snell already knew about the meteor. Yes, he would be along in the morning. Yes, he would bring geiger counters;

he would also test for metal and electromagnetism. But what was this about spaceships?

He had no doubt (he said) that a night's rest – an hour or two of forgetfulness of that landslide – would cure John of *that* hallucination!

In the morning John called for Ellen, got her to cut school, and set off for the crater. On the way Ellen shoved a newspaper beneath his nose.

STAR-GAZER SEES MARTIANS

"Huh . . ." he said, and kept his eyes on the road.

There was a notice up at the crater: "No Admittance Without Authorization." From the jeeps strewn about at all angles it was clear that the army was in control. A grey-haired, bespectacled man came down the slope, wrung John's hand, and kissed Ellen's cheek.

"Well, Doctor Snell, this is nice!"

"John, I'd never have guessed that my star pupil was going to join the saucer-spotters – the spaceship fans!"

John's spirits fell at once; a deep depression stole over him.

"But Doctor Snell, I *did* see it! If only we could get together quietly and talk about it . . ."

"I'd quit talking here, at any rate. The place is thick with reporters, all hot after The Man Who Saw The Monsters. How about you, Ellen? See any bug-eyes yourself?"

"No," she answered. "I didn't. But listen here, Doctor Snell, if John says a thing it's true."

John stole a grateful glance at her. This was sheer love and loyalty; he knew only too well the doubts she really felt.

"I can prove there's a spaceship down there," he said at length," if I can get you to help me dig it out."

"My poor dumb dope! There's a meteor down there – it all checks – the metallic dust, the fusion from heat, the angle of contact. It's a very big one – maybe as big as the famous

26

one that fell in prehistoric times in Arizona. Someday we'll dig it out. But not until we've been able to raise half a million bucks from somewhere. For, boy, that meteor's in plenty deep; since you got out of the pit last night there's been another fall, and it's now got enough stuff on top of it to bury the White House."

"I've been hoping I'd run into you, Putnam!"

It was the Sheriff, who came scrambling from the crater and dusted himself down.

"What's the matter, Matt? Have I been breaking the law?"

"You might call it that. Ellen's supposed to be teachin' school. If you want to drive yourself crazy seeing Martians, that's your lookout; but leave Ellen out of it – she's got her job."

"Listen, I – "

"No, you listen. I knew Ellen when she was a crawler. I also knew her pop. I was his deputy – "

He broke off as a crowd of reporters and camera men came from the pit.

"There's the guy!"

"That's John Putnam!"

"Say, Mr Putnam, what about this monster you saw last night?"

"Quick!" Ellen said. She grabbed his arm. "He's nothing to say, boys!" she yelled; and together they ran down the slope to the car.

John drove savagely. "What do you know? Snell agrees with the Sheriff that I'm crazy."

"I just wish we'd found one of them!" she sighed. "Just one little monster to toss into the Sheriff's office, and maybe another for dear Doctor Snell's bedroom!"

The road was a long, smooth rib in the desert. The telegraph poles danced past tirelessly. Suddenly the blankness ahead contained life; a friendly reminder that other people existed. A work truck stood by the road; two figures were perched and busy on one of the poles.

John stopped the car.

"Hiya, Frank! George!"

Frank was an elderly engineer; George his young assistant. Both had called in the first place at John's shack to fix the telephone, and had often been there since as guests to squint through the telescope and talk science-fiction.

"Well, where'd you two come from?" Frank grunted. "Thought you'd be all day back at that crater."

"I don't much like the show over there."

"Heard they'd got you going, John. Don't let 'em ride you, boy."

"Have you two seen anything unusual this morning?" John asked.

George said: "You mean like another meteor?"

"No, I don't mean that."

"Well, we ain't, have we, Frank? Although I sure have been hearing things."

"Hearing what things?"

"Like this," George said. He was strapped right on the top of the telegraph pole with a handphone plugged in. "Come up and listen."

"Darndest noise ever," he added, as John swarmed up the ladder and took the phone. "Any ideas?"

John did not answer. The noise was not music, but it might have been a kind of chant. It hovered between the boundaries of low and high frequency, so that some of it was a faint rumble almost too deep for the ear, and some of it again was so high that only a bat could have registered it properly. Of sound on the normal audio-band between these extremes there was none.

It was like an utterly alien creature – an other-worldly creature – talking to itself! The thought smote John softly between the eyes; but he said nothing except: "Now it's gone."

"Well, that's the way – comes and goes. Had enough?"

"Yes. Didn't know what it was, anyway."

The Meteor

Frank said: "Sounded to me like someone was pluggin'
in. George, why don't we drive up the line and take a
squint?"

"Anything you say, boss."

"We'll have a look the other way," John told them. "I'll
let you know if we spot anyone."

*

The creature was half a Joshua tree, half a rivulet of slime.
There was no one about. It was relaxing!

Mimicry, although as natural to its race as running to a
hare, was still a conscious effort. It was pleasant, when
events allowed, to let the acquired shape melt – to allow it to
relapse a little into the running glob of mist and mucus that
was its natural self.

It had experimented. It had been for a short time a
coyote. Then a rabbit. Then a telegraph pole. But those
were mere sports. There was only one form which could
manipulate the repair and digging-out of the spaceship, and
that was the useful arrangement of a central trunk with two
extensions, the whole mounted on a pair of legs, which was
the property of this strange planet's ruling race – Man! But
first it had to catch and study Man. Even a mimic had to
know his subject.

*The Joshua tree dissolved completely as a work truck, full
of ladders and wire, came into sight. A pool and an eye and a
few tentacles strewed themselves across the road and waited.*

*

The car stopped.

"Did you see something, John?"

"No, there's nothing. Only . . . I had a strange feeling."
He shrugged. "I'd better get back to Frank and George and
tell them we saw nothing."

29

"Oh, but they won't need . . ."

"We promised."

He backed and turned. Soon, far ahead like a toy, the works truck came and went in the lakes of heat-haze that flowed from the desert. As he drew nearer a tight core of foreboding grew in John's chest. He braked the convertible beside the truck. It was empty; both doors were flapping open, and he stumbled out on to the road, scanning the flat horizons . . .

Ellen, beside him, said: "Perhaps . . . perhaps they went off into the desert."

"And left both doors open?"

There was an outcrop of rock a quarter of a mile into the desert. John took her hand, tensely leading her towards it. Yes – the haze and dancing bands of light had been playing tricks – there *was* a man beside the rock.

"George!"

"Hello."

"Where's Frank?"

"He . . . went off to look around."

"I couldn't see you at first. The sun . . ."

"Yes," George said. "The sun. The beautiful sun."

And he lifted his head and stared, stared at the sun. Unblinking!

*

The Sheriff was sitting in his office. He had left the army men and the scientist and the reporters to talk and scramble at the crater; it had been time for him to go back and attend to the peace of Sand Rock.

The door from the sunlit street burst open. John and Ellen came in breathlessly.

"You're coming right out with us, Matt. Bring your gun!"

"Listen," he said patiently. "The school principal's been here. You're supposed to be teachin' school, Ellen."

"Oh, cut it out, Matt! You listen to John – it's important."

Putnam was gabbling out the story of the two telephone engineers. ". . . And then we found George," he finished. "Yet somehow he wasn't like George. He was like a man so shocked . . . a man shocked right out of his personality. He talked like someone else, not George – his voice was lifeless. And . . . and . . ."

"Something had happened to his eyes," Ellen put in. "He kept staring at the sun and didn't blink!"

"We tried to ask him where Frank was. He said, 'Just around.' Imagine saying that in the desert! Then we tried to get him to come with us, but he wouldn't. We left him standing there like crazy – the sun beating down and him staring at it, unblinking!"

Matt Warren tilted back his chair.

"Has this anything to do with your Martian monsters? If so, I ain't buying."

"How do I know? It's utterly queer, that's all. Seems to me George went nuts. There was no sign of Frank. Maybe George had knocked him out and he was lying on the sand somewhere – you can't see far in that dazzle. But if so, what was it sent George nuts?"

"Only one answer to that!" the Sheriff said. "Your monsters!" He was grinning and looking at the window.

"Do you really think so?" Ellen asked.

"Oh, sure! But before we discuss it, Putnam, would you mind opening that door and just look over them two guys passing down the street?"

"What . . .?" John crossed to the street-door and opened it.

"Hi!" he yelled. He was out of the door in an instant, chasing after the two figures.

George and Frank! Just turning the corner . . . but their backs were unmistakable.

He reached the corner. It was the entrance to a narrow alley leading off Main Street; there was a lot of scaffolding where a new building, finished except for the paintwork, stood flush with the alley. The clean, unpainted door was the only one ajar. He pushed it.

George and Frank were standing in the hall.

Their eyes glowed!

He said: "George! Frank!"

"Keep away," Frank said.

"Where've you been? What happened back there? If anything's wrong I want to help."

"Stand back."

The voice – was it Frank's or George's? – was like a diaphragm fed with an air pump; there was nothing in it of flesh and blood. The voice of a robot telling someone's weight in return for a coin in a slot.

Two pairs of eyes glowed . . .

"Whoever you are," John whispered, ". . . whatever you are . . . I want to help you."

"Then keep away. We do not want to hurt you – or anyone. Your friends are alive. They will not be harmed if you keep away – give us time . . ."

"Time for what?"

"Or terrible things will happen," said the voice, ignoring his question. "Terrible to you, because undreamed of. Undreamed of because never experienced. Never experienced because not of your world."

Putnam's muscles relaxed, seemed to obey an impulse not of his body or mind. He stepped back dutifully to let the pair come out. They passed him without a sideways glance and walked like marionettes to the head of the alley. Then they turned the corner.

With a half sob he flung his stupefied self into action – sprang after them. He saw them walking the centre of the street, left right! left right! Sinister toy men! The dazzle swallowed them – the bright mouth of Main Street where the buildings finished and the desert almost instantly began.

The Meteor

*

The voice of the radio announcer was self-satisfied and hearty.

"Well, folks! No one has yet turned up any bug-eyed monsters . . . so it must be set down as another of those hoaxes . . . another case of saucers on the brain . . . this time by a young publicity-seeking astronomer. Of course, if he *should* bring a Martian to your favourite radio station, this network would be only too pleased to give our visitor the freedom of the air – even if he could only honk . . ."

John cut the radio so savagely that the set rocked.

"Don't let it get you, John dear."

"We sit!" he snorted. "We wait! Things are happening – folks are disappearing – everyone *knows* there's something queer going on – and nothing's done! There's no money to clear a few tons of rock and settle doubts for good!"

Two days had passed since his strange encounter in the alley. Although it was still possible for radio announcers to treat the whole matter as light entertainment, the climate of the town itself was somewhat more tense.

George's wife had already been to the Sheriff to say that her husband was missing. Frank's mother had come forward with the same story. Two prospectors, who had been working at the Excelsior Mine for the past week, had not shown up at their lodgings in town. The army, it was true, had pulled out that afternoon, uninterested and intact; only Doctor Snell still remained at the mine.

The telephone rang.

"Putnam speaking."

"This is Matt. Putnam, I apologise!"

"What goes on?"

"Doctor Snell's car is still at the crater. But Snell's missing."

"Now are you ready to believe me?"

"I'm trying, or I wouldn't have called you."

33

"You've got to believe there's a ship buried out there – that at least some of our visitors from space got out before the ship was covered over."

"Sure, I'm trying to believe just that. There's another thing, Putnam – the hardware store's been raided. Nothing taken except electrical gear."

"It all adds up! What happened to George and Frank's telephone truck? That's never been found, has it? Don't you see? – they want electrical spares."

"Listen, Putnam, I'm coming round to your way of thinking, but other folks aren't. They'd think I was crazy like you if I spilled this stuff around. So it's just you and me together. I'm coming out to your place right away and we'll get up to that crater and pry a bit."

Five minutes later the Sheriff's car braked outside and there came the sound of an impatient horn.

"Ellen, you stay here. I guess we'll both have room for some ham and eggs when we get back."

"John! There's danger out there . . ."

"I'm glad someone's realising that at last; but I'll be careful, don't worry."

He kissed her.

*

The rim of the crater shimmered. The bodywork of the empty car at the foot of the hill was too hot for the hand; visible heat made the background move like jelly; vultures wheeled in the hot blue bowl of the sky.

"Well, he's not here," Matt said, "and it's a cinch he wouldn't leave without his car. I'd give a lot to have things back to what they were yesterday, with me calling you a fool!"

Together they crossed the rim and climbed down into the jumble of boulders within the crater. The heat seemed to pulse slowly as in an oven; it was the driving blood in their own bodies that gave the impression.

The Meteor

"There's nothing here," Matt grunted. "At least, whatever's here is buried too deep for any gear in Sand Rock to tackle. But where in heck is Doctor Snell? Another thing – " He turned to John almost fiercely. "If these monsters of yours *have* kidnapped Doctor Snell, not to mention two prospectors and a coupla telephone linesmen, what they done with 'em? There just ain't no place to hide in this county 'cept Sand Rock; the desert's got a way of frying a guy by day and freezing him by night. It sure is a poor break for those guys."

They searched; they poked among the rocks while the heat blistered their feet through the soles of their boots. And at last they had to admit that the crater contained no clue. Sorrowfully they got into the Sheriff's baking hot car and drove away, leaving the scientist's empty car behind.

"Stop a moment," John said.

He had caught a glimpse of something black against the crumbly hill. The Sheriff backed the car and he jumped out.

It was a small heap of burnt-out chassis parts.

"I'd bet my bottom dollar that *that* was George and Frank's telephone truck!"

"Could be," Matt frowned, sucking his teeth. "The plot thickens."

*

"What now?" John asked as they sped back towards his shack.

"It's not a local job. I got my duty, and that's to tell police headquarters in Flagstaff; and if I didn't do that today I'd be all set for losing my badge."

"Whew! The monsters from space are in for some publicity, after all."

"Aw, people don't take to that stuff, even if you give 'em real monsters with their cornflakes."

They drew up outside John's shack.

35

"So long, Matt. Call me if there's anything."

"I sure will. Give my love to Ellen and tell her I apologise for being snooty."

John watched the car rattle off towards town. He turned with a sigh to his front door; and then he remembered the ham and eggs.

"Darn! Hey, Ellen . . ."

There was no answer.

The room was a shambles. There was a glistening trail of filmy stuff on the carpet.

Slime.

*

"Hello! Matt? Listen, they've got Ellen!"

"What's that? How? Where?"

He babbled the story into the phone. "Come back here right away! We must go up to the crater . . ."

"But that's crazy! Nothing passed us on the road."

"Everything's crazy. We're just not dealing with things of this world."

"I'll be right over – soon as I've got a deputy and posse."

"Matt, listen to me. For heck's sake – no posse. Just you and me."

"Now you're nuts."

"It's something that struck me. What if those creatures mean no harm? What if they kidnap people for some reason we haven't guessed – like for study, the way we catch zoo animals? See? Violence might be the worst line at present. . ."

"I don't see," Matt answered, "but in case there's a thousandth chance of you being right I'll come alone for Ellen's sake."

Again the arrival of the Sheriff's car; again the rush over the grey, hot road towards the crater. A white-faced Putnam; a scowling Sheriff who said, as he wrenched the car around a bend: "It's enough to send a guy bat-dreams.

36

What'll we find when we get there? Just the crater – a hole full of rock to the brim. And what'll we be able to do? Nothing!"

"While I was waiting for you I thought of something. Something a kid could have thought of but we didn't. The Excelsior Mine! I guess th're must be a way through the workings, and that's where we'll find Ellen and the others."

"The mine's a long way from the crater. They think the main tunnels all fell in years ago. Besides, the workings are down to be searched tonight if those two prospectors haven't shown up by then."

Away to the left, where the low hill petered out in the flatness of the desert floor, was the entrance to the old mine. Matt drove towards it and braked where the black hole of the tunnel could be seen.

"It doesn't go in very far," he said. "I've got a flash-lamp – come on . . ."

"I'm going in alone," John told him.

"But listen . . ."

"I want you to do this for me, Matt. I've a hunch it would be best for Ellen. So will you stay here?"

"Well, if that's the way you want it . . ."

*

The alien world pressed against the beings from Ool and was terrifying. Space itself was a lesser horror. Out there between the worlds it was like a cocoon; a spaceship did not seem to be anything but a speck, hanging for ever against a multitude of changeless stars, and it was possible to fall into the illusion of timelessness. But here on this hostile planet all was hideous labour and emergency Labour made the more bitter because of homesickness for the vaporous and lightweight world of Ool.

That the ship had buried itself beneath a huge quantity of the dense material of this world had been at first a matter for despair. The beings were built entirely differently from any living form on the Earth. Their bodies were mere globs of molecules surrounding a fixed and yellow eye. And whilst an Earth-type creature – man or beast – would adapt *the body for certain actions, such as flexing the muscles or arching the spine, the beings from Ool would actually* change *theirs. To watch such a creature at work would be to see bits of it flow from a liquid to a gaseous state or from solid to jelly according to the work in hand!*

The beings had plenty of brain but little strength. The civilisation of Ool was rich in science, but here, lost and broken on an alien planet, there was nothing to use against the stubborn mass of rock except their frail bodies and a few ray guns, the use of which might easily start another landslide.

It had been the Commander who had thought of the idea of changing their bodies into those of men. It seemed clear that a body native to the planet would be the right sort to deal with a problem like the landslide – with the massed rocks which were so hard and heavy compared with the vapours and light soils of Ool.

It had also been the Commander who had ordered the crew to strike out horizontally from the buried ship with the ray guns in order to clear working space around it. In that way they had found a link with the galleries of the old mine.

And now, having probed and seeped into the bodies of the few humans who had come their way, a gang was at work, slowly raying a space around the ship, renewing the circuits of the electronic computor that formed its heart, testing the superstructure . . .

A strange gang . . .

Three Georges. A half-dozen Franks.

Two Ellens . . .

*

The Meteor

John poked the flashlight into the mouth of the mine and followed its beam. His feet crunched on hard flint; his movements sent tiny pebbles down the walls and on to his head. Soon he had to bend; later came a time when he was on all fours, pushing the beam into impenetrable darkness. He shivered, although the sweat was running into his eyes. Obviously this was a place for coyotes and rabbits; nothing else could find lodging in here . . .

Then his ears caught the rumblings.

A muffled thunder, turning into minute ground tremors; and at the same time – more continuous, if fainter – a tap, tap, tap.

He scrambled forward, to bring his forehead crashing against the roof. The gallery had narrowed to a mere warren. He kept his head down and crawled a few more yards, until his torch showed a blank surface, which he felt with his hands and knew for the end of the passage.

For minutes he lay there in his torn, dusty clothing, listening to his own breathing and the distant tapping and occasional low rumble. Then he turned gingerly, sensing that his knees were bruised and sticking through tears in his pants, and started back the way he had come. At once came a pitter-patter of flints and dust on the crown of his head; a small cascade that grew until, with a sick apprehension, he put his head down, covered it with his hands and waited in the blackness for the inevitable.

It came. It was as if someone had hit him heavily with a baseball bat, and his lungs were full of dust, and over his body ran like liquid fear the thought of being buried alive. He heaved – more in panic than anything else – and the loose stuff slid off his back, and he wriggled in his yearning for light and air and freedom to move freely wherever he wanted to go.

But there was light. He went for it like a moth, ignoring in his frenzy the fresh torrent of earth and rock that bounced against his ears. He remembered butting with his head, wrenching his legs away from a weight that would have pinned them down; and then he found himself lying half in and half out of a gaping hole, and the sky was above with vultures weaving.

He stood up, feeling weak. He had come right through the hill and he shuddered at the recollection.

A figure was standing halfway up the slope, staturesque amongst the boulders.

"Ellen!" he yelled, and plunged forward.

*

Up the hillside he ran, a scarecrow figure, breathless and nearly spent, the rocks bruising his legs, the yearning of thirst on his tongue.

"Ellen!"

The figure had gone.

He reached the spot. Leathery growths of cactus – stones jagged as glass.

The vultures overhead were silent witnesses as he sat down suddenly, sweat cold and prickly on him, feeling the silence like something tangible.

Then he saw the hole.

It was a rectangle half the height of a man, and the timber shoring told him what it was. Another entrance to the mine!

He had lost his torch. He blundered into the hole shouting "Ellen! Ellen! Ellen!"

The darkness met him like black water, and the sound of his own voice dwindled as if he were shouting into a thick curtain of cotton wool . . .

And suddenly he froze, transfixed by something un-guessed – the never-experienced. His mind was free, the muscles of his body unfettered and ready to move him on; yet a voice was telling him to stop.

A voice inside his head; but the voice of someone else.

A voice that spoke to him without sound, without words.

A voice of pure *thought*, intruding into his own brain.

"Stay where you are," the voice said.

In the stunned depths of his mind he knew that he was meeting the strange science of telepathy. Some other brain was thinking directly into his mind!

He heard his own physical voice croak: "Where's Ellen?"

"Safe," said the voice inside him.

"Come out into the open – out where I can see you!"

"No."

"What do you want? What are you really doing?"

"We are repairing our ship to leave your world. We need to be left alone."

"You've kidnapped and stolen," he thought. And he felt the answering thought of the other as if he had spoken aloud.

"But we meant no harm. By nightfall we will have left your planet, upon which we crashed by chance. We are living forms like yourselves . . ."

"Then why are you hiding?"

"Yours is an isolated world. You have never met any type of intelligence other than yourselves. Nearer the centre of our star-galaxy all types of intelligence meet and co-operate, but you have always been alone. You would be horrified at the sight of us . . . you would want to kill us, because we are so very different from yourselves."

"All I understand is that you've taken my friends . . . and now the woman."

"We make use of their bodies, but they are safe. They will return to you when we have freed our ship. But if you bring your people here to destroy us the captives will be destroyed, too."

"Stand out in the sun!" John signalled.

"In time perhaps . . ."

"Let me see you now!"

"No, let us stay apart."

41

"I've got to see you as you really are. Come out – or I can't take the responsibility of protecting you."

A pause.

"Very well."

John backed into the sun. The hole gaped black. And then he screamed . . .

*

The Sheriff milled around his car, mopping his neck frequently with a handkerchief. He made off suddenly towards the hill; thought better of it; came back and sat for a moment in the sparse shade of the car. All the time he was shooting anxious glances towards the mouth of the mine and his foot was scrabbing impatiently in the dust.

Then he started up and began to run. He met John fifty yards from the jalopy and grabbed the reeling body in time to prevent it from falling.

"Where's Ellen?"

"She's . . . safe . . ." John panted.

"Where? What have they done to you?"

"Nothing."

"Men don't look the way you look for nothing."

"I . . . I saw them, Matt! Horrible!"

"And you left Ellen with them?" Matt was shouting into the white face.

"She's safe . . . as long as we don't interfere."

Haltingly he poured his story into the incredulous ears of the other. "You see?" he finished. "They're mad to get away because they know we'd kill them if we could. And we would! We'd kill them because they're different. Like when we squash spiders – but this time it would be with even more cause! We're just not advanced enough to stand the impact of other types of living beings with better brains than ourselves!

"That," he added, "is why they've been hiding behind other people's faces."

He had told all he knew. Now he looked into Matt's face, expecting to find some understanding there; but what he saw was a typical human face – the face of a lord of creation, brave, stubborn . . .

"All I know is this," Matt grunted." They've got five people over there, and it's up to us to get 'em out."

"When are you going to stop being a badge and do some thinking?"

"A thing's wrong – so someone's got to set it right. Okay! You won't set it right! But I will, see?"

"Matt, listen to me! They weren't fooling! They need a few more hours. If you go to them with violence now . . . they'll kill Ellen!"

He lunged with two tired and would-be restraining hands. Matt's hand flashed up and caught the front of his shirt.

"Look at you – you're all washed up. You're hysterical. Remember what I am? I'm the Sheriff – someone responsible for the law around here. And the law says there's to be a posse to clear those devils out!"

John's despairful fist caught Matt's chin a glancing blow. Matt had expected it and was ready. John was dimly aware of hitting the dust, of being lifted and dumped into the car. When he came to himself in the rattling car he knew a stupefying feeling of contempt for himself.

The rushing air revived him; the guilt inside him blossomed into an intolerable growth; here in Matt was truly boneheaded conduct – conduct asking for disaster – and he was letting himself be pushed around.

Matt was concentrating on his driving. John advanced his hand slowly to the shaking door of the car and stole a glance at the road. He knew the spot ahead where there was a bank of soft, crash-breaking sand . . .

When the time came he was out of the speeding car like an acrobat and turning over and over on the soft sand; and then he staggered up and began to run across the desert at right angles to the road.

When he was out of breath he turned. Far away stood the car with Matt beside it waving both arms at him. He waved his arms back, almost grinning . . .

*

It was a long way back to the hills. The sun was low in the sky by the time he reached the spot where the collapsed gallery gave on to the hillside. Passing the pile of earth, from which he had emerged earlier that day like a crushed and frightened rabbit, his foot struck something metallic. The torch! He pocketed it thankfully

Higher. Here was the real entrance to the mine. He went into the blackness, holding the beam in front of him, trying not to think of the nightmare thing he had seen there, trying not to open his mind to the voices he expected to sound within it at any moment. His brain cringed!

But nothing happened; and the passage seemed to be widening.

Suddenly it was an almost circular chamber hewn out of rock; and at the same time he heard the sounds of work around the buried spaceship – the tapping and scraping, like the activities of underground dwarfs in fairy tales.

And then he heard a sound like an intake of breath. He swung the torch.

"Who's there?"

His beam flashed across the space.

"Ellen!"

She stood there, ten yards from him, unhurt, cool.

"Ellen! Are you all right? I . . ."

Then she spoke. Or didn't speak. The voice was not a sound – not words – but a set of questionings popping thought-like into his head:

"Why have you come back? Who have you brought with you? Why do you wish to destroy us?"

He felt weak. He had lost her. This was not Ellen; or if it

was Ellen's body in front of him, something else was in possession.

He said: "I came back to warn you. Some men of my world are on their way here . . ."

"I know" – her thought-voice said inside him – "there are a dozen cars on the road from the town this minute."

"I tried to stop them . . ."

"We are not yet ready. Not quite ready."

"Take me to . . . to your friends. I want to help."

"Come."

He followed her; and soon the ground sloped, the walls widened and the work-sounds became a roar. There was light, blue and vibrant – the naked light of energy – and a prickling went over him as he breathed an air like the aftermath of storm, all washed clean with electricity.

For the second time in his life he saw the spaceship, the six-sided globe with its hull aglow, as if the contained force of its motors was a sort of lifeblood making its plates flush like flesh.

Around the ship the rock and earth had been cleared; above it the massed debris shut out the sun. Busy round the open port, through which strange mechanisms could be glimpsed, were a dozen figures familiar as home. He recognised the backs of Doctor Snell, of Frank . . . and then one of the figures turned and came towards him. He nearly collapsed . . .

He stared open-jawed at *himself*!

*

The other-John – the man with the face he had never seen except in mirrors – came swiftly to him and gazed without curiosity. The sad thought of the other-John came to birth in his head:

"So the men of your world are on their way, and will destroy us?"

He answered with another statement. "You are not *me* . . . and *that* is not Ellen."

"All we took are safe. But if those others of your world come to destroy us they will be destroyed themselves. There is enough power here to tear your world apart."

"Listen to me," John said. "There's still a way."

"Is there? All we need is time."

John gazed past his double to the saffron-glowing space-ship, which seemed to leap and tremble as if ready that instant to break its bonds of rock and thunder into the sky; at the busy figures – so like his friends and yet so obviously not his friends – at the brilliantly-lit port with its strange glimpse of a motive-force fit to hurl this massive thing to the outer stars. And his inner ear almost heard the sound of arrival of Matt's car and the cars of the posse. But that was impossible; it was his time-sense that told him they must by now be at the foot of the hill . . .

"Give me back the people of my world," he said. "– the girl and the men; between us we shall stop those others, and you will fly away in peace."

"How can I trust you?"

"Didn't you say you could tear the earth apart? If we attack you, you could reach out and destroy us. Why are you so . . . so afraid of us?"

"Because you might force us to kill. Our world is very old; our memories are longer than yours; and we have grown out of the habit of killing and don't like such a thing forced upon us."

"You are wiser than the best of us," John said: and then a longing struck him, and he added: "Will you change into your natural form and let me see you as you are?"

Before his eyes he watched the image of himself melt drooling into gas and liquid; watched the great yellow eye materialise, the whipcord tendons and liver-coloured tentacles wave. He smiled in the sudden, sure knowledge that

46

all his loathing, his small-town horror, had vanished and would never come back.

"Remember us when you get to the stars," he said, "and come back in a thousand years. And now, there's no time to lose – give me my friends and let me get out of here!"

Thoughts in this place ran like speech. John was dimly aware that the human forms about the ship had vanished; instead were the now familiar glob-creatures, some already slithering into the open port. The vibrations of the ship shook the earth; but when he heard an actual human voice the sound shook him to the depths of his being.

"John! Oh, John!"

Ellen had darted, released from the rocky spaces behind the ship. She was in his arms, and the unmistakably solid and human forms of Snell, the two telephone men and the pair of missing prospectors were about him.

"Quick!" he said. "No explanations – we've to get back up the shaft – or we'll all be dead!"

*

The posse climbed the hill – Matt, his deputy, a crowd of the grim and worthy citizens of Sand Rock.

"Hear anything?"

"Sure, Matt – kind o' vibrations."

"Matt, I'm sure scared – don't mind admittin'."

"Well," Matt grunted, "guess none of us feel so good."

"What's best to do?"

"We goin' to the crater, or to the old workings?"

"I reckon we might look at the crater first," Matt said.

"What's that?" The deputy was pointing into the heavy dusk.

With a crunch of rock a whole crowd of people came diagonally down the hill.

"Matt, stop! Don't go near that crater!"

"Putnam! What in jeepers . . . and Ellen! Why . . ."

"It's all right! We're all here. But we've got to clear off quickly, because – "

He dragged Ellen down – everyone dropped down – as a dull, deep explosion heaved the ground beneath them and made the hill shake and dance and throw bits of itself overside like droplets.

The explosion ended in a loud, continuous blare too deep to be called a scream – a noise that grated inside the very bones of their bodies and made every face grimace.

"Are *they* down there?" Matt gasped. "Well, I guess that takes care of 'em!"

"Yes," John repeated. "That takes care of them. But don't get up . . ."

There came a sound like the ground being sick, and they all sensed rather than saw that the piled rocks which had lain in the crater were now being flung into the night sky like dust. They lay cowering, expecting the crushing blows. Not far away the ground-rocks splintered as the stuff came down.

Seconds seemed like years as they waited.

And like a whirlwind the great bright thing came rushing from the core of the hill, vertically upwards, and shot in dwindling fire into the starbright air, printing a fiery and fast-fading streak against the background of the hills.

The humans lay there for minutes.

Matt rose to his feet and spoke soberly.

"They've gone."

"For good, John?" It was Ellen, whispering.

"Not for good," John said. "It wasn't quite the right point in history for us to meet. But they'll be back a thousand years from now."

*

Far above the atmosphere, speeding from the planet, the Commander spoke to the Astrogator:

"Sometime we'll go back."

"In a short time they'll have space-travel themselves. They might come to us."

The Commander gave the Oolean version of a shudder. He said: "It's easier to make spaceships than friends."

THE CONQUEST OF SPACE

(Paramount, 1955)
Starring: Walter Brooke, Eric Fleming
& William Hopper
Directed by Byron Haskin
Screenplayed based on "Life On Mars"
by Werner von Braun

Not to be outdone by the other major studios, Paramount
Pictures in 1955 bought the rights to a story by a man who
was then actually involved in helping to make space flight a
reality, Werner von Braun (1912–1977), a German-born
rocket scientist who had earlier designed the infamous V2
rockets which bombed London at the end of the Second World
War. Von Braun had, in fact, turned his youthful enthusiasm
for the works of Jules Verne and H.G. Wells into practical
research, but after the fall of Germany he was recruited by the
Americans to work with their own scientists on space exploration. The V2 which he had seen used with such destruc-
tive purpose now became the prototype for a whole new
generation of rockets which would later take men to the
moon and launch probes to the other planets. The film-maker
charged with bringing to the cinema screen Von Braun's
vision of a journey to Mars was the resourceful George
Pal who, just as he had done when making *Destination
Moon*, again surrounded himself with experts including
Chesley Bonestell, Will Ley and designers Hal Pereira and
J. McMillan Johnson – all of whom now had the added
benefit of working in technicolour. To direct, Pal hired Byron
Haskins, who likewise brought a special skill to the job having
previously been the head of the Special Effects department at
the rival Warner Brothers studios. In the movie, the journey of
the rocket ship through space was brought to life by Haskins

with a series of notable effects sequences – including a space burial with the corpse falling slowly towards the sun – and culminating in an evocative red landscape which had been specialy envisioned by Chesley Bonestell to represent the surface of Mars. Sadly, the pictures subsequently sent back to earth by NASA's orbiting spacecraft have shown the reality to be rather different. This, however, does nothing to spoil a viewing of the picture today, or of reading the story on which it was based by the man who probably did more than anyone else to realise man's long dream of conquering space. . .

Mckay sat easily in his seat on the flight deck, watching Bill Squire beside him at the controls of *Goddard*, the big rocket-nosed glider which had launched them from the expedition's cargo ship orbiting 620 miles out from the surface of Mars. The glider was following a free-coasting spiral around the red planet, and McKay felt a slight forward pull on his shoulder straps with the retarding effect of air drag in the weak Martian atmosphere.

He glanced down through binoculars from their present height of ninety-six miles at the multicoloured spectacle beneath, then back at Squire whose eyes were fixed on the dials in front of him. This was no longer space flight. He was using aircraft controls.

The long ellipse carried them out of the Martian day and into night as *Goddard* winged downwards. But half an hour later the night sky became a dusky cyclorama shaded to purple, and from purple to blue. At last the glider emerged into full sunlight.

McKay looked around at the ten astronauts who had been his companions on the deep-space voyage of 260 days from the artificial satellite *Lunetta*, poised in orbit above Earth. With the exception of Sterling, the brilliant young archeologist, these men were all experienced pioneers of the space age.

No emotion showed in their faces, but McKay, leader of this first expedition to explore a distant planet, guessed that all of them shared the same apprehension. A landing on unknown terrain without a prepared runway was tricky business. No better man for it than Bill Squire, but who knew what the surface of Mars would be like? Pulverized rock? Sand? Lava dust? How would the skis of the tandem landing gear behave when they touched down? Would the surface hold, or would the treads break through brittle crust, bringing them to a catastrophic stop?

They were on course. The altimeter showed 2,500 feet, and McKay studied the terrain, picking out features from the pilot's contour map.

The ground was coming up fast now, and Squire was turning the nose of the glider south. McKay reached up to tighten the shoulder straps and turned to nod at the men behind him. Then he braced for contact, which would come at 120 miles an hour.

Dust rose in a cloud outside *Goddard's* windows with the first impact and there were two or three stunning jolts as the skis bumped over the surface. But the great glider gradually rumbled to a stop, steadied by its outrigger skids. Squire grinned – he'd put the first ship down on Mars!

McKay unbuckled his straps and stood up. "Nice landing, Bill," he said, and turned to face the others. "Now don't get excited. We'll try some knee bends before we go outside. Quickest way I know to shake out the after-effects of weightlessness. And we are going to need our strength."

He put the crew through calisthenics and then had them close the helmet visors of their pressure suits. One by one they worked their way through the airlock and assembled on the wing, twelve adventurers in space suits, the first Earthmen to scan Mars' desolate landscape. For their base they had picked the area called Libya, south of Moeris Lacus and directly athwart the Martian equator.

"It's like desert country in our southwest," said Duncan Ross, their geologist, into his helmet microphone.

"Rugged," McKay agreed. "Surface seems to be mostly reddish-yellow sand." He turned to the pilot. "You got us here, Bill, so you should be the first man to touch down. Jump, boy!"

"Not with my legs as weak as they are," Squire protested. "I'm going to slide." He dropped to the trailing-edge flaps and coasted part of the eighteen feet to the ground. "Nothing to it," he said into his microphone. "Gravity's too weak to let you drop hard." McKay could see him grinning. "Hey!" Bill called. "That was the first message from Mars!"

McKay laughed and turned to John Berger, the radio operator. "Get inside and flash *Oberth*," he said to the radio operator. *Oberth* was the mother ship with a crew of three, which would continue to orbit above the planet until the expedition was ready to return to earth, 449 days from now. "Tell Phil Boyer it was a perfect landing with all personnel and equipment intact," he said. "Tell him we're proceeding now to set up camp."

The others were on the ground when McKay jumped to join them. Spottswood and Burke, the engineers, had opened the cargo bay and were lowering two tractors from the yawning belly. The others were erecting the hermetic tent which contained light cots, chairs and cooking equipment. The tent would be inflated by the standard "spaceman's atmosphere" of forty per cent. oxygen and sixty per cent. helium in which space suits could be replenished.

"Let's get the return rocket erected," McKay said. "Detach the forward section of *Goddard* from the wings," he ordered.

Under Spottswood's skilled direction the tractors hooked on, and soon a gap appeared between the slim fore part of the glider's body and its thicker rear section. Cables were attached to the bullet-shaped nose, and the tractors drew it upright, settling it on four levelling jacks. Guy wires secured the sleek return rocket against heavy winds.

McKay inspected the job with satisfaction.

"Now we know we can get away fast in case of trouble," he said. "Not that we'll find any." But this was an intrusion into unexplored territory, and George McKay remembered the tales he had read since childhood about hostile monsters on Mars.

Herbert Breitstein, the chemist, was preparing dinner when they entered the pressure tent. This would be the first food they would eat normally with knives and forks since they left *Lunetta* nearly nine months before. But the others were too tired to care much. They took off their space suits in the air-conditioned interior, ate a quick meal around the table and then, after McKay had detailed the order in which they would stand watch during the night, the men lay down on their aluminium cots. McKay breathed a quick prayer of thanks for their safe landing and then he was asleep . . .

They were up shortly after dawn, and at breakfast McKay gave orders for the day. "I'll take the Number One tractor and look around a bit. Departure in half an hour," he said. "Sterling, Ross and Burke will go with me. Spottswood, I want you and the others to make a thorough check of *Goddard's* communication equipment. We'll keep in touch with the base by radio, and Berger will relay every message back to *Oberth*. All clear ?"

Two hours later their lumbering tractor was approaching a conical out-cropping of the bright yellow mountain range which formed one side of the valley where they had set up their base. McKay was at the controls. Suddenly Sterling called from the back seat, "Colonel, would you stop a minute while I put my glasses on that ridge?"

McKay braked the treads, and Sterling stood up in the pressurized interior. "It *is* – I swear there's a spidery-looking ancient temple up there," he said excitedly. "It's like a Grecian ruin."

The others brought up their glasses. "You're right," Duncan Ross said. "That thing was built! Funny – the columns are so thin that any good breeze would bring the whole thing down."

"I guess Martian gravity's your answer to that," McKay said. "It didn't take long to prove there was life on this planet once." He felt a tingle of excitement. Was there still life around here? For a moment he wondered if they had been foolhardy not to bring any weapons along with them.

They churned forward, Sterling trying desperately to keep his binoculars steady against the pitching and yawing. Then he almost shouted. "Behind that ruin and to the right – there's something shaped like an oversized army hut."

McKay changed course and put on more speed till they had come within fifty yards of the structure. All of them surveyed the curving walls.

"It looks remarkably unlike anything ancient," McKay said. "We'll investigate." He reached for his space helmet and nodded to Sterling and Ross. "Burke, you guard the tractor," he ordered, "while the three of us do a reconnaissance. If there's trouble, radio the base and start back immediately to report what's happened."

He dropped through the airlock, with Sterling and Ross close behind, and they approached the odd structure cautiously. Ross tapped the material of the exterior with his geologist's hammer.

"Hard as granite," he said.

They continued around the building. After a short distance the three explorers stopped. A set of perfect steps was cut at the point where the building's end curved away from the semicylindrical main portion.

"Stay here," McKay said. "I'm going up."

They saw him climb the steps to the rim of a rounded roof. Suddenly he stopped abruptly. For over a minute they saw him stare down, motionless. Finally, his staccato voice resounded from their helmet earphones. "Sterling and Ross, come up at once," he said. "I'm standing beside a heavy glass roof. There are machines below, I think – fourteen big red casings that could be turbine housings. The interior seems covered with silvery-white metal." Suddenly his voice recovered from the excitement, and he inquired in the tone of an experienced radio operator: "Burke, do you read me? Over."

"Loud and clear," came back Burke's awed voice.

"Good, just keep the tape-recorder running. This is something for keeps."

Sterling and Ross were beside him now, peering into the interior. "Over by that furthest casing," Sterling said hoarsely. "There's someone moving. See him, Ross?"

The figure came slowly towards them, unaware of the Earthmen. He appeared to be checking the gauges which were visible on the machines. There was not only life on Mars – they had run into an outpost of a highly developed Martian civilization! But McKay kept his voice steady as he droned out a description of the subterranean installation into his helmet microphone, which was heard not only by Burke but by the party at the base camp.

". . . an undersized, dark-haired man – repeat 'man'. Definitely human in appearance. Fair, white skin, beardless, dressed in an oriental-looking long white tunic with gay coloured stitching."

Ross broke in as the creature came into full view. "Look at the size of that head," he muttered. "If what's inside is all brains we can learn plenty here!"

"Suppose he sees us?" Sterling whispered.

"We want him to," McKay answered. "We're bound to run into Martians sooner or later." He looked sharply at the others. "Anybody worried?"

"No, sir," Ross said stolidly, while young Sterling swallowed dryly and shook his head.

"Let's make him see us," McKay said. He rapped gently on the glass with the hasp of his knife. Below them the man stopped and looked up, momentarily startled. Then he waved his hand in what seemed a friendly gesture. McKay talked constantly into his microphone so that every detail would be recorded by both Burke and the party at the base. He waved back at the Martian, pointed to himself and his companions, then towards the level where the figure stood. The Martian considered for a moment, then he smiled and pointed to the end of the building where the three explorers stood. He walked in that direction and disappeared through a door.

"Seems friendly enough," Ross said. "But will he let us in?"

The answer came a moment later when a panel slid back beside them at the top of the steps. The opening widened rapidly until it became a rectangular door within which they could see the Martian behind a curving sheet of glass. He beckoned them to come through the opening.

McKay nodded, spoke a final, full message into his microphone to tell the others what was happening. Then the three men stepped inside, and the door slid rapidly shut behind them.

"I don't like this," Sterling began apprehensively, as the Martian continued to stare at them through the glass.

McKay cautioned him sharply. "Steady, Pete. We'll take it as it comes. Look at your pressure gauge. We're in an airlock."

The indicator showed four-sevenths of their space-suit pressure, and Ross drew a gas-analyzer from his belt: 39 per cent, oxygen, .3 per cent. carbon dioxide. The remainder was some sort of neutral gas.

"I hope it's nitrogen," Ross muttered.

McKay hoped so, too.

The hissing of the entering pressure ceased, and the glass partition slid out of sight. The man smiled, bowed and placed his hand over the left side of his chest. The three explorers repeated the gesture and went in. The glass partition closed at the push of a button, and the platform began to sink. Presently they stepped out on to the floor of the red machines.

The Martian led them the length of the great hall. As they strode along, McKay glanced anxiously at his pressure indicator and decided to risk the atmosphere. He depressurized his suit, took off his helmet and gulped a deep breath. Nothing happened, and he made a gesture to the others that everything was all right and for them to do the same.

They now entered a long corridor. It glowed with soft light which seemed to come evenly from the walls, roof and floor, for there were neither visible artificial light sources nor windows.

"They've found the secret of the firefly!" Sterling said wonderingly. "Light without heat."

The corridor ended in a large room hung with crimson textiles. Seated at a long, ebony-coloured table was an elderly Martian, dignified and imposing. Beside him was a younger man. They both rose as the little party entered. They placed their hands over their left chests and bowed solemnly, motioning the newcomers to be seated.

Their guide now began to talk to his chief, in a low, musical voice, occasionally interrupted by what were obviously questions. McKay was no linguist, and he glanced at Sterling who spoke a dozen languages easily. But the young archeologist shook his head and smiled nervously.

"Do you suppose they're talking about what to do with us?" he asked.

McKay shrugged his shoulders. "We'll know soon," he said. As he spoke the elderly Martian turned to look at him questioningly across the table. McKay drew a pencil from his pocket and made motions of writing.

The Martian twisted a knob at the edge of the table, and a white, luminescent rectangle appeared in front of McKay. McKay began to sketch the solar system, and the Martians watched as he traced the ellipse of the space-ship's flight. Then they smiled, indicating that they understood, and the young Martian opened a cabinet door and turned a dial. There was a low-pitched hum, interrupted by a recording of Phil Boyer's voice as the party in *Goddard* left *Oberth* the day before, and McKay's reply, "Happy orbiting, Phil."

Instantly the Martians looked at McKay questioningly. There was something impenetrable about their politeness. No wonder they had greeted their visitors calmly. They had listened in on the expedition's radio traffic and recorded it!

McKay wondered if they caught the meaning of the messages. "You understood?" he asked in English.

All three looked blank. Then the chief Martian brought out a large sheet which contained a schematic drawing marked in circled symbols and shaped like a pyramid. He pointed to one of the circles on the baseline and then to himself. Next he indicated a large circle at the apex of the pyramid and made a sweeping gesture, uttering a word which sounded like "Ahla". He pointed to his visitors and again said "Ahla."

"That's a government organization chart if I've ever seen one," Sterling said. "To think that we've come all the way across the solar system only to get tangled up in red tape! I think Ahla's the head man, and our ancient friend plans to send us to him – through channels, of course!"

McKay produced an astronomer's map of Mars that he had brought along and spread it on the table. McKay guessed it must seem pretty crude, but he pointed to Libya, where they had landed. The Martians nodded. Then he handed the pencil to the white-haired Martian and said, "Ahla," in a questioning tone.

His host took the pencil and drew a circle in the very centre of Lacus Solis. "Ahla," he repeated firmly. He placed his finger on Libya and drew it across the map till it paused at the circle. Then he pointed to the Earthmen.

"Ahla must be the chief city, not the name of the head man," McKay said to Ross and Sterling. "His attitude is so positive I think he's got some kind of transport. It's a good two thousand miles from here."

He stepped forward and made a gesture of speaking into a microphone. Instantly the young Martian handed McKay an instrument like any standard microphone.

"McKay to Tractor One and base," McKay droned. "Over."

John Berger's voice cut in. "Base to Colonel McKay – just a moment, sir." And then there was Bill Squire. "Are you all right, George? Over."

"Everything's fine," McKay said. "We're in this big building you've heard about. There are three Martians down here. We've had a map exercise, and they want us to go to Ahla, which seems to be the name of their capital. It's in Lacus Solis. Over."

Squire was obviously agitated. "That's two thousand miles from here. How are you going to get there? Over."

"I haven't the slightest idea, but so far these people seem remarkably friendly. No evidence of coercion or hostility. No weapons about. They're fantastically advanced technologically. And, Bill, they're wonderfully impressive people. There's a calmness about them that makes me think this civilization is old – very old. Over."

"But suppose they're just luring you to visit their king – or whatever he is. Leaving the rough stuff to high authority. Have you thought of that one? Over."

"I've thought of that one – and a lot more," said McKay crisply. "I don't see what else there is to do but go to Ahla. Our directive from Washington was to explore Mars. There are millions of dollars riding on this expedition, and I think we're on the edge of a magnificent discovery. We'll see it through. Burke, you're to return to base. All of you will wait till I can communicate again. Better post a double guard tonight. The Martians know where you are now. That's all, Bill. You're in command."

While McKay was speaking, the chief Martian had been giving instructions to their guide. Now the younger man stepped forward and signified they were ready. McKay and the others followed their guide into an elevator.

Down they went into the mass of Mars. But at last the car came to a gentle stop, and they were ushered into a gleaming, vault-like chamber about seventy feet long and ten feet high. Along one wall was a series of round windows, their lower rims touching the floor. They peered through.

Duncan Ross laughed excitedly. "This is enough to make any New Yorker feel at home," he said. "It's a subway!"

"But no rails," objected Sterling. "Same firefly illumination as upstairs. How do you suppose they do it?"

Behind one of the windows they saw a compartment equipped with fixed, comfortable chairs. The Martian turned a small handle, and the glass rose into the ceiling. They went inside, and the Martian motioned them to the chairs, which were equipped with seat belts.

Their guide seated himself in the forward end of the compartment before a small control panel. They heard his voice against the microphone, then a buzzer sounded, and the platform door slid down silently, followed by the compartment door itself.

They could see over the Martian's shoulder through another round window into the gleaming white tunnel ahead. The Martian flipped a few switches on the control panel and listened to a voice which came back through his radio telephone. Then he moved back, smiling reassuringly, to strap himself into a seat beside them.

Presently there were three bright flashes from the panel, followed in a few moments by a bright orange-red flash, and they were pressed into their seats by an acceleration like the effect of a rocket blast-off. But there was no noise whatsoever.

McKay punched his stop watch. His experienced feelings told him that he was undergoing not less than three G's pressure, and it continued for twenty seconds. This meant that they were moving at supersonic speed. But the question was – how?

His engineering mind could guess part of the solution. The compartment was pressurized, but the tunnel had been emptied of all atmosphere. *They were moving through a vacuum!*

There was absolutely no sound – no clicking of rail joints, no motor hum. Maybe the Martian could enlighten him further, in spite of the language barrier.

McKay took out a notebook and quickly sketched a streamlined train. Then he touched the Martian's arm, pointed to the sketch, indicated the wheels and rails. He waved his arm and pointed ahead. The Martian nodded and took the notebook and pencil. He worked rapidly, and on the opposite page appeared an engineering drawing. A wheel was sketched and crossed out. No wheels! A rail appeared under the wheel and was also crossed out.

The Martian's sketch then showed the secret of the transportation system. At each end of their car was an electric magnet with its poles on either side of a supporting rail in the roof of the tunnel. They kept their car magnetically suspended without bodily contact between magnet and rail. McKay was overcome with admiration at the device which provided such a free-floating frictionless support. Electronically the magnetizing current was so controlled that the width of the gap remained constant, regardless of load or forward motion.

He nodded to show that he had understood, for the sketch also explained what gave their car its propulsion. It was an application of the solenoid gun principle which ballistic experts on Earth had dreamed of for years, but had never succeeded in putting to practical use. A never-ending chain of coils one ahead of the other was energized in programmed succession. Surrounded by the coils, but attached to the roof of their car was a string of permanent magnets which was pulled through the coils as they were energized. This was substantially an electric motor's armature moving in a straight line instead of rotating. They were travelling almost as fast as a space rocket, but with a minimum expenditure of power as there were no friction losses.

McKay turned to Ross. "The minds that could develop this subway system could have put a space ship on earth years ago," he said. "I wonder why they didn't."

Far down the tunnel McKay saw the lighted windows of what must be a station appear and pass them so rapidly that the flash of light was almost imperceptible. There must be an automatic block-signal system of unparalleled efficiency, for no operator, however smart the Martians were, could cope with this enormous speed. Yes, their voyage was obviously controlled by some mechanism outside. Occasionally they slowed, then went on as the next block opened up.

McKay wondered how long it would take them to reach Lacus Solis. He glanced at the stop watch. They had been in motion one hour and fifty-three minutes. But who knew just how fast they were travelling?

Sterling had been dozing but now he woke up and leaned forward. "I wonder what this Ahla is like," he said. "Maybe our friend can show us." He took out his own notebook and, remembering the spidery temple, drew a city of thinly columned buildings and houses, with wide, tree-lined streets. Martians in fanciful spacesuits walked about. He showed it to their guide. "Ahla?" he said. "Ahla?"

The Martian looked in bewilderment for a moment. Then he laughed and shook his head. He took the notebook and worked busily for ten minutes, then handed it back.

"Ahla's underground!" Sterling cried. "See? A big vertical city with central squares in layers and parks at the top open to the sky but enclosed with domed glass roofs. Do you suppose the whole Martian population lives underground?"

"I've suspected it," McKay said. "I think Mars once had atmosphere enough to breathe, which explains that Grecian ruin. The change came gradually so that there was time to prepare technologically for an underground existence."

Sterling shivered. "It's uncanny," he said, "and we're going to be on Mars for more than a year. How do you two manage to keep calm with what we're going through? I don't mind admitting I'm scared."

McKay put a hand on his shoulder. "All right, Sterling," he said. "Just don't sound off. We're all a little scared in space. We keep it to ourselves so we don't infect others with our own fears."

It was twenty minutes later when the car gradually slowed, and the Martian signalled that their journey was to end. They were gliding soundlessly through a maze of switch-points. Outside they could see a marshalling yard with cars like their own, and bigger, windowless cars apparently designed for freight.

They moved to the windows to look out on the scene. Ahead, they saw a brightly lit area and a platform on which a crowd was clustered. They were still too far away to tell, but it seemed to McKay that they were all wearing tunics or robes.

"Ahla?" he said to their guide, who nodded vigorously.

McKay smiled and the guide smiled back. McKay could see no trace of guile in his face, but he found himself tense as the car slid along the platform.

"I'll go first," he said to Sterling and Ross. "Wait inside the car. If everything goes all right, follow me out."

Sterling moved up to his side.

"I'm not disobeying an order, Colonel," he said, "but if the Martians intend to clobber you, there's nothing to prevent them from clobbering us. Let's go together."

McKay smiled. "Good man, Pete," he said.

The inner door slid upwards. There was a hiss, and the outer door opened. The noise of many voices and of strange unearthly music swelled from the platform. Their guide jumped out and stood, bowing deferentially.

For just a moment McKay hesitated on the threshold of this climax to adventure. Then the three explorers stepped out into Ahla, the subterranean capital of Mars.

As the Earthmen left the car which had sped them 2,000 miles to Ahla through the subterranean tunnels of Mars, McKay's eyes swept the crowd of men and women on the platform. There might have been a hundred Martians, all dressed in some form of Grecian garment. McKay read eager curiosity in their faces – also calmness and complete absence of hostility.

"It's going to be okay," he said to Sterling and Ross. "We've got a reception committee!"

The music and voices ceased as an elderly Martian stepped forward. McKay advanced to meet him, with his companions just behind. When the Earthmen bowed and placed their hands over their hearts, a quick look of pleasure lighted the Martian's face, and he repeated the gesture. At the same time, a soft, welcoming "Ah" swelled from the crowd.

The Martian held out a handsome jewelled chain, similar to one he was wearing. McKay leaned down, and the dignitary hung it round his neck. Then, smiling warmly, he embraced the Earthman. The moment called for a token of goodwill in return. McKay wore a wrist watch, and he offered it now. The Martian seemed delighted and indicated that the Earthmen were to accompany him.

The three explorers, followed by their guide from the Libya station, advanced through the crowd. McKay studied the faces on each side. The tallest of the men was no more than five-feet-five, the women much smaller. They were by no means an unattractive race. They were slim and graceful and, except for the size of their heads, would have attracted no special notice on Earth if they wore conventional clothes. The dark hair of the men was close-cropped, but the women wore theirs long and pinned in a thick, heavy coil which covered the back of the head. They appraised their visitors calmly and talked softly among themselves.

From the station the party walked down a broad corridor which opened on a huge circular plaza, surrounded entirely by a window-studded wall some thirty storeys high. A solid roof covered the area at a height of perhaps 300 feet. The plaza was packed, and their host signalled a halt and spoke to the crowd. The people clapped, and again the sound of their massed "Ahs" swelled up, while the explorers bowed and stretched out their hands in greeting.

"They're wonderful!" Ross murmured.

Young Sterling said eagerly, "Their features are almost early Roman. And you know, some of these girls are really attractive. I'm sure you'd soon get accustomed to the size of their heads."

There were no vehicles of any sort in the plaza, and they could see no streets leading from it as the official who had become their host conducted them to a big gate leading into one of the "buildings" which surrounded it. There he spoke to the Martian from Libya and left them with gestures of farewell.

They passed through a sort of lobby. Then their guide took them down a corridor and, before they knew what had happened, they found themselves in the living room of a small apartment. A pretty maid appeared almost immediately with a tray of unfamiliar dishes and smilingly indicated that the explorers were to seat themselves.

"Tastes good anyway," Ross said. "I'd forgotten how hungry I was."

Sterling said, "I bet it's synthetic food of some sort – but not bad." He frowned a little. "First thing tomorrow I'm going to start learning Martian. It's a terrible handicap not to be able to talk with these people."

"With these girls, you mean," laughed McKay.

While they were eating and joking, their guide reappeared and motioned McKay to follow him. He took him into a small room and made him sit down in front of a table covered with green velvet. Then the guide left. Suddenly McKay saw Bill Squire sitting across the table from him.

"What on Mars are you doing here?" McKay shouted.

"I am not here at all, Colonel," Squire replied. "We are just talking over the Mars telephone."

It was a stunning experience. There was a life-size Bill Squire, in full colour and 3-D, sitting at the same velvet-covered table just four or five feet away speaking to him, yet it was nothing but an electronic illusion.

"The guys from the pumping station – that's what that subterranean installation in Libya really is – came over to our camp and indicated you had a message for us," Squire went on. "We decided you'd be unable to get in touch with us through anything but their own communication system and might need some assistance. That's why I left camp and took the chance of entering the pumping station."

McKay smiled. "These people must have figured you'd like to know what happened to us. Well, we're in Ahla, and you can cancel the guard duty, Bill. These are the friendliest people I've ever met. Pass this to *Oberth* for transmission to Earth. Tell them that tomorrow we'll begin a daily half-hour broadcast. Over and out."

When McKay opened the door of the telephone room, Sterling called excitedly from one of the bedrooms. "Look, Colonel," he said, pointing to a small disc. "Pillow-speakers. There's one with every bed. I'll bet they are going to give us a lesson in first-grade Martian while we're asleep."

"I hope it works," McKay said. "I've never used one of these things, but they're being tried out on Earth by some researchers to cram information through the subconscious.

I wonder how they are going to do it though, since they can't speak English. Anyway, I have confidence that they know what they're doing. This could cut down the language barrier in no time . . ."

When McKay awoke the next morning, the guide came into the bedroom. The man spoke, and sounds which had been gibberish the day before translated instantly in McKay's startled mind.

"Good morning," the Martian said. "I am Karis. Do you understand me?"

McKay astonished himself by replying in simple Martian. "Yes, I understand you. My name is George McKay. My companions are Peter Sterling and Duncan Ross."

"Thank you," said Karis politely. "I will wake them now. I am to be your personal aide while you are on Mars." He smiled. "You speak Martian very well," he said, "but we are using only easy words. In a few nights the pillow-speaker will teach you all of our language."

After breakfast, the Earthmen were taken on a sight-seeing tour of the capital. Everywhere they met with unfailing courtesy. Karis explained the layout of the city as they stood before a model in the Municipal Building. A cutaway section showed that Ahla was twenty miles in diameter and exactly circular. The depth in the city centre was just under a mile, and its hub was composed of fifteen circular plazas, layered one above the other, and each a thousand feet in diameter.

Ahla had no streets, but from the rim of each plaza tubes of the radial metropolitan transit system extended to residential sections in all directions and to the many parks. These, they could see from the model, were vast subterranean open spaces in the top floor of the city, with transparent plexidomes to let in the sun.

The cleanliness of Ahla astounded the visitors. There was no dust, Karis explained, because it was removed by the central air-conditioning system, which also controlled the temperature and humidity. There were no streets, automobiles, pedestrian problems or crowded trains.

All that week, the Earthmen were kept busy with inspections and receptions. At a hospital they witnessed an operation in which a man whose arm had been destroyed in an accident was given another.

"We have a stock-pile of all parts of the body," explained a doctor matter-of-factly. "They are willed to us."

The Earthmen found the school they visited that afternoon more exhilarating. In one classroom six-year-olds were studying chemistry. A lecturer was rushing through the subject at terrifying speed. Within thirty minutes he covered the periodic system of elements and the mystery of electrical cohesion of atoms when forming molecules.

"We don't expect them to remember all this," the teacher explained as they left the room. "We just give them a grasp of the fundamentals. Learning in detail takes place at night through the pillow-speakers."

Each day McKay spent half an hour broadcasting a report to the base for transmission to Earth via the orbiting ship, *Oberth*. Each night their knowledge of Martian was increased through more advanced language tapes fed into their pillow-speakers. Sterling busied himself creating tapes in English at the request of the professors, so that Martians could learn one of the languages of Earth.

On the fifth day of their visit, McKay was amused to have two little girls greet him on Plaza 12 with "Good morning, Earthman." There was hardly a trace of Martian accent.

The other members of the expedition were being brought to Ahla that afternoon, leaving only the radio operator and two engineers at the base. But they had not arrived before McKay, Sterling and Ross had to leave the hotel.

That evening, Karis had arranged to take them to the house of Oraze, the leading astronomer of Mars. The Earthmen followed him into a subway station across the plaza. It was their first experience with the local transit system. They entered one of the small cars passing the platform at a walking pace, and Karis dialled a three-digit combination on a panel. They moved slowly to a point where unused cars were rotated back to the platform, but their own car flew down a straight tunnel until it reached a circular gallery. The number of this gallery, Karis explained, was controlled by the first digit he dialled.

"Now, you see, the car is being detached from its track and raised to the level where Oraze lives," he said. "The floor level is what the second digit of the dial directs."

The Earthmen watched out the window as their car passed nine levels till it came to Plaza 15.

"This is the top level," Karis pointed out. "Oraze lives here because as an astronomer he must be able to look out at the sky. His observatory is in the nearby park."

The car shot off to the left down the circular gallery and came to a stop at the location indicated by the third digit. As they left the car, its doors closed, and it started automatically on the return journey.

Oraze greeted them at the subway door of his spacious, modern-appearing apartment, and through a window in the entrance hall McKay could see the unblinking stars bright in the dark velvet firmament. The astronomer appeared to be a man in his fifties. He introduced his wife Linnith, his son Omi and his pretty daughter Arum.

Entering the dining room, the Earthmen and the Martians seated themselves at a table which was bare except for a dark red tablecloth. Omi handed each of them a small disc, and Linnith dimmed the illumination. A colour television screen lighted, and upon it in slow procession passed the dishes that were available. Each person pushed the buttons of his disc when he saw something he liked. The Earthmen were now familiar with Martian food, though this was their first try at selecting it electronically.

Presently there was a clicking sound. Linnith opened a door in the wall behind which were seven shining trays with the dishes each person had ordered. Spoons, forks, knives and napkins were also provided.

"It is a tubular delivery system," Arum explained, "which reaches every house in Ahla. I like it because there is no dish-washing. We return everything by the tubes."

Later Oraze produced a globe of Earth and talked astronomy with the Earthmen, while Linnith and the young people listened.

The Earth, moving around the sun through an orbit inside that of Mars, appeared to Martians as the Morning or Evening Star, Oraze explained, just as Venus appears to inhabitants of Earth. This, he added apologetically, makes observation by Martians more difficult than for Earth's astronomers when they study Mars.

Yet Martian observation, in spite of this and the curtain caused by Earth's more extended cloud cover, was remarkably advanced. They had determined seasonal, climatic and temperature data quite accurately, and their estimate of the composition of Earth's atmosphere was vastly superior to the information McKay had been given about Mars.

Martian science had conceived no very high opinion of the intelligence of Earthlings, the explorers learned, though Oraze added politely that this was probably because they had no knowledge of the kind of lives people on Earth led.

"Our conclusions," he said, "were based mainly on the fact that we saw you have our scarcest commodity – water – in ample supply. We couldn't conceive of a civilization which would permit deserts to exist when so much water is available to make them bloom like the many fertile areas on Earth we observed through our telescopes."

"Well, it's true that we are still stupid enough to have deserts," McKay said. "But you must admit, Oraze, that we know enough technology to put men on Mars."

"This seems a good time to clear up a mystery," Duncan Ross said. "Have you Martians ever visited Earth?"

"You may put your mind at rest," Oraze replied. "Martians feel no urge to storm the heavens. The centuries have dulled us in our subterranean burrows, and we are few who direct the attention of our fellow citizens to the stars."

"But how can that be," Ross pursued, "when all your people are so religious – so illuminated by a light that seems to come from heaven itself?"

"Our Martian God does not live in heaven," Oraze said softly. "A few of our better folk still keep Him in their hearts. But, in the minds of the majority, He has gradually been forgotten."

"But this whole planet is bursting with creative energy!" Peter protested. "Don't the easier living conditions on Earth tempt some of your adventurous souls?"

"Ah, but where are the adventurers?" asked Oraze resignedly. "You Earthmen have been impressed by super-ficialities. All our technological refinements are a screen for an age-weary, languid, satiated culture.

"You have told me that a few pioneering races civilized your globe a few centuries ago. The same thing happened here tens of thousands of years ago. Wars and revolutions preceded the present stable planetary government. Then came a long period of advancing civilization and culture. Living standards improved despite the inroads of erosion and drought. The fine arts advanced to unheard-of perfection. Mass production of consumer goods almost wiped out the differences between rich and poor.

"When we had to go underground five thousand years ago, our technology was advanced to the point where it could provide all these marvels you have seen. But when this subterranean paradise was completed, the mainspring of Martian endeavour, divine discontent, began to flag. The adventurous spirit died, and we are now a planet of peace-seeking and easeful people, content to rest on the laurels of our ancestors. The spirit of adventure has been drowned in a sea of organization."

He paused contemplatively and then went on. "There is no escaping the laws of nature," he said. "The demands of millions of beings can be fulfilled only by the production of millions of articles, each from an identical mould. Standardization and yet more standardization is necessary. Eventually that means standardization of tastes and desires – and, yes, even of opinions.

"Our food this evening was available to all five million Ahlans. Our tablecloth is one of the ten types you can buy on this planet. Our clothes, our shoes, our habits – all are the same. This is the major tragedy of our lives. It presses upon all of us like a horrible nightmare. Inwardly we constantly battle the dull, grey uniformity our civilization imposes upon us.

"The advance of technology is primarily responsible for our planetary peace and plenty. But with it has come a soul-destroying equivalence of everything by which we live, and a conformity that makes it very unappealing for a young Martian to become different or outstanding."

McKay and the others were deeply moved by the emotion which had stirred Oraze out of his Martian calm as he spoke.

"Do you feel that something of this sort will happen to Earth's civilization in time?" McKay asked.

Oraze looked up and spoke slowly. "Yours is still a young planet and vast parts of it are still untouched deserts or jungles," he said. "If you can preserve your pioneering spirit and develop these areas, you still have several hundred years of creative activity ahead of you. But thereafter the Law of Nature will catch up with you, too." He paused. "How can you escape it? Your global population is increasing alarmingly, you tell me. How can the people be fed and clothed except by mass production?"

"And must mass production always lead to standardization?" Ross asked.

"I can only say that it has seemed so to us," Oraze observed. "Maybe we made a grave mistake when we built that TransMars Subway System. It made global transportation so cheap and so fast that our people, regardless of their cultural origin and heritage, migrated to the big cities where they found it easiest to make a living. Within a few generations this development destroyed the old values of home-grown customs and beliefs, for most newcomers were only too eager to abandon their old standards and embrace the glib, conformist, big-city culture in their place. Perhaps, if we had not promoted this trend, we would not have lost the spirit of adventure and life would be different here." Oraze laid his hand on McKay's arm. "If your visit could inspire our people, stir their laggard spirits – what a blessing you would have brought!"

The Earthmen were thoughtful on their trip back to the centre of Ahla. Even Karis seemed sad.

"Oraze is right in saying that your coming here may give us a rebirth of adventure," he said. "People talk about nothing but your expedition. It is as though you had come in an enchanted ship."

McKay laughed. "When are you going to produce my other men from your enchanted subway?" he asked.

"I think we shall find them at the hotel now," Karis said.

He was right. And McKay immediately set up a schedule so that their observation of every phase of life on Mars would be stored in notebooks before their departure. Before, the 449 days they would have to spend on a barren Mars, or at least in orbit around Mars, had seemed a lonely prospect. The date of departure was fixed by the necessity of leaving Mars when the Earth was at a certain point on its orbit. Now, when they had made the amazing discovery that Mars was bustling with life, a year and three months seemed too short a span.

"The only way we can carry out our mission," McKay said, "is to split up. Every man will do the jobs his field of knowledge fits him for. We'll want to do some surface exploration, too."

"That is easy," Karis said. "But you will find the exhibits and museums in our big parks have a complete record of what life was like before we were driven underground."

They spent most of the weeks that followed studying elaborate exhibits. Answers to all the questions which Earth's scientists had asked since Mars was first sighted in space went into their notebooks.

Interspersed with their studies of Martian history were visits to Martian industrial cities where they saw the underground factories that provided the population of 800 million with food and consumer goods, as well as the nuclear power stations which energized the technological wonders of the planet.

But the Earthmen were impatient to get their own surface exploration started. McKay, Sterling, Ross and Karis made up the party.

They took the tractor up to Plaza 15, then transferred it to the last-stage freight elevator, which was equipped with an airlock at the summit, where they donned spacesuits for the first time in weeks. Karis opened the big hatch, and they looked out on rugged mountain terrain. There was a small level area in front of the exit and then the land rose sharply on all sides to a small plateau.

"Tough going," McKay said doubtfully. "You three go ahead on foot. I'll follow in the tractor."

He went through the tractor's airlock and started the reactor-powered turbine drive, while Sterling, Ross and Karis set out for the rise, loping easily in the weak Martian gravity McKay could hear them talking through his helmet receiver. Ross called back that the surface was volcanic.

"Seems hard enough," he said.

Sterling and Karis had already disappeared over the rim when the tractor began the climb. McKay lumbered to the top and braked to survey the scene around him. Far over to the left were the ruins of the ancient surface city, an enormous pile of jumbled masonry on a desolate plain.

McKay moved forward gingerly. He reached the edge of the plateau and, as he eased the big machine over, the crust gave way with a sudden crunch. The tractor plunged through the volcanic surface, jolted hard on solid rock and slid crazily downwards.

McKay braked hard, but the treads refused to grip on the scurrying stones. The controls were almost ineffective, and he fought them with all his intelligence. Unless he could stop the tractor or turn it aside in a few seconds, the ponderous machine would crash through the dome of the park, and plunge into the city of Ahla.

Dust from the avalanche rose in a yellow cloud around the tractor, and McKay could see only dimly that Karis was braced in front of him with an enormous boulder. As the wind blew the dust aside, McKay saw the nearness of the park's canopy and he alternately braked and released the brake, hoping to stop the slipping treads, praying they would catch traction.

Then he saw Karis bend down suddenly and he felt the right tread of the tractor lift. For a moment it balanced there uncertainly. Then the machine slowly turned in spite of its locked controls. It skirted the rim of the plexidome by no more than a yard. Then it was free and out on the open plain, and McKay cut the power. Karis came running up as McKay dropped through the air lock and shook his hand gratefully.

"You are quite safe now," the Martian said simply. "I am glad."

McKay wondered if these people ever lost their Olympian calm.

"Karis, you did the only thing that could save me," he said. "Marvellous how you handled that huge rock. You put it at the right side of the tread so the tractor was forced to the left."

Karis smiled. "A simple enough decision," he said. "It is not difficult to move large boulders in our Martian gravity."

Peter Sterling came running to join them, and they lumbered three miles across the plain to the ruins of ancient Ahla, which had been built on the surface thousands of years before. But all they could see were columns, foundations and a few reasonably intact but completely bare buildings.

"The people had plenty of time to strip the city," Karis said. "Anything of value and all the records were taken underground. Mars was already in a high state of civilization so, contrary perhaps to your expectations, you will find nothing primitive here.

"Over there to the right used to be an airport and you can still see the shells of some of our ancient jet aircraft. Oh yes, Martians used to fly a great deal. When we went underground, aviation was abandoned because our underground transport system was so much more efficient. The only flying machines we use now are a fleet of duct-fan aircraft from which the engineers observe the progress of the polar melts. But they are assigned to pumping stations near the poles."

One of the great belts of vegetation extended on both sides of the abandoned city as far as they could see. It was these fields, the explorers learned, which Earth's astronomers had called "canals".

"One thing we haven't thoroughly understood," McKay said, "is just how your water cycle works. I can see that, when the snow in the polar zones melts, you pump the water to the cities. But how do you return the water to the atmosphere so that new snow can fall at the poles?"

"Why, it's quite simple," Karis said. "Under each of these fields there are porous tile pipes. Into them our great cities pump their sewage and interior condensation. You see, they must get rid of exactly the same amount of water as we supply to them. Otherwise they would soon be flooded. Well, the waste water is absorbed by the roots of the plants and drawn up into the stems and leaves. This moisture escapes into our parched atmosphere, and strong winds of autumn carry it to the poles. There it is precipitated as snow, and in the spring the snow melts. The water is caught in big basins and flows through conduits to reservoirs situated all over the planet."

A sudden shadow darkened the sun. Karis looked up quickly. "It is one of our dust storms," he said. "I think we should return now so that we are back in the city before it strikes."

Already they could feel the wind rising as they re-entered the tractor and started back. Swirls of reddish-yellow dust eddied across the plain, and they saw Ross looking anxious behind his space helmet as they approached the plateau. The geologist had found an easier route up the jagged side, and there was no trouble getting back to the summit hatch.

As they emerged on Plaza 15 and drove the tractor to the freight elevator, Peter Sterling laughed suddenly.

"I must be going Martian," he said. "I've just realized I'm glad to be underground."

The fact was that they had all come to feel very much at home in the subterranean life of Mars. As the weeks sped by, McKay felt a great sense of accomplishment in the amount of information they had stored in their notebooks. Their research had covered the entire complex of Martian science, technology and history. Detailed descriptive blueprints and pictures were microfilmed for easy storage on the return rocket, *Goddard*, so that Earth's scientists could study and evaluate their findings later.

Now that he felt less pressed, McKay increased his broadcast time to Earth. From messages relayed to him by their orbiting interplanetary passenger ship, *Oberth*, Earth was insatiable in its appetite for every scrap of information he could send. And the most insistent of

Earth's demands was that the expedition bring back some of the marvellous Martians.

This was a subject McKay had not discussed with any of his Martian hosts. He tried it out on Karis one afternoon when they were on their way to the sports stadium to watch an athletic event.

"How would you like to come back to Earth with us, Karis?" he said.

"I should like that very much," the Martian said. "But I would not suggest it until you expressed the wish yourself."

"We're having lunch with Ansanto, the head of your Academy of Science, tomorrow," McKay said. "I'll bring it up then."

"Ansanto will be pleased," Karis said, as they left their car and joined a stream of Martians moving towards the stadium.

They entered the great oval amphitheatre and found their seats. McKay looked around the packed arena, then down at the young men and women who would be competing in a programme of field events. Their tanned bodies were almost naked and beautifully knit.

Karis explained that athletic superiority combined with physical symmetry made up the Martian ideal. "We strive to develop the whole body to achieve perfection in our men," he said. "It is true of our women, too."

McKay could believe they had succeeded. He watched the contests in growing wonder as the athletes jumped, threw weights and ran faster than he had ever seen before. He knew that the feeble Martian gravity had a lot to do with it, but it still astonished him to see a handsome young Martian maiden with the body of a goddess soar more than forty feet to win the high jump. Looking around the stadium at the spectators, dressed in their Grecian costumes and raising their "Ahs" of approval, he could imagine himself back in Earth's Golden Age in Greece, when the Olympic games were young.

Werner von Braun

Making notes for tomorrow's broadcast to Earth, McKay wrote: "We were impressed by the inner pride and enthusiasm with which the women presented their perfections. Despite their costumes, which verged upon nudism, there was not the slightest suggestion of that over-emphasis of the sensual which on Earth so frequently accompanies exposure of the female body. These women had beautiful bodies and they exhibited them in athletic excellence with no other purpose."

Next morning McKay went to the station of the trans-planetary system with Karis, and they took one of those supersonic subway cars for Laroni, a small town beneath the moss fields of Lacus Lunae. It turned out that Laroni was largely inhabited by artists, writers and philosophers whose individualities were expressed in what was, for Mars, a wide variety of decorative schemes and furnishings in their dwellings.

McKay was much impressed by Ansanto's breadth of mind and extensive historical knowledge as they talked during luncheon. He realised that here was a man with a perspective on the development of the planet such as few possessed.

After luncheon, the Earthman lost no time in proposing that the return flight include three Martians chosen by the Academy.

Ansanto's benign countenance lit up. "We have been hoping there could be such an invitation," he said quickly. "Yes, of course, Martians will go with you. You have reborn in us the spirit of adventure."

They discussed the type of men best suited for the Earth journey.

"I leave that to you, sir," McKay said, "but it would give us great pleasure if Karis might be one of the three."

Ansanto looked at the young Martian in some surprise.

"Karis is not a scientist," he began, "and yet – yes, I think Karis must go with you. He reflects the thoughts of our people." He smiled at Karis. "We shall discuss at the Academy our other two space pioneers. Their names will be announced at the dinner we plan in your honour before you leave us."

Time was growing short now, but McKay was confident that he and his companions had completed their studies. The Earthmen shuttled frequently between Ahla and their base camp, carrying the records of their observations, containers of microfilm and the samples of Martian life – clothing, shoes, packages of synthetic food, specialized tools, and reels of exposed film they had taken of life on Mars.

Martian engineers and mechanics had been assigned to help Spottswood and Burke in checking *Goddard* against the day of departure. Spottswood reported a week before take-off that they were ready.

Riding back to Ahla in one of the supersonic cars late that afternoon, McKay turned to Karis.

"What would you say was the most important achievement of your Martian technology?" he asked.

"Limitless electric power," Karis answered promptly. "Without this, our existence would be impossible." He drew from a pocket of his tunic some Martian currency and pointed to the symbols on the notes of different denominations. In very much the same way as the value of a dollar is based on the gold standard, Karis' bills were based on varying amounts of the Martian equivalent of kilowatt hours. "You see," Karis said, "electrical energy units are the standard of value on Mars. They are responsible for our material welfare – the clothes we wear, the food we eat, the air we breathe. It is electrical power which has reduced our standard work day to only four hours."

It occurred to McKay that, in an advanced technological civilization, where physical labour is virtually non-existent and the total production level is directly related to the total level of available electrical power, a kilowatt currency seemed to have a built-in mechanism against inflation: when a new generating station was built, more money would go into circulation to keep balance with the increased productivity.

"I am really impressed by what you have accomplished with electrification, Karis, but I have even greater respect for the intelligent way your people use their leisure," McKay said. "Everyone I meet seems to be following a creative hobby – painting, sculpture, sports activities, music, writing. Our folks back home could really learn a lot from you in this respect, too. You know, our scientists and engineers knock themselves out making life more comfortable, but all too many people just don't know what to do with their spare time."

"I think your people will improve in the art of cultured leisure as technology continues to free them from manual work," Karis said. "There is something eminently satisfying in working with your hands, but after centuries of enslavement to manual work many people have to learn to be proud of their hands again. Here on Mars there is practically no manual labour any more. Our machine tools are perfected to the stage where there is little more to making new machines than feeding instructions into a computer. We no longer have stenographers on Mars. You have seen our offices where we use mechanical transcription direct from the voice. Yes, we need to be creative with our hands again to make us forget what Oraze told you that night and what Ansanto repeated today – the greyness of standardization."

"Did you go to one of the universities, Karis?" McKay asked.

"My examination results were not good enough," Karis said, "and our testing system indicated that I should be more useful if I went through a technical school. I do not regret it. I have a good life. I am twenty-five now, and I am the deputy supervisor of the pumping station where you found me. It is not bad for one ten years out of technical school."

"I sometimes wonder," McKay said, as he watched a station flick past, "whether your Martian system is wise in racing children through school as fast as it does. We are much slower on Earth. Our children begin school at five, yours at three. But we do not feel that so young a child is able to understand all the advanced science you teach your youngsters by the time they are eight. And it seems incredibly young for boys and girls to enter the university or technical school at the age of twelve."

"But you do not use pillow-speakers, I believe," Karis said. "As you found when you learned Martian, all the drudgery of memorization is performed by the pillow-speaker. When the process of cramming knowledge is handled mechanically, then the child is free to think – to understand."

That evening, back in Ahla, McKay assembled all the Earthmen who were not at the base. One by one McKay questioned them and was relieved to find that none of the scientists felt his observations were incomplete.

The interesting thing was that none of these men appeared particularly eager to leave Mars. Their year and three months had created friendships for all of them among the Martians and developed a fascination for this technologically-driven life.

The 449th day when they must leave Mars was a Saturday, and on Thursday evening the Earthmen went up to Plaza 40 on their last trip through Ahla's transport system. The entire party of twelve had been summoned to this final banquet, and *Goddard*, the return rocket, was left in the care of Martian engineers.

The explorers entered the magnificent Academy of Science Building where they were received by Ardri, the Martian chief of state, and his ministers, as well as the principal intellectuals of the planet. After dinner, there was

a programme of speeches. Ardri welcomed them to this
final ceremony and called on McKay, who tried to express
the thanks of all the Earthmen for the hospitality of the
Martians.

Then Ansanto rose to give the address of the evening.
"Brothers from Earth," he said, "the inspiration behind
your daring journey across the solar system was far more
than the urge to perform a technical feat, magnificent as it
was. That inspiration brought you here so you might fulfil a
mission that must have been planned by the Creator
Himself.

"The meaning of that mission can only be that God
willed that the living beings He has formed after His image
and spread throughout the universe shall establish contact
and learn to work together for His greater glory.

"Your voyage is indeed a great technical accomplishment
that has made a profound impression on millions of
Martians. But you have told us that people on Earth have
been even more impressed by the messages that you have
sent them about what you found here. So let me give you a
word of warning and advice from an old man who is a
citizen of an even older planet.

"The history of this planet has taught us that idolatry of
our technical accomplishments constitutes the worst evil
with which we threaten our race and our civilization.
Worshipping those accomplishments renders man sterile
and incapable of meeting the demands of the future. If we
worship scientific achievement, we kill humility, and of
humility alone can be born any further progress, scientific
or otherwise.

"Man should worship none but God, if he would fulfil his
mission in this life. Thus, and thus only, can we create the
ethical foundation on which a technological civilization can
be built from which all mankind can benefit."

Ansanto then called the roll of the Earthmen and, as each
walked to the rostrum, Ardri hung about his neck Mars'

highest decoration for scientific achievement. He then called up Granat and Koras, the two scientists who had been nominated to accompany the expedition back to Earth, and with them he summoned Karis, who walked proudly to receive the accolade of this man.

When they were all seated again, Ansanto called loudly, "Roll back the canopy!"

The ceiling slid away soundlessly and, as they looked through the transparent dome to the star-studded firmament, they saw a light brighter than the brightest star move slowly across the heavens.

"I have the honour to report," said Ansanto, "that, inspired by your visit, Mars has made its first venture into space. That light you see up there is an artificial satellite that was launched only this afternoon. When you Earthmen return to Mars, there will be a space station up there in orbit waiting to receive you."

It was all over then, and they said farewell. Oraze came up to McKay. "So it is good-bye for now," he said as he embraced McKay. "But we shall meet again. I feel sure of it."

A few hours later the Earthmen were in the subway cars, speeding down the straight tunnel, on their final journey to the base camp in Libya.

Karis woke them in the morning. The two Martian scientists had arrived and the party set out in the transplanetary cars.

In a little more than two hours they were back at the station under the floor of the red machines. The elevator carried them to the level where they had first glimpsed life on Mars. Their old friends, the superintendent and his assistant greeted them. McKay and his men donned their pressure suits, walked to the elevator, were lifted to the airlock and soon the little party was back on the surface of Mars.

At 0651 next morning McKay felt the blast and the acceleration which lifted their rocket ship into the clear, rarified Martian atmosphere. *Goddard* rose smoothly, and soon the flight track tilted into an easterly direction. After a little over two minutes the roar of the rocket engines subsided and an hour later the orbiting interplanetary ship *Oberth*, which would carry them back to Earth, slid into view . . .

A few days after that they were counting down the last minutes as *Oberth* was readied for the long return voyage across the solar system. McKay lay in his contour chair and, between careful checks of his instrument board, took a last glimpse at the vast reddish and greenish disc with the great white south polar cap that had been their second home for over a year.

Down there was an exciting civilization, undreamed of till their expedition found it.

He felt an immense sense of satisfaction, a deep assurance of what would come from this conjunction of intelligence between the planets Mars and Earth.

John Berger, at the radio, tore a sheet from his pad and passed it up to McKay. "Message from Radio Ahla," he said.

McKay read it to the expedition:

"Mars sends its blessings to your flight, its greetings to all people of Earth. Carry in your ship our remembrance and our promise of swift reunion. – Ardri."

PANIC IN THE YEAR ZERO

> (American International, 1962)
> Starring: Ray Milland, Jean Hagen & Mary Mitchell
> Directed by Ray Milland
> Based on the story "Lot" by Ward Moore

The exploding of the Atom Bomb at Hiroshima in 1945 not surprisingly inspired a whole group of novels and films of varying degrees of conviction and paranoia in which the Earth was threatened with cataclysmic destruction. The first of these was *The Beginning or the End* (1946) in which Brian Donlevy (who would later star in the film version of *Quatermass*) played a troubled scientist involved in building the Bomb in the Manhattan Project. This was followed by the "Red menace" of *Invasion U.S.A.* (1952) starring Gerald Mohr and Dan O'Herlihy, and Stanley Kramer's *On The Beach* (1959) based on Nevil Shute's novel about a world destroyed by radioactivity, with Gregory Peck, Ava Gardner and Anthony Perkins. For a number of critics the best picture of this kind was *Panic In The Year Zero* which focused on a typical American family and how they came to terms with life after an atomic war. Though to some others it was a cynical and particularly violent film for its time, it can now be seen as a forerunner of today's no-holds-barred extravaganzas such as *The Terminator* in which the central character abandons all the traditional ideals of humanity and shoots first and asks questions afterwards. *Panic in the Year Zero*, which was directed by its star, was starkly photographed in a grainy black and white style that added to the harshness of the ruined landscape of Los Angeles brilliantly created by special effects designer Daniel Heller. Ward Moore (1903–1978), the author of "Lot", the story on which the film was based, was curiously not credited for his contribution, although he was already well

Ward Moore

known as a writer of a number of best-selling mainstream
novels and the creator of a pair of classic SF books, *Greener
Than You Think* (1947) about a mutated grass that overruns
the world, and *Bring The Jubilee* (1953), a time travel story in
which a man from the future has the chance to change the
course of the American Civil War. First published in *The
Magazine of Fantasy and Science Fiction* in 1953, "Lot" has
been described by Brian Aldiss as "one of the most notable
stories describing nuclear holocaust and its consequences",
and it is perhaps therefore not so surprising that it should also
have inspired a landmark movie.

Mr Jimmon even appeared elated, like a man about to set
out on a vacation.

"Well, folks, no use waiting any longer. We're all set. So
let's go."

There was a betrayal here; Mr Jimmon was not the kind
of man who addressed his family as "folks".

"David, you're sure . . .?"

Mr Jimmon merely smiled. This was quite out of character; customarily he reacted to his wife's habit of posing
unfinished questions – after seventeen years the unuttered
and larger part of the queries were always instantly known to
him in some mysterious way, as though unerringly projected
by the key in which the introduction was pitched, so that not
only the full wording was communicated to his mind, but the
shades and implications which circumstance and humour
attached to them – with sharp and querulous defence. No
matter how often he resolved to stare quietly or use the still
more effective, Afraid I didn't catch your meaning, dear, he
had never been able to put his resolution into force. Until this
moment of crisis. Crisis, reflected Mr Jimmon, still smiling
and moving suggestively towards the door, crisis changes
people. Brings out underlying qualities.

It was Jir who answered Molly Jimmon, with the adolescent's half-whine of exasperation. "Aw furcrysay Mom,

what's the idea? The highways'll be clogged tight. What's the good figuring out everything heada time and having everything all set if you're going to start all over again at the last minute? Get a grip on yourself and let's go."

Mr Jimmon did not voice the reflexive, That's no way to talk to your mother. Instead he thought, not unsympathetically, of woman's slow reaction time. Asset in childbirth, liability behind the wheel. He knew Molly was thinking of the house and all the things in it: her clothes and Erika's, the TV set – so sullenly ugly now, with the electricity gone – the refrigerator in which the food would soon begin to rot and stink, the dead stove, the cellarful of cases of canned stuff for which there was no room in the station wagon. And the Buick, blocked up in the garage, with the air thoughtfully let out of the tyres and the battery hidden.

Of course the house would be looted. But they had known that all along. When they – or rather he, for it was his executive's mind and training which were responsible for the Jimmons' preparation against this moment – planned so carefully and providentially, he had weighed property against life and decided on life. No other decision was possible.

"Aren't you at least going to phone Pearl and Dan?"

Now why in the world, thought Mr Jimmon, completely above petty irritation, should I call Dan Davisson? (Because of course it's *Dan* she means – My Old Beau. Oh, he was nobody then, just an impractical dreamer without a penny to his name; it wasn't for years that he was recognized as a Mathematical Genius; now he's a professor and all sorts of things – but she automatically says Pearl-and-Dan, not Dan.) What can Dan do with the square root of minus nothing to offset M equals whatever it is, at this moment? Or am I supposed to ask if Pearl has all her diamonds? Query, why doesn't Pearl wear pearls, only diamonds? My wife's friends, heh heh, but even the subtlest intonation won't label them when you're entertaining an important client and Pearl and Dan.

And why should I phone? What sudden paralysis afflicts her? Hysteria?

"No," said Mr Jimmon. "I did not phone Pearl and Dan."

Then he added, relenting, "Phone's been out since."

"But," said Molly.

She's hardly going to ask me to drive into town. He selected several answers in readiness. But she merely looked towards the telephone helplessly (she ought to have been fat, thought Mr Jimmon, really she should, or anyway plump; her thinness gives her that air of competence), so he amplified gently, "They're unquestionably all right. As far away from it as we are."

Wendell was already in the station wagon. With Waggie hidden somewhere. Should have sent the dog to the humane society; more merciful to have it put to sleep. Too late now; Waggie would have to take his chance. There were plenty of rabbits in the hills above Malibu, he had often seen them quite close to the house. At all events there was no room for a dog in the wagon, already loaded to within a pound of its capacity.

Erika came in briskly from the kitchen, her brown jodhpurs making her appear at first glance even younger than fourteen. But only at first glance; then the swell of hips and breast denied the childishness the jodhpurs seemed to accent.

"The water's gone, Mom. There's no use sticking around any longer."

Molly looked incredulous. "The water?"

"Of course the water's gone," said Mr Jimmon, not impatiently, but rather with satisfaction in his own foresight. "If It didn't get the aqueduct, the mains depend on pumps. Electric pumps. When the electricity went, the water went too."

"But the water," repeated Molly, as though this last catastrophe was beyond all reason – even the outrageous logic which It brought in its train.

Jir slouched past them and outside. Erika tucked in a strand of hair, pulled her jockey cap downward and sideways, glanced quickly at her mother and father, then followed. Molly took several steps, paused, smiled vaguely in the mirror and walked out of the house.

Mr Jimmon patted his pockets; the money was all there. He didn't even look back before closing the front door and rattling the knob to be sure the lock had caught. It had never failed, but Mr Jimmon always rattled it anyway. He strode to the station wagon, running his eyes over the springs to reassure himself again that they really hadn't overloaded it.

The sky was overcast; you might have thought it one of the regular morning high fogs if you didn't know. Mr Jimmon faced south-east, but It had been too far away to see anything. Now Erika and Molly were in the front seat; the boys were in the back lost amid the neatly packed stuff. He opened the door on the driver's side, got in, turned the key and started the motor. Then he said casually over his shoulder, "Put the dog out, Jir."

Wendell protested, too quickly, "Waggie's not here."

Molly exclaimed, "Oh, David . . ."

Mr Jimmon said patiently, "We're losing pretty valuable time. There's no room for the dog; we have no food for him. If we had room we could have taken more essentials; those few pounds might mean the difference."

"Can't find him," muttered Jir.

"He's not here. I tell you he's not here," shouted Wendell, tearful voiced.

"If I have to stop the motor and get him myself we'll be wasting still more time and gas." Mr Jimmon was still detached, judicial. "This isn't a matter of kindness to animals. It's life and death."

Erika said evenly, "Dad's right, you know. It's the dog or us. Put him out, Wend."

"I tell you – " Wendell began.

"Got him!" exclaimed Jir. "Okay, Waggie! Outside and good luck."

The spaniel wriggled ecstatically as he was picked up and put out through the open window. Mr Jimmon raced the motor, but it didn't drown out Wendell's anguish. He threw himself on his brother, hitting and kicking. Mr Jimmon took his foot off the gas, and as soon as he was sure the dog was away from the wheels, eased the station wagon out of the driveway and down the hill towards the ocean.

"Wendell, Wendell, stop," pleaded Molly. "Don't hurt him, Jir."

Mr Jimmon clicked on the radio. After a preliminary hum, clashing static crackled out. He pushed all five buttons in turn, varying the quality of unintelligible sound. "Want me to try?" offered Erika. She pushed the manual button and turned the knob slowly. Music dripped out.

Mr Jimmon grunted. "Mexican station. Try something else. Maybe you can get Ventura."

They rounded a tight curve. "Isn't that the Warbinns'?" asked Molly.

For the first time since It happened, Mr Jimmon had a twinge of impatience. There was no possibility, even with the unreliable eye of shocked excitement, of mistaking the Warbinns' blue Mercury. No one else on Rambla Catalina had one anything like it, and visitors would be most unlikely now. If Molly would apply the most elementary logic!

Besides, Warbinn had stopped the blue Mercury in the Jimmon driveway five times every week for the past two months – ever since they had decided to put the Buick up and keep the wagon packed and ready against this moment – for Mr Jimmon to ride with him to the city. Of course it was the Warbinns'.

"*. . . advised not to impede the progress of the military. Adequate medical staffs are standing by at all hospitals. Local civilian defence units are taking all steps in accordance . . .*"

"Santa Barbara," remarked Jir, nodding at the radio with an expert's assurance.

Mr Jimmon slowed, prepared to follow the Warbinns down to 101, but the Mercury halted and Mr Jimmon turned out to pass it. Warbinn was driving and Sally was in the front seat with him; the back seat appeared empty except for a few things obviously hastily thrown in. No foresight, thought Mr Jimmon.

Warbinn waved his hand vigorously out the window and Sally shouted something.

"*. . . panic will merely slow rescue efforts. Casualties are much smaller than originally reported . . .*"

"How do they know?" asked Mr Jimmon, waving politely at the Warbinns.

"Oh, David, aren't you going to stop? They want something."

"Probably just to talk."

"*. . . to retain every drop of water. Emergency power will be in operation shortly. There is no cause for undue alarm. General . . .*"

Through the rear-view mirror Mr Jimmon saw the blue Mercury start after them. He had been right then, they only wanted to say something inconsequential. At a time like this.

At the junction with U.S. 101, five cars blocked Rambla Catalina. Mr Jimmon set the handbrake, and steadying himself with the open door, stood on tiptoe twistedly, trying to see over the cars ahead. 101 was solid with traffic which barely moved. On the southbound side of the divided highway a stream of vehicles flowed illegally north.

"Thought everybody was figured to go east," gibed Jir over the other side of the car.

Mr Jimmon was not disturbed by his son's sarcasm. How right he'd been to rule out the trailer. Of course the bulk of the cars were headed eastward as he'd calculated; this sluggish mass was nothing compared with the countless ones which must now be blocking the roads to Pasadena; Alhambra, Garvey, Norwalk. Even the northbound refugees were undoubtedly taking 99 or regular 101 – the highway before them was really 101 Alternate – he had picked the most feasible exit.

The Warbinns drew up alongside. "Hurry didn't do you much good," shouted Warbinn, leaning forward to clear his wife's face.

Mr Jimmon reached in and turned off the ignition. Gas was going to be precious. He smiled and shook his head at Warbinn; no use pointing out that he'd got the inside lane by passing the Mercury, with a better chance to seize the opening on the highway when it came. "Get in the car, Jir, and shut the door. Have to be ready when this breaks."

"If it ever does," said Molly. "All that rush and bustle. We might just as well . . ."

Mr Jimmon was conscious of Warbinn's glowering at him and resolutely refused to turn his head. He pretended not to hear him yell, "Only wanted to tell you you forgot to pick up your bumper-jack. It's in front of our garage."

Mr Jimmon's stomach felt empty. What if he had a flat now? Ruined, condemned. He knew a burning hate for Warbinn – incompetent borrower, bad neighbour, thoughtless, shiftless, criminal. He owed it to himself to leap from the station wagon and seize Warbinn by the throat . . .

"What did he say, David? What is Mr Warbinn saying?"

Then he remembered it was the jack from the Buick; the station wagon's was safely packed where he could get at it easily. Naturally he would never have started out on a trip like this without checking so essential an item. "Nothing," he said, "nothing at all."

"*. . . plane dispatches indicate target was the Signal Hill area. Minor damage was done to Long Beach, Wilmington,*

94

and San Pedro. All non-military air traffic warned from Mines Field . . ."

The smash and crash of bumper and fender sounded familiarly on the highway. From his look-out station he couldn't see what had happened, but it was easy enough to reconstruct the impatient jerk forward that caused it. Mr Jimmon didn't exactly smile, but he allowed himself a faint quiver of internal satisfaction. A crash up ahead would make things worse, but a crash behind – and many of them were inevitable – must eventually create a gap.

Even as he thought this, the first car at the mouth of Rambla Catalina edged on to the shoulder of the highway. Mr Jimmon slid back in and started the motor, inching ahead after the car in front, gradually leaving the still uncomfortable proximity of the Warbinns.

"Got to go to the toilet," announced Wendell abruptly.

"Didn't I tell you – ! Well, hurry up! Jir, keep the door open and pull him in if the car starts to move."

"I can't go here."

Mr Jimmon restrained his impulse to snap, Hold it in then. Instead he said mildly, "This is a crisis, Wendell. No time for niceties. Hurry."

". . . the flash was seen as far north as Ventura and as far south as Newport. An eye-witness who has just arrived by helicopter . . ."

"That's what we should have had," remarked Jir. "You thought of everything except that."

"That's no way to speak to your father," admonished Molly.

"Aw heck, Mom, this is a crisis. No time for niceties."

"You're awful smart, Jir," said Erika. "Big, tough, brutal man."

"Go down, brat," returned Jir, "your nose needs wiping."

"As a matter of record," Mr Jimmon said calmly, "I thought of both plane and helicopter and decided against them."

"I can't go. Honest, I just can't go."

"Just relax, darling," advised Molly. "No one is looking."

". . . *fires reported in Compton, Lynwood, Southgate, Harbour City, Lomita, and other spots are now under control. Residents are advised not to attempt to travel on the overcrowded highways as they are much safer in their homes or places of employment. The civilian defence . . .*"

The two cars ahead bumped forward. "Get in," shouted Mr Jimmon.

He got the left front tyre of the station wagon on the asphalt shoulder – the double lane of concrete was impossibly far ahead – only to be blocked by the packed procession. The clock on the dash said 11.04. Nearly five hours since It happened, and they were less than two miles from home. They could have done better walking. Or on horseback.

". . . *All residents of the Los Angeles area are urged to remain calm. Local radio service will be restored in a matter of minutes, along with electricity and water. Reports of fifth column activities have been greatly exaggerated. The FBI has all known subversives under . . .*"

He reached over and shut it off. Then he edged a daring two inches further on the shoulder, almost grazing an aggressive Cadillac packed solid with cardboard cartons. On his left a Model A truck shivered and trembled. He knew, distantly and disapprovingly, that it belonged to two painters who called themselves man and wife. The truckbed was loaded high with household goods; poor, useless things no looter would bother to steal. In the cab the artists passed a quart beer bottle back and forth. The man waved it genially at him; Mr Jimmon nodded discouragingly back.

The thermometer on the mirror showed 90. Hot all right. Of course if they ever got rolling . . . I'm thirsty, he thought; probably suggestion. If I hadn't seen the thermometer. Anyway I'm not going to paw around in back for the canteen. Forethought. Like the arms. He cleared his throat. "Remember there's an automatic in the glove compartment. If anyone tries to open the door on your side, use it."

"Oh, David, I . . ."

Ah, humanity. Non-resistance. Gandhi. I've never shot at anything but a target. At a time like this. But they don't understand.

"I could use the rifle from back here," suggested Jir. "Can I, Dad?"

"I can reach the shotgun," said Wendell. "That's better at close range."

"Gee, you men are brave," jeered Erika. Mr Jimmon said nothing; both shotgun and rifle were unloaded. Foresight again.

He caught the hiccuping pause in the traffic instantly, gratified at his smooth coordination. How far he could proceed on the shoulder before running into a culvert narrowing the highway to the concrete he didn't know. Probably not more than a mile at most, but at least he was off Rambla Catalina and on 101.

He felt tremendously elated. Successful.

"Here we go!" He almost added, Hold on to your hats.

Of course the shoulder too was packed solid, and progress, even in low gear, was maddening. The gas consumption was something he did not want to think about; his pride in the way the needle of the gauge caressed the F shrank. And gas would be hard to come by in spite of his pocketful of ration coupons. Black market.

"Mind if I try the radio again?" asked Erika, switching it on.

Mr Jimmon, following the pattern of previous success, insinuated the left front tyre on to the concrete, eliciting a disapproving squawk from the Pontiac alongside. ". . . *sector was quiet. Enemy losses are estimated . . .*"

"Can't you get something else?" asked Jir. "Something less dusty?"

"Wish we had TV in the car," observed Wendell. "Joe Tellifer's old man put a set in the back seat of their Chrysler."

"Dry up, squirt," said Jir. "Let the air out of your head."

"Jir!"

"Oh, Mom, don't pay attention! Don't you see that's what he wants?"

"Listen, brat, if you weren't a girl, I'd spank you."

"You mean, if I wasn't your sister. You'd probably enjoy such childish sex-play with any other girl."

"Erika!"

Where do they learn it? marvelled Mr Jimmon. These progressive schools. Do you suppose . . .?

He edged the front wheel further in exultantly, taking advantage of a momentary lapse of attention on the part of the Pontiac's driver. Unless the other went berserk with frustration and rammed into him, he practically had a cinch on a car-length of the concrete now.

"Here we go!" he gloried. "We're on our way."

"Aw, if I was driving we'd be half-way to Oxnard by now."

"Jir, that's no way to talk to your father."

Mr Jimmon reflected dispassionately that Molly's ineffective admonitions only spurred Jir's sixteen-year-old brashness, already irritating enough in its own right. Indeed, if it were not for Molly, Jir might . . .

It was of course possible – here Mr Jimmon braked just short of the convertible ahead – Jir wasn't just going through a "difficult" period (What was particularly difficult about it? he inquired, in the face of all the books Molly suggestively left around on the psychological problems of growth. The boy had everything he could possibly want) but was the type who, in different circumstances drifted well into – well, perhaps not exactly juvenile delinquency, but . . .

". . . *in the Long Beach-Wilmington-San Pedro area. Comparison with that which occurred at Pittsburgh reveals that this morning's was in every way less serious. All fires are now under control and all the injured are now receiving medical attention . . ."*

"I don't think they're telling the truth," stated Mrs Jimmon.

He snorted. He didn't think so either, but by what process had she arrived at that conclusion?

"I want to hear the ball game. Turn on the ball game, Rick," Wendell demanded.

Eleven sixteen, and rolling northward on the highway. Not bad, not bad at all. Foresight. Now if he could only edge his way leftward to the southbound strip they'd be beyond the Santa Barbara bottleneck by two o'clock.

"The lights," exclaimed Molly, "the taps!"

Oh no, thought Mr Jimmon, not that too. Out of the comic strips.

"Keep calm," advised Jir. "Electricity and water are both off – remember?"

"I'm not quite an imbecile yet, Jir. I'm quite aware everything went off. I was thinking of the time it went back on."

"Furcrysay, Mom, you worrying about next month's bills *now*?"

Mr Jimmon, nudging the station wagon ever leftward formed the sentence: You'd never worry about bills, young man, because you never have to pay them. Instead of saying it aloud, he formed another sentence: Molly, your talent for irrelevance amounts to genius. Both sentences gave him satisfaction.

The traffic gathered speed briefly, and he took advantage of the spurt to get solidly in the left-hand lane, right against the long island of concrete dividing the north from the southbound strips. "That's using the old bean, Dad," approved Wendell.

Whatever slight pleasure he might have felt in his son's approbation was overlaid with exasperation. Wendell, like

99

Jir, was more Manville than Jimmon; they carried Molly's
stamp on their faces and minds. Only Erika was a true
Jimmon. Made in my own image, he thought pridelessly.

"I can't help but think it would have been at least
courteous to get in touch with Pearl and Dan. At least
try. And the Warbinns . . ."

The gap in the concrete divider came sooner than he
anticipated and he was on the comparatively unclogged
southbound side. His foot went down on the accelerator
and the station wagon grumbled earnestly ahead. For the
first time Mr Jimmon became aware how tightly he'd been
gripping the wheel; how rigid the muscles in his arms,
shoulders and neck had been. He relaxed part-way as he
adjusted to the speed of the cars ahead and the speedometer
needle hung just below 45, but resentment against Molly (at
least courteous), Jir (no time for niceties), and Wendell (not
to go), rode up in the saliva under his tongue. Dependent.
Helpless. Everything on him. Parasites.

At intervals Erika switched on the radio. News was
always promised immediately, but little was forthcoming,
only vague, nervous attempts to minimize the extent of the
disaster and soothe listeners with allusions to civilian
defence, military activities on the ever-advancing front,
and comparison with the destruction of Pittsburgh, so
vastly much worse than the comparatively harmless detonation at Los Angeles. Must be pretty bad, thought
Mr Jimmon; cripple the war effort . . .

"I'm hungry," said Wendell.

Molly began stirring around, instructing Jir where to find
the sandwiches. Mr Jimmon thought grimly of how they'd
have to adjust to the absence of civilized niceties: bread and
mayonnaise and lunch meat. Live on rabbit, squirrel,
abalone, fish. When Wendell grew hungry he'd have to
get his own food. Self-sufficiency. Hard and tough.

At Oxnard the snarled traffic slowed them to a crawl
again. Beyond, the juncture with the main highway north

kept them at the same infuriating pace. It was long after two when they reached Ventura, and Wendell, who had been fidgeting and jumping up and down in the seat for the past hour, proclaimed, "I'm tired of riding."

Mr Jimmon set his lips. Molly suggested, ineffectually, "Why don't you lie down, dear?"

"Can't. Way this crate is packed, ain't room for a grasshopper."

"Verry funny. Verrrry funny," said Jir.

"Now, Jir, leave him alone! He's just a little boy."

At Carpenteria the sun burst out. You might have thought it the regular dissipation of the fog, only it was almost time for the fog to come down again. Should he try the San Marcos Pass after Santa Barbara, or the longer, better way? Flexible plans, but . . . Wait and see.

It was four when they got to Santa Barbara and Mr Jimmon faced concerted though disorganized rebellion. Wendell was screaming with stiffness and boredom; Jir remarked casually to no one in particular that Santa Barbara was the place they were going to beat the bottleneck oh yeh; Molly said, Stop at the first clean-looking gas station. Even Erika added, "Yes, Dad, you'll really have to stop."

Mr Jimmon was appalled. With every second priceless and hordes of panic-stricken refugees pressing behind, they would rob him of all the precious gains he'd made by skill, daring, judgement. Stupidity and shortsightedness. Unbelievable. For their own silly comfort – good lord, did they think they had a monopoly on bodily weaknesses? He was cramped as they and wanted to go as badly. Time and space which could never be made up. Let them lose this half-hour and it was quite likely they'd never get out of Santa Barbara.

"If we lose a half-hour now we'll never get out of here."

"Well, now, David, that wouldn't be utterly disastrous, would it? There are awfully nice hotels here and I'm sure it would be more comfortable for everyone than your idea of camping in the woods, hunting and fishing . . ."

He turned off State; couldn't remember the name of the parallel street, but surely less traffic. He controlled his temper, not heroically, but desperately. "May I ask how long you would propose to stay in one of these awfully nice hotels?"

"Why, until we could go home."

"My dear Molly . . ." What could he say? My dear Molly, we are never going home, if you mean Malibu? Or: My dear Molly, you just don't understand what is happening?

The futility of trying to convey the clear picture in his mind. Or any picture. If she could not of herself see the endless mob pouring, pouring out of Los Angeles, searching frenziedly for escape and refuge, eating up the substance of the surrounding country in ever-widening circles, crowding, jam-packing, overflowing every hotel, boarding-house, lodging, or private home into which they could edge, agonizedly bidding up the price of everything until the chaos they brought with them was indistinguishable from the chaos they were fleeing – if she could not see all this instantly and automatically, she could not be brought to see it at all. Any more than the other aimless, planless, improvident fugitives could see it.

So, my dear Molly; nothing.

Silence gave consent to continued expostulation. "David, do you really mean you don't intend to stop at all?"

Was there any point in saying, Yes I do? He set his lips still more tightly and once more weighed San Marcos Pass against the coast route. Have to decide now.

"Why, the time we're waiting here, just waiting for the cars up ahead to move would be enough."

Could you call her stupid? He weighed the question slowly and justly, alert for the first jerk of the massed cars all around. Her reasoning was valid and logical if the laws of physics and geometry were suspended. (Was that right – physics and geometry? Body occupying two different positions at the same time?) It was the facts which were illogical – not Molly. She was just exasperating.

By the time they were half-way to Gaviota or Goleta – Mr Jimmon could never tell them apart – foresight and relentless sternness began to pay off. Those who had left Los Angeles without preparation and in panic were dropping out or slowing down, to get gas or oil, repair tyres, buy food, seek rest rooms. The station wagon was steadily forging ahead.

He gambled on the old highway out of Santa Barbara. Any kind of obstruction would block its two lanes; if it didn't he would be beating the legions on the wider, straighter road. There were stretches now where he could hit 50; once he sped a happy half-mile at 65.

Now the insubordination crackling all around gave indication of simultaneous explosion. "I really," began Molly, and then discarded this for a fresher, firmer start. "David, I don't understand how you can be so utterly selfish and inconsiderate."

Mr Jimmon could feel the veins in his forehead begin to swell, but this was one of those rages that didn't show.

"But, Dad, would ten minutes ruin everything?" asked Erika.

"Monomania," muttered Jir. "Single track. Like Hitler."

"I want my dog," yelped Wendell. "Dirty old dog-killer."

"Did you ever hear of cumulative – " Erika had addressed him reasonably; surely he could make her understand? "Did you ever hear of cumulative . . ." What was the word? Snowball rolling downhill was the image in his mind. "Oh, what's the use?"

The old road rejoined the new; again the station wagon was fitted into the traffic like parquetry. Mr Jimmon, from an exultant, unfettered – almost – 65 was imprisoned in a treadmill set at 38. Keep calm; you can do nothing about it,

he admonished himself. Need all your nervous energy. Must
be wrecks up ahead. And then, with a return of satisfaction:
if I hadn't used strategy back there we'd have been with
those making 25. A starting-stopping 25.

"It's fantastic," exclaimed Molly. "I could almost believe
Jir's right and you've lost your mind."

Mr Jimmon smiled. This was the first time Molly had
ever openly showed disloyalty before the children or sided
with them in their presence. She was revealing herself.
Under pressure. Not the pressure of events; her incredible
attitude at Santa Barbara had demonstrated her incapacity
to feel that. Just pressure against the bladder.

"No doubt those left behind can console their last moments with pride in their sanity." The sentence came out
perfectly formed, with none of the annoying pauses or
interpolated "ers" or "mmphs" which could, as he knew
from unhappy experience, flaw the most crushing rejoinders.

"Oh, the end can always justify the means for those who
want it that way."

"Don't they restrain people – "

"That's enough, Jir!"

Trust Molly to return quickly to fundamental hypocrisy;
the automatic response – his mind felicitously grasped the
phrase, conditioned reflex – to the customary stimulus. She
had taken an explicit stand against his common sense, but
her rigid code – honour thy father; iron rayon the wrong
side; register and vote; avoid scenes; only white wine with
fish; never re-hire a discharged servant – quickly substituted
pattern for impulse. Seventeen years.

The road turned away from the ocean, squirmed inland
and uphill for still slower miles; abruptly widened into a
divided, four lane highway. Without hesitation Mr Jimmon
took the southbound side; for the first time since they had
left Rambla Catalina his foot went down to the floorboards
and with a sigh of relief the station wagon jumped into
smooth, ecstatic speed.

Improvisation and strategy again. And, he acknowledged generously, the defiant example this morning of those who'd done the same thing in Malibu. Now, out of re-established habit the other cars kept to the northbound side even though there was nothing coming south. Timidity, routine, inertia. Pretty soon they would realize sheepishly that there was neither traffic nor traffic cops to keep them off, but it would be miles before they had another chance to cross over. By that time he would have reached the comparatively uncongested stretch.

"It's dangerous, David."

Obey the law. No smoking. Keep off the grass. Please adjust your clothes before leaving. Trespassers will be. Picking California wildflowers or shrubs is forbidden. Parking 45 min. Do not.

She hadn't put the protest in the more usual form of a question. Would that technique have been more irritating? Isn't it *dangerous*, Day-vid? His calm conclusion: it didn't matter.

"No time for niceties," chirped Jir.

Mr Jimmon tried to remember Jir as a baby. All the bad novels he had read in the days when he read anything except *Time* and the *New Yorker*, all the movies he'd seen before they had a TV set, always prescribed such retrospection as a specific for softening the present. If he could recall David Alonzo Jimmon, junior, at six months, helpless and lovable, it should make Jir more acceptable by discovering some faint traces of the one in the other.

But though he could recreate in detail the interminable, disgusting, trembling months of that initial pregnancy (had he really been afraid she would die?) he was completely unable to reconstruct the appearance of his first-born before the age of . . . It must have been at six that Jir had taken his baby sister out for a walk and lost her. (Had Molly permitted it? He still didn't know for sure.) Erika hadn't been found for four hours.

The tidal screeching of sirens invaded and destroyed his thoughts. What the devil . . .? His foot lifted from the gas pedal as he slewed obediently to the right, ingrained reverence surfacing at the sound.

"I told you it wasn't safe! Are you really trying to kill us all?"

Whipping over the rise ahead, a pair of motor-cycles crackled. Behind them snapped a long line of assorted vehicles, fire-trucks and ambulances mostly, interspersed here and there with olive drab army equipment. The cavalcade flicked down the central white line, one wheel in each lane. Mr Jimmon edged the station wagon as far over as he could; it still occupied too much room to permit the free passage of the onrush without compromise.

The knees and elbows of the motor-cycle policemen stuck out widely, reminding Mr Jimmon of grasshoppers. The one on the near side was headed straight for the station wagon's left front fender; for a moment Mr Jimmon closed his eyes as he plotted the unswerving course, knifing through the crust-like steel, bouncing lightly on the tyres, and continuing unperturbed. He opened them to see the other officer shoot past, mouth angrily open in his direction while the one straight ahead came to a skidding stop.

"Going to get it now," gloated Wendell.

An old-fashioned parent, one of the horrible examples held up to shuddering moderns like himself, would have reached back and relieved his tension by clouting Wendell across the mouth. Mr Jimmon merely turned off the motor.

The cop was not indulging in the customary deliberate and ominous performance of slowly dismounting and striding towards his victim with ever more menacing steps. Instead he got off quickly and covered the few feet to Mr Jimmon's window with unimpressive speed.

Heavy goggles concealed his eyes; dust and stubble covered his face. "Operator's licence!"

Lot

Mr Jimmon knew what he was saying, but the sirens and the continuous rustle of the convoy prevented the sound from coming through. Again the cop deviated from the established routine; he did not take the proffered licence and examine it incredulously before drawing out his pad and pencil, but wrote the citation, glancing up and down from the card in Mr Jimmon's hand.

Even so, the last of the vehicles – *San Jose F.D.* – passed before he handed the summons through the window to be signed. "Turn around and proceed in the proper direction," he ordered curtly, pocketing the pad and buttoning his jacket briskly.

Mr Jimmon nodded. The officer hesitated, as though waiting for some limp excuse. Mr Jimmon said nothing.

"No tricks," said the policeman over his shoulder. "Turn around and proceed in the proper direction."

He almost ran to his motor-cycle, and roared off, twisting his head for a final stern frown as he passed, siren wailing. Mr Jimmon watched him dwindle in the rear-view mirror and then started the motor. "Gonna lose a lot more than you gained," commented Jir.

Mr Jimmon gave a last glance in the mirror and moved ahead, shifting into second. "David!" exclaimed Molly horrified, "you're not turning around!"

"Observant," muttered Mr Jimmon, between his teeth.

"Dad, you can't get away with it," Jir decided judicially.

Mr Jimmon's answer was to press the accelerator down savagely. The empty highway stretched invitingly ahead; a few hundred yards to their right they could see the north-bound lanes ant-clustered. The sudden motion stirred the traffic citation on his lap, floating it down to the floor. Erika leaned forward and picked it up.

"Throw it away," ordered Mr Jimmon.

Molly gasped. "You're out of your mind."

"You're a fool," stated Mr Jimmon calmly. "Why should I save that piece of paper?"

"Isn't what you told the cop." Jir was openly jeering now.

"I might as well have, if I'd wanted to waste conversation. I don't know why I was blessed with such a stupid family – "

"May be something in heredity after all."

If Jir had said it out loud, reflected Mr Jimmon, it would have passed casually as normal domestic repartee, a little ill-natured perhaps, certainly callow and trite, but not especially provocative. Muttered, so that it was barely audible, it was an ultimate defiance. He had read that far back in pre-history, when the young males felt their strength, they sought to overthrow the rule of the Old Man and usurp his place. No doubt they uttered a preliminary growl or screech as challenge. They were not very bright, but they acted in a pattern; a pattern Jir was apparently following.

Refreshed by placing Jir in proper Neanderthal setting, Mr Jimmon went on, "– None of you seem to have the slightest initiative or ability to grasp reality. Tickets, cops, judges, juries mean nothing any more. There is no law now but the law of survival."

"Aren't you being dramatic, David?" Molly's tone was deliberately aloof, adult to excited child.

"I could hear you underline words, Dad," said Erika, but he felt there was no malice in her gibe.

"You mean we can do anything we want now? Shoot people? Steal cars and things?" asked Wendell.

"There, David! You see?"

Yes, I see. Better than you. Little savage. This is the pattern. What will Wendell – and the thousands of other Wendells (for it would be unjust to suppose Molly's genes and domestic influence unique) – be like after six months of anarchy? Or after six years?

Survivors, yes. And that will be about all: naked, primitive, ferocious, superstitious savages. Wendell can read and write (but not so fluently as I or any of our generation at his age); how long will he retain the tags and scraps of progressive schooling?

And Jir? Detachedly Mr Jimmon foresaw the fate of Jir. Unlike Wendell, who would adjust to the new conditions, Jir would go wild in another sense. His values were already set; they were those of television, high school dating, comic strips, law and order. Released from civilization, his brief future would be one of guilty rape and pillage until he fell victim to another youth or gang bent the same way. Molly would disintegrate and perish quickly. Erika . . .

The station wagon flashed along the comparatively unimpeded highway. Having passed the next crossover, there were now other vehicles on the southbound strip, but even on the northbound one, crowding had eased.

Furiously Mr Jimmon determined to preserve the civilization in Erika. (He would teach her everything he knew (including the insurance business?)) . . . ah, if he were some kind of scientist, now – not the Dan Davisson kind, whose abstract speculations seemed always to prepare the way for some new method of destruction, but the . . . Franklin? Jefferson? Watt? Protect her night and day from the refugees who would be roaming the hills south of Monteray. The rifle ammunition, properly used – and he would see that no one but himself used it – would last years. After it was gone – presuming fragments and pieces of a suicidal world hadn't pulled itself miraculously together to offer a place to return to – there were the two hunting bows whose steel-tipped shafts could stop a man as easily as a deer or mountain lion. He remembered debating long, at the time he had first begun preparing for It, how many bows to order, measuring their weight and bulk against the other precious freight and deciding at last that two was the satisfactory minimum. It must have been in his subconscious mind all along that of the whole family Erika was the only other person who could be trusted with a bow.

"There will be – " he spoke in calm and solemn tones, not to Wendell, whose question was now left long behind, floating on the gas-greasy air of a sloping valley growing with live-oaks, but to a larger, impalpable audience, "– there will be others who will think that because there is no longer law or law enforcement – "

"You're being simply fantastic!" She spoke more sharply than he had ever heard her in front of the children. "Just because It happened to Los Angeles – "

"And Pittsburgh."

"All right. And Pittsburgh, doesn't mean that the whole United States has collapsed and everyone in the country is running frantically for safety."

"Yet," added Mr Jimmon firmly, "yet, do you suppose they are going to stop with Los Angeles and Pittsburgh, and leave Gary and Seattle standing? Or even New York and Chicago? Or do you imagine Washington will beg for armistice terms while there is the least sign of organized life left in the country?"

"We'll wipe Them out first," insisted Jir in patriotic shock. Wendell backed him up with a machine gun "Brrrrr".

"Undoubtedly. But it will be the last gasp. At any rate it will be years, if at all in my lifetime, before stable communities are re-established – "

"David, you're raving."

"Re-established," he repeated. "So there will be many others who'll also feel that the dwindling of law and order is license to kill people and steal cars 'and things'. Naked force and cunning will be the only means of self-preservation. That was why I picked out a spot where I felt survival would be easiest; not only because of wood and water, game and fish, but because it's nowhere near the main highways, and so unlikely to be chosen by any great number."

"I wish you'd stop harping on that insane idea. You're just a little too old and flabby for pioneering. Even when

110

you were younger you were hardly the rugged, outdoor type."

No, thought Mr Jimmon, I was the sucker type. I would have gotten somewhere if I'd stayed in the bank, but like a bawd you pleaded; the insurance business brought in the quick money for you to give up your job and have Jir and the proper home. If you'd got rid of it as I wanted. Flabby, *flabby*! Do you think your scrawniness is so enticing?

Controlling himself, he said aloud, "We've been through all this. Months ago. It's not a question of physique, but of life."

"Nonsense. Perfect nonsense. Responsible people who really know its effects . . . Maybe it was advisable to leave Malibu for a few days or even a few weeks. And perhaps it's wise to stay away from the larger cities. But a small town or village, or even one of those ranches where they take boarders.

"Aw, Mom, you agreed. You know you did. What's the matter with you anyway? Why are you acting like a drip?"

"I want to go and shoot rabbits and bears like Dad said," insisted Wendell.

Erika said nothing, but Mr Jimmon felt he had her sympathy; the boys' agreement was specious. Wearily he debated going over the whole ground again, patiently pointing out that what Molly said might work in the Dakotas or the Great Smokies but was hardly operative anywhere within refugee range of the Pacific Coast. He had explained all this many times, including the almost certain impossibility of getting enough gasoline to take them into any of the reasonably safe areas; that was why they'd agreed on the region below Monterey, on California State Highway I, as the only logical goal.

A solitary car decorously bound in the legal direction interrupted his thoughts. Either crazy or has mighty important business, he decided. The car honked disapprovingly as it passed, hugging the extreme right side of the road.

111

Passing through Buellton the clamour again rose for a pause at a filling station. He conceded inwardly that he could afford ten or fifteen minutes without strategic loss since by now they must be among the leaders of the exodus; ahead lay little more than the normal travel. However, he had reached such a state of irritated frustration and consciousness of injustice that he was willing to endure unnecessary discomfort himself in order to inflict a longer delay on them. In fact it lessened his own suffering to know the delay was needless, that he was doing it, and that his action was a just – if inadequate – punishment.

"We'll stop this side of Santa Maria," he said. "I'll get gas there."

Mr Jimmon knew triumph: his forethought, his calculations, his generalship had justified themselves. Barring unlikely mechanical failure – the station wagon was in perfect shape – or accident – and the greatest danger had certainly passed – escape was now practically assured. For the first time he permitted himself to realize how unreal, how romantic the whole project had been. As any attempt to evade the fate charted for the multitude must be. The docile mass perished; the headstrong (but intelligent) individual survived.

Along with triumph went an expansion of his prophetic vision of life after reaching their destination. He had purposely not taxed the cargo capacity of the wagon with transitional goods; there was no tent, canned luxuries, sleeping bags, lanterns, candles, or any of the paraphernalia of camping midway between the urban and nomadic life. Instead, besides the weapons, tackle, and utensils, there was in miniature the List For Life On A Desert Island: shells and cartridges, lures, hooks, nets, gut, leaders, flint and steel, seeds, traps, needles and thread, government pamphlets on curing and tanning hides and the recognition of edible weeds and fungi, files, nails, a judicious stock of simple medicines. A pair of binoculars to spot intruders. No coffee, sugar, flour; they would begin living immediately as they would have to in a month or so in any case, on the old, half-forgotten human cunning.

"Cunning," he said aloud.

"What?"

"Nothing. Nothing."

"I still think you should have made an effort to reach Pearl and Dan."

"The telephone was dead, Mother."

"At the moment, Erika. You can hardly have forgotten how often the lines have been down before. And it never takes more than half an hour till they're working again."

"Mother, Dan Davisson is quite capable of looking after himself."

Mr Jimmon shut out the rest of the conversation so completely he didn't know whether there was any more to it or not. He shut out the intense preoccupation with driving, with making speed, with calculating possible gains. In the core of his mind, quite detached from everything about him, he examined and marvelled.

Erika. The cool, inflexible, adult tone. Almost indulgent, but so dispassionate as not to be. One might have expected her to be exasperated by Molly's silliness, to have answered impatiently, or not at all.

Mother. Never in his recollection had the children ever called her anything but Mom. The "Mother" implied – oh, it implied a multitude of things. An entirely new relationship, for one. A relationship of aloofness, or propriety without emotion. The ancient stump of the umbilical cord, black and shrivelled, had dropped off painlessly.

She had not bothered to argue about the telephone or point out the gulf between "before" and now. She had not even tried to touch Molly's deepening refusal of reality. She had been . . . indulgent.

Not "Uncle Dan", twitteringly imposed false avuncularity, but striking through it (and the façade of "Pearl and")

and aside (when I was a child I . . . something . . . but now I have put aside childish things); the wealth of implicit assertion. As yes, Mother, we all know the pardonable weakness and vanity; we excuse you for your constant reminders, but Mother, with all deference, we refuse to be forced any longer to be parties to middle age's nostalgic flirtatiousness. One could almost feel sorry for Molly.

. . . middle age's nostalgic flirtatiousness . . .

. . . *nostalgic* . . .

Metaphorically Mr Jimmon sat abruptly upright. The fact that he was already physically in this position made the transition, while invisible, no less emphatic. The nostalgic flirtatiousness of middle age implied – might imply – memory of something more than mere coquetry. Molly and Dan.

It all fitted together so perfectly it was impossible to believe it untrue. The impecunious young lovers, equally devoted to Dan's genius, realizing marriage was out of the question (he had never denied Molly's shrewdness; as for Dan's impracticality, well, impracticality wasn't necessarily uniform or consistent. Dan had been practical enough to marry Pearl and Pearl's money) could have renounced . . .

Or not renounced at all?

Mr Jimmon smiled; the thought did not ruffle him. Cuckoo, cuckoo. How vulgar, how absurd. Suppose Jir were Dan's? A blessed thought.

Regretfully he conceded the insuperable obstacle of Molly's conventionality. Jir was the product of his own loins. But wasn't there an old superstition about the image in the woman's mind at the instant of conception? So, justly and rightly Jir was not his. Nor Wendell, for that matter. Only Erika, by some accident. Mr Jimmon felt free and lighthearted.

"Get gas at the next station," he bulletined.

"The next one with a clean rest room," Molly corrected.

Invincible. The Earth-Mother, using men for her purposes: reproduction, clean rest rooms, nourishment, objects of culpability, *Homes and Gardens*. The bank was my life; I could have gone far but: Why, David – they pay you less than the janitor! It's ridiculous. And: I can't understand why you hesitate; it isn't as though it were a different type of work.

No, not different; just more profitable. Why didn't she tell Dan Davisson to become an accountant; that was the same type of work, just more profitable? Perhaps she had and Dan had simply been less befuddled. Or amenable. Or stronger in purpose? Mr Jimmon probed his pride thoroughly and relentlessly without finding the faintest twinge of retrospective jealousy. Nothing like that mattered now. Nor, he admitted, had it for years.

Two close-peaked hills gulped the sun. He toyed with the idea of crossing over to the northbound side now that it was uncongested and there were occasional southbound cars. Before he could decide the divided highway ended.

"I hope you're not planning to spend the night in some horrible motel," said Molly. "I want a decent bath and a good dinner."

Spend the night. Bath. Dinner. Again calm sentences formed in his mind, but they were blown apart by the unbelievable, the monumental obtuseness. How could you say, It is absolutely essential to drive till we get there? When there were no absolutes, no essentials in her concepts? My dear Molly, I.

"No," he said, switching on the lights.

Wendy, he knew, would be the next to kick up a fuss. Till he fell mercifully asleep. If he did. Jir was probably debating the relative excitements of driving all night and stopping in a strange town. His voice would soon be heard.

The lights of the combination wayside store and filling-station burned inefficiently, illuminating the deteriorating false-front brightly and leaving the gas pumps in shadow. Swallowing regret at finally surrendering to mechanical and human need, and so losing the hard-won position; relaxing, even for a short while, the fierce initiative that had brought them through in the face of all probability; he pulled the station wagon alongside the pumps and shut off the motor. About half-way – the worst half, much the worst half – to their goal. Not bad.

Molly opened the door on her side with stiff dignity. "I certainly wouldn't call this a *clean* station." She waited for a moment, hand still on the window, as though expecting an answer.

"Crummy joint," exclaimed Wendell, clambering awkwardly out.

"Why not?" asked Jir. "No time for niceties." He brushed past his mother who was walking slowly into the shadows.

"Erika," began Mr Jimmon, in a half-whisper.

"Yes, Dad?"

"Oh . . . never mind. Later."

He was not himself quite sure what he had wanted to say; what exclusive, urgent message he had to convey. For no particular reason he switched on the interior light and glanced at the packed orderliness of the wagon. Then he slid out from behind the wheel.

No sign of the attendant, but the place was certainly not closed. Not with the lights on and the hoses ready. He stretched, and walked slowly, savouring the comfortably painful uncramping of his muscles, towards the crude out-house labelled "Men". Molly, he thought, must be furious.

When he returned, a man was leaning against the station wagon. "Fill it up with ethyl," said Mr Jimmon pleasantly, "and check the oil and water."

The man made no move. "That'll be five bucks a gallon." Mr Jimmon thought there was an uncertain tremor in his voice.

"Nonsense; I've plenty of ration coupons."

"Okay." The nervousness was gone now, replaced by an ugly truculence. "Chew'm up and spit'm in your gas tank. See how far you can run on them."

The situation was not unanticipated. Indeed, Mr Jimmon thought with satisfaction of how much worse it must be closer to Los Angeles; how much harder the gouger would be on later supplicants as his supply of gasoline dwindled. "Listen," he said, and there was reasonableness rather than anger in his voice, "we're not out of gas. I've got enough to get to Santa Maria, even to San Luis Obispo."

"Okay. Go on then. Ain't stopping you."

"Listen. I understand your position. You have a right to make a profit in spite of government red tape."

Nervousness returned to the man's speech. "Look, whyn't you go on? There's plenty other stations up ahead."

The reluctant bandit. Mr Jimmon was entertained. He had fully intended to bargain, to offer $2 a gallon, even to threaten with the pistol in the glove compartment. Now it seemed mean and niggling even to protest. What good was money now? "All right," he said, "I'll pay you $5 a gallon."

Still the other made no move. "In advance."

For the first time Mr Jimmon was annoyed; time was being wasted. "Just how can I pay you in advance when I don't know how many gallons it'll take to fill the tank?"

The man shrugged.

"Tell you what I'll do. I'll pay for each gallon as you pump it. In advance." He drew out a handful of bills; the bulk of his money was in his wallet, but he'd put the small bills in his pockets. He handed over a five. "Spill the first one on the ground or in a can if you've got one."

"How's that?"

Why should I tell him; give him ideas? As if he hadn't got them already. "Just call me eccentric," he said. "I don't want the first gallon from the pump. Why should you care? It's just five dollars more profit."

For a moment Mr Jimmon thought the man was going to refuse, and he regarded his foresight with new reverence. Then he reached behind the pump and produced a flat-sided tin in which he inserted the flexible end of the hose. Mr Jimmon handed over the bill, the man wound the handle round and back – it was an ancient gas pump such as Mr Jimmon hadn't seen for years – and lifted the drooling hose from the can.

"Minute," said Mr Jimmon.

He stuck two fingers quickly and delicately inside the nozzle and smelled them. Gas all right, not water. He held out a ten-dollar bill. "Start filling."

Jir and Wendell appeared out of the shadows. "Can we stop at a town where there's a movie tonight?"

The handle turned, a cog-toothed rod crept up and retreated, gasoline gurgled into the tank. Movies, thought Mr Jimmon, handing over another bill; movies, rest rooms, baths, restaurants. Gouge apprehensively lest a scene be made and propriety disturbed. In a surrealist daydream he saw Molly turning the crank, grinding him on the cogs, pouring his essence into insatiable Jir and Wendell. He held out $20.

Twelve gallons had been put in when Molly appeared. "You have a phone here?" he asked casually. Knowing the answer from the blue enamelled sign not quite lost among less sturdy ones advertising soft drinks and cigarettes.

"You want to call the cops?" He didn't pause in his pumping.

"No. Know if the lines to L.A." – Mr Jimmon loathed the abbreviation – "are open yet?" He gave him another ten.

"How should I know?"

Mr Jimmon beckoned his wife around the other side of the wagon, out of sight. Swiftly but casually he extracted the contents of his wallet. The 200 dollar bills made a fat lump. "Put this in your bag," he said. "Tell you why later.

118

Meantime why don't you try and get Pearl and Dan on the phone? See if they're okay?"

He imagined the puzzled look on her face. "Go on," he urged. "We can spare a minute while he's checking the oil."

He thought there was a hint of uncertainty in Molly's walk as she went towards the store. Erika joined her brothers. The tank gulped: gasoline splashed on the concrete. "Guess that's it."

The man became suddenly brisk as he put up the hose, screwed the gas cap back on. Mr Jimmon had already disengaged the hood; the man offered the radiator a squirt of water, pulled up the oil gauge, wiped it, plunged it down, squinted at it under the light, and said, "Oil's OK."

"All right," said Mr Jimmon. "Get in Erika."

Some of the light shone directly on her face. Again he noted how mature and self-assured she looked. Erika would survive – and not as a savage either. The man started to wipe the windshield. "Oh, Jir," he said casually, "run in and see if your mother is getting her connexion. Tell her we'll wait."

"Aw furcrysay. I don't see why I always – "

"And ask her to buy a couple of boxes of candy bars if they've got them. Wendell, go with Jir, will you?"

He slid in behind the wheel and closed the door gently. The motor started with hardly a sound. As he put his foot on the clutch and shifted into low he thought Erika turned to him with a startled look. As the station wagon moved forward, he was sure of it.

"It's all right, Erika," said Mr Jimmon, "I'll explain later." He'd have lots of time to do it.

2001: A SPACE ODYSSEY

(MGM, 1968)
Starring: Keir Dullea, Gary Lockwood
& William Sylvester
Directed by Stanley Kubrick
Script by Arthur C. Clarke from his story
"Sentinel of Eternity"

Few other films have had quite such an impact on movie history in general or been more influential on the Space Movies genre in particular than Stanley Kubrick's visually overwhelming *2001: A Space Odyssey* which, a quarter of a century after it was made, still remains the benchmark against which all pictures of this kind are judged. It was by far the most ambitious SF film of its time and by spanning human history from prehistoric times to the year 2001 emphasised that man was still very much in the infancy of his development and was, in all probability, the "property" of vastly superior alien intelligences. But human beings were not actually at the core of the story – that distinction belonged to a space ship's super-computer, HAL 9000, which increasingly ran amok during the course of the journey, killing all the astronauts bar one before it reached the appointed rendezvous with an alien sentinel. HAL's demise during the climax to the picture has been called "one of the longest and most poignant death scenes in film history" (*The Times*) and actually won the superbrain – whose voice was that of actor Douglas Rain – an Oscar. Although *2001* was very much Kubrick's vision and he was responsible for many of the picture's remarkable innovations, the special effects owed a great deal to the team of Douglas Trumbell, a veteran of space documentary, and his fellow film technicians, Wally Veevers, Con Pederson and Tom Howard. This monumental film actually

Sentinel of Eternity

originated from a brief story, "The Sentinel of Eternity" by Arthur C. Clarke (1917–), the English-born SF writer who has been lavished with awards for his best-selling novels and praised by scientists for the prescience of his ideas. Clarke used the tale – which he had originally published in *10 Story Fantasy* in September 1951 – as the basis for his script which he worked on in 1966; but he was thereafter little involved in the lengthy and extremely costly filming of the picture during the next two years when Kubrick gave full vent to his imagination and skill as a film maker to create a wholly believable space voyage to Jupiter. Audiences around the world had seen nothing like the wonders he brought to the screen – and movie special effects, also, have never been the same since.

The next time you see the full moon high in the South, look carefully at its right-hand edge and let your eye travel upwards along the curve of the disc. Round about 2 o'clock you will notice a small, dark oval; anyone with normal eyesight can find it quite easily. It is the great walled plain, one of the finest on the Moon, known as the Mare Crisium – the Sea of Crises. Three hundred miles in diameter, and almost completely surrounded by a ring of magnificent mountains, it had never been explored until we entered it in the late summer of 1996.

Our expedition was a large one. We had two heavy freighters which had flown our supplies and equipment from the main lunar base in the Mare Serenitatis, five hundred miles away. There were also three small rockets which were intended for short-range transport over regions which our surface vehicles couldn't cross. Luckily, most of the Mare Crisium is very flat. There are none of the great crevasses so common and so dangerous elsewhere, and very few craters or mountains of any size. As far as we could tell, our powerful caterpillar tractors would have no difficulty in taking us wherever we wished.

121

Arthur C. Clarke

I was geologist – or selenologist, if you want to be pedantic – in charge of the group exploring the southern region of the Mare. We had crossed a hundred miles of it in a week, skirting the foothills of the mountains along the shore of what was once the ancient sea, some thousand million years before. When life was beginning on Earth, it was already dying here. The waters were retreating down the flanks of those stupendous cliffs, retreating into the empty heart of the Moon. Over the land which we were crossing, the tideless ocean had once been half a mile deep, and now the only trace of moisture was the hoarfrost one could sometimes find in caves which the searing sunlight never penetrated.

We had begun our journey early in the slow lunar dawn, and still had almost a week of Earth-time before nightfall. Half a dozen times a day we would leave our vehicle and go outside in the spacesuits to hunt for interesting minerals, or to place markers for the guidance of future travellers. It was an uneventful routine. There is nothing hazardous or even particularly exciting about lunar exploration. We could live comfortably for a month in our pressurized tractors, and if we ran into trouble we could always radio for help and sit tight until one of the spaceships came to our rescue. When that happened there was always a frightful outcry about the waste of rocket fuel, so a tractor sent out an SOS only in a real emergency.

I said just now that there was nothing exciting about lunar exploration, but of course that isn't true. One could never grow tired of those incredible mountains, so much steeper and more rugged than the gentle hills of Earth. We never knew, as we rounded the capes and promontories of that vanished sea, what new splendors would be revealed to us. The whole southern curve of the Mare Crisium is a vast delta where a score of rivers had once found their way into the ocean, fed perhaps by the torrential rains that must have lashed the mountains in the brief volcanic age when the Moon was young. Each of these ancient valleys was an invitation, challenging us to climb into the unknown uplands beyond. But we had a hundred miles still to cover, and could only look longingly at the heights which others must scale.

We kept Earth-time aboard the tractor, and precisely at 22.00 hours the final radio message would be sent out to Base and we would close down for the day. Outside, the rocks would still be burning beneath the almost vertical sun, but to us it was night until we awoke again eight hours later. Then one of us would prepare breakfast, there would be a great buzzing of electric shavers, and someone would switch on the short-wave radio from Earth. Indeed, when the smell of frying bacon began to fill the cabin, it was sometimes hard to believe that we were not back on our own world – everything was so normal and homey, apart from the feeling of decreased weight and the unnatural slowness with which objects fell.

It was my turn to prepare breakfast in the corner of the main cabin that served as a galley. I can remember that moment quite vividly after all these years, for the radio had just played one of my favourite melodies, the old Welsh air, *David of the White Rock*. Our driver was already outside in his spacesuit, inspecting our caterpillar treads. My assistant, Louis Garnett, was up forward in the control position, making some belated entries in yesterday's log.

As I stood by the frying pan, waiting, like any terrestrial housewife, for the sausages to brown, I let my gaze wander idly over the mountain walls which covered the whole of the southern horizon, marching out of sight to east and west below the curve of the Moon. They seemed only a mile or two from the tractor, but I knew that the nearest was twenty miles away. On the Moon, of course, there is no loss of detail with distance – none of that almost imperceptible haziness which softens and sometimes transfigures all far-off things on Earth.

123

Those mountains were ten thousand feet high, and they climbed steeply out of the plain as if ages ago some subterranean eruption had smashed them skywards through the molten crust. The base of even the nearest was hidden from sight by the steeply curving surface of the plain, for the Moon is a very little world, and from where I was standing the optical horizon was only two miles away.

I lifted my eyes towards the peaks which no man had ever climbed, the peaks which, before the coming of Terrestrial life, had watched the retreating oceans sink sullenly into their graves, taking with them the hope and the morning promise of a world. The sunlight was beating against those ramparts with a glare that hurt the eyes, yet only a little way above them the stars were shining steadily in a sky blacker than a winter midnight on Earth.

I was turning away when my eye caught a metallic glitter high on the ridge of a great promontory thrusting out into the sea thirty miles to the west. It was a dimensionless point of light, as if a star had been clawed from the sky by one of those cruel peaks, and I imagined that some smooth rock surface was catching the sunlight and heliographing it straight into my eyes. Such things were not uncommon. When the Moon is in her second quarter, observers on Earth can sometimes see the great ranges in the Oceanus Procellarum burning with a blue-white iridescence as the sunlight flashes from their slopes and leaps again from world to world. But I was curious to know what kind of rock could be shining so brightly up there, and I climbed into the observation turret and swung our four inch telescope round to the west.

I could see just enough to tantalize me. Clear and sharp in the field of vision, the mountain peaks seemed only half a mile away, but whatever was catching the sunlight was still too small to be resolved. Yet it seemed to have an elusive symmetry, and the summit upon which it rested was curiously flat. I stared for a long time at that glittering

124

enigma, straining my eyes into space, until presently a smell of burning from the galley told me that our breakfast sausages had made their quarter-million mile journey in vain.

All that morning we argued our way across the Mare Crisium while the western mountains reared higher in the sky. Even when we were out prospecting in the spacesuits, the discussion would continue over the radio. It was absolutely certain, my companions argued, that there had never been any form of intelligent life on the Moon. The only living things that had ever existed there were a few primitive plants and their slightly less degenerate ancestors. I knew that as well as anyone, but there are times when a scientist must not be afraid to make a fool of himself.

"Listen," I said at last, "I'm going up there, if only for my own peace of mind. That mountain's less than twelve thousand feet high – that's only two thousand under Earth gravity – and I can make the trip in twenty hours at the outside. I've always wanted to go up into those hills, anyway, and this gives me an excellent excuse."

"If you don't break your neck," said Garnett, "you'll be the laughing-stock of the expedition when we get back to Base. That mountain will probably be called Wilson's Folly from now on."

"I *won't* break my neck," I said firmly. "Who was the first man to climb Pico and Helicon?"

"But weren't you rather younger in those days?" asked Louis gently.

"That," I said with great dignity, "is as good a reason as any for going."

We went to bed early that night, after driving the tractor to within half a mile of the promontory. Garnett was coming with me in the morning; he was a good climber, and had often been with me on such exploits before. Our driver was only too glad to be left in charge of the machine.

At first sight, those cliffs seemed completely unscalable, but to anyone with a good head for heights, climbing is easy on a world where all weights are only a sixth of their normal value. The real danger in lunar mountaineering lies in overconfidence; a six hundred foot drop on the Moon can kill you just as thoroughly as a hundred foot fall on Earth.

We made our first half on a wide ledge about four thousand feet above the plain. Climbing had not been very difficult, but my limbs were stiff with the unaccustomed effort, and I was glad of the rest. We could still see the tractor as a tiny metal insect far down at the foot of the cliff, and we reported our progress to the driver before starting on the next ascent.

Hour by hour the horizon widened and more and more of the great plain came into sight. Now we could look for fifty miles out across the Mare, and could even see the peaks of the mountains on the opposite coast more than a hundred miles away. Few of the great lunar plains are as smooth as the Mare Crisium, and we could almost imagine that a sea of water and not of rock was lying there two miles below. Only a group of crater-pits low down on the skyline spoilt the illusion.

Our goal was still invisible over the crest of the mountain, and we were steering by maps, using the Earth as a guide. Almost due east of us, that great silver crescent hung low over the plain, already well into its first quarter. The sun and the stars would make their slow march across the sky and would sink presently from sight but Earth would always be there never moving from her appointed place, waxing and waning as the year and seasons passed. In ten days' time she would be a blinding disc bathing these rocks with her midnight radiance, fifty-fold brighter than the full moon. But we must be out of the mountains long before night, or else we would remain among them forever.

Sentinel of Eternity

Inside our suits it was comfortably cool, for the refrigeration units were fighting the fierce sun and carrying away the body-heat of our exertions. We seldom spoke to each other, except to pass climbing instructions and to discuss our best plan of ascent. I do not know what Garnett was thinking, probably that this was the craziest goose-chase he had ever embarked upon. I more than half agreed with him, but the joy of climbing, the knowledge that no man had ever gone this way before and the exhilaration of the steadily widening landscape gave me all the reward I needed.

I don't think I was particularly excited when I saw in front of us the wall of rock I had first inspected through the telescope from thirty miles away. It would level off about fifty feet above our heads, and there on the plateau would be the thing that had lured me over these barren wastes. It was, almost certainly, nothing more than a boulder splintered ages ago by a falling meteor, and with its cleavage planes still fresh and bright in this incorruptible unchanging silence.

There were no hand-holds on the rock face, and we had to use a grapnel. My tired arms seemed to gain new strength as I swung the three-pronged metal anchor round my head and sent it sailing up towards the stars. The first time, it broke loose and came falling slowly back when we pulled the rope. On the third attempt, the prongs gripped firmly and our combined weights could not shift it.

Garnett looked at me anxiously. I could tell that he wanted to go first, but I smiled back at him through the glass of my helmet and shook my head. Slowly, taking my time, I began the final ascent.

Even with my spacesuit, I weighed only forty pounds here, so I pulled myself up hand over hand without bothering to use my feet. At the rim I paused and waved to my companion, then I scrambled over the edge and stood upright, staring ahead of me.

You must understand that until this very moment I had been almost completely convinced that there could be nothing strange or unusual for me to find here. Almost, but not quite; it was that haunting doubt that had driven me forwards. Well, it was a doubt no longer, but the haunting had scarcely begun.

I was standing on a plateau perhaps a hundred feet across. It had once been smooth – too smooth to be natural – but falling meteors had pitted and scored its surface through immeasurable aeons. It had been levelled to support a glittering, roughly pyramidal structure, twice as high as a man, that was set in the rock like a gigantic, many-faceted jewel.

Probably no emotion at all filled my mind in those first few seconds. Then I felt a great lifting of my heart, and a strange, inexpressible joy. For I loved the Moon, and now I knew that the creeping moss of Aristarchus and Eratosthenes was not the only life she had brought forth in her youth. The old, discredited dream of the first explorers was true. There had, after all, been a lunar civilization – and I was the first to find it. That I had come perhaps a hundred million years too late did not distress me; it was enough to have come at all.

My mind was beginning to function normally, to analyze and to ask questions. Was this a building, a shrine – or something for which my language had no name? If a building, then why was it erected in so uniquely inaccessible a spot? I wondered if it might be a temple, and I could picture the adepts of some strange priesthood calling on their gods to preserve them as the life of the Moon ebbed with the dying oceans, and calling on their gods in vain.

I took a dozen steps forward to examine the thing more closely, but some sense of caution kept me from going too near. I knew a little of archaeology, and tried to guess the cultural level of the civilization that must have smoothed this mountain and raised the glittering mirror surfaces that still dazzled my eyes.

The Egyptians could have done it, I thought, if their workmen had possessed whatever strange materials these far more ancient architects had used. Because of the thing's smallness, it did not occur to me that I might be looking at the handiwork of a race more advanced than my own. The idea that the Moon had possessed intelligence at all was still almost too tremendous to grasp, and my pride would not let me take the final, humiliating plunge.

And then I noticed something that set the scalp crawling at the back of my neck – something so trivial and so innocent that many would never have noticed it at all. I have said that the plateau was scarred by meteors; it was also coated inches deep with the cosmic dust that is always filtering down upon the surface of any world where there are no winds to disturb it. Yet the dust and the meteor scratches ended quite abruptly in a wide circle enclosing the little pyramid, as though an invisible wall was protecting it from the ravages of time and the slow but ceaseless bombardment from space.

There was someone shouting in my earphones, and I realized that Garnett had been calling me for some time. I walked unsteadily to the edge of the cliff and signalled him to join me, not trusting myself to speak. Then I went back towards that circle in the dust. I picked up a fragment of splintered rock and tossed it gently towards the shining enigma. If the pebble had vanished at that invisible barrier I should not have been surprised, but it seemed to hit a smooth, hemispherical surface and slid gently to the ground.

I knew then that I was looking at nothing that could be matched in the antiquity of my own race. This was not a building, but a machine, protecting itself with forces that had challenged Eternity. Those forces, whatever they might be, were still operating, and perhaps I had already come too close. I thought of all the radiations man had trapped and tamed in the past century. For all I knew, I might be as irrevocably doomed as if I had stepped into the deadly, silent aura of an unshielded atomic pile.

I remember turning then towards Garnett, who had joined me and was now standing motionless at my side. He seemed quite oblivious to me, so I did not disturb him but walked to the edge of the cliff in an effort to marshal my thoughts. There below me lay the Mare Crisium – Sea of Crises, indeed – strange and weird to most men, but reassuringly familiar to me. I lifted my eyes towards the crescent Earth, lying in her cradle of stars, and I wondered what her clouds had covered when these unknown builders had finished their work. Was it the steaming jungle of the Carboniferous, the bleak shoreline over which the first amphibians must crawl to conquer the land – or, earlier still, the long loneliness before the coming of life?

Do not ask me why I did not guess the truth sooner – the truth that seems so obvious now. In the first excitement of my discovery, I had assumed without question that this crystalline apparition had been built by some race belonging to the Moon's remote past, but suddenly, and with overwhelming force, the belief came to me that it was as alien to the Moon as I myself.

In twenty years we had found no trace of life but a few degenerate plants. No lunar civilization, whatever its doom, could have left but a single token of its existence.

I looked at the shining pyramid again, and the more remote it seemed from anything that had to do with the Moon. And suddenly I felt myself shaking with a foolish, hysterical laughter, brought on by excitement and over-exertion: for I had imagined that the little pyramid was speaking to me and was saying: "Sorry, I'm a stranger here myself."

It has taken us twenty years to crack that invisible shield and to reach the machine inside those crystal walls. What we could not understand, we broke at last with the savage might of atomic power and now I have seen the fragments of the lovely, glittering thing I found up there on the mountain.

They are meaningless. The mechanisms – if indeed they are mechanisms – of the pyramid belong to a technology that lies far beyond our horizon, perhaps to the technology of para-physical forces.

The mystery haunts us all the more now that the other planets have been reached and we know that only Earth has ever been the home of intelligent life. Nor could any lost civilization of our own world have built that machine, for the thickness of the meteoric dust on the plateau has enabled us to measure its age. It was set there upon its mountain before life had emerged from the seas of Earth.

When our world was half its present age, *something* from the stars swept through the Solar System, left this token of its passage, and went again upon its way. Until we destroyed it, that machine was still fulfilling the purpose of its builders; and as to that purpose, here is my guess.

Nearly a hundred thousand million stars are turning in the circle of the Milky Way, and long ago other races on the worlds of other suns must have scaled and passed the heights that we have reached. Think of such civilizations, far back in time against the fading afterglow of Creation, masters of a universe so young that life as yet had come only to a handful of worlds. Theirs would have been a loneliness we cannot imagine, the loneliness of gods looking out across infinity and finding none to share their thoughts.

They must have searched the star-clusters as we have searched the planets. Everywhere there would be worlds, but they would be empty or peopled with crawling, mindless things. Such was our own Earth, the smoke of the great volcanoes still staining its skies, when that first ship of the peoples of the dawn came sliding in from the abyss beyond Pluto. It passed the frozen outer worlds, knowing that life could play no part in their destinies. It came to rest among the inner planets, warming themselves around the fire of the Sun and waiting for their stories to begin.

Those wanderers must have looked on Earth, circling safely in the narrow zone between fire and ice, and must have guessed that it was the favorite of the Sun's children. Here, in the distant future, would be intelligence; but there were countless stars before them still, and they might never come this way again.

So they left a sentinel, one of millions they have scattered throughout the universe, watching over all worlds with the promise of life. It was a beacon that down the ages has been patiently signalling the fact that no one had discovered it.

Perhaps you understand now why that crystal pyramid was set upon the Moon instead of on the Earth. Its builders were not concerned with races still struggling up from savagery. They would be interested in our civilization only if we proved our fitness to survive – by crossing space and so escaping from the Earth, our cradle. That is the challenge that all intelligent races must meet, sooner or later. It is a double challenge, for it depends in turn upon the conquest of atomic energy and the last choice between life and death.

Once we had passed that crisis, it was only a matter of time before we found the pyramid and forced it open. Now its signals have ceased, and those whose duty it is will be turning their minds upon Earth. Perhaps they wish to help our infant civilization. But they must be very, very old, and the old are often insanely jealous of the young.

I can never look now at the Milky Way without wondering from which of those banked clouds of stars the emissaries are coming. If you will pardon so commonplace a simile, we have broken the glass of the fire-alarm and have nothing to do but to wait.

I do not think we will have to wait for long.

LOGAN'S RUN

(MGM/United Artists, 1976)
Starring: Michael York, Jenny Agutter & Peter Ustinov
Directed by Michael Anderson
Based on *Logan's Run* by William F. Nolan
& George C. Johnson

Logan's Run is another SF story which now enjoys an international cult reputation because of the movie it inspired, the TV series which followed, and the literary sequels which co-author William F. Nolan has written. The story is also set in the twenty-first century where the computer is all-powerful – now it actually rules the population and has solved the problem of over-population by ordering the mandatory death of men and women as soon as they reach the age of 21. To enforce this ruling, there exists a crack force of Sandmen who hunt down and kill anyone who tries to escape, those referred to as "runners". Logan, when first met, is a Sandman: cunning, efficient and a crack shot. But his ideals are put to the test when he reaches the fatal age just at the time when he has fallen in love with a beautiful girl, Jessica. The couple decide to become runners – and Logan soon comes to realise that he needs all his old resourcefulness to outwit the elite corps of killers to which he once belonged. According to his American creator, the respected and prolific author William F. Nolan (1928), the unique concept for *Logan's Run* came to him by simply reversing the old saying, "Life begins at Forty". Bill, who was formerly a commercial artist, worked on the original story with his friend, George Clayton Johnson, and although their novel was published in 1967, almost a decade passed before it was finally brought to the screen. But patience has been rewarded, and Bill has subsequently watched Logan (whom he named after the phone exchange of the Kansas City home where he grew up) become a "pop culture" hero with his own fan club, magazines, books and even games and puzzles inspired by the Sandman's world. The original novel has been followed by two sequels – both solo efforts by Bill – *Logan's World* (1977) and *Logan's Search* (1980), which together complete the trilogy. In order to represent the original movie and the TV series (which starred Gregory Harrison and Heather Menzies), the author has selected the following episode from *Logan's World*, and also provided these notes by way of introduction . . .

"*Logan's World* is, of course, a direct sequel to *Logan's Run*. Ten years have passed and the great computer that ruled the youth society, The Thinker, with its system of compulsory death at 21, has been destroyed and the force of Sandmen (DS or Deep Sleep operatives) have been disbanded. Logan and Jessica are now living with the Wilderness People beyond the destroyed cities and have a young son, Jag. When the boy becomes ill, Logan sets out to find a proper medicine for him, but while he is away, a gypsy band kill Jag and kidnap Jessica. When Logan discovers the dead boy he is convinced that Jess is also dead and is plunged into a deep depression. He decides to go to New York to obtain a large dosage of the drug R-11 as a way to recapture the love of his wife and son – despite being warned that the drug is extremely dangerous and he might never 'come out' or even die. He rejects the warning, declaring that without Jess and Jag, 'I'm dead already.' In this episode of Logan's extraordinary saga he again meets Dia, a young blind girl, who is a telepath, and Jonath, the leader of the Wilderness People. Now read on . . ."

Logan had taken a mazecar to the New York Complex on leave from DS school when he was sixteen to pairmate with a female who lived there. She was an older woman of twenty, a year away from Sleep and into young Sandmen. Gonzales 2 had told Logan about her, told him she was something really special. Chinese. Sexually astonishing.

Gonzales had been correct. Her voracious sensual appetites had drained Logan, left him anxious to return to duty. The pleasure with her had been so intense it was akin to pain. New York was different then: glittering, swarming with citizens, a world mecca for exotic living.

Now it was dark ruins.

But it had something Logan wanted far more than he had wanted the Chinese girl. It had R-11.

In 2010, when Mayor Margaret Hatch had ordered the Central Park fill-in, construction of the Green Giants had begun. Taking their name from the fact that they were replacing the last bit of open greenery in New York City, the Giants were designed to accommodate three million, a bold step in reducing the city's acute housing crisis. In height, they were taller than the Empire State and each was a self-contained miniature city, with every comfort and convenience. To get space in one, you hocked your soul, and signed a lifetime lease.

The first three-mile complex was a converted Giant. But, eventually, the outdated skytowers were torn down and replaced.

Nostalgia prevailed. As a memorial to the past, one of the Green Giants was allowed to remain standing, dwarfed by the three-mile city dwellings around it.

Yet it lived again when the Thinker died. Its precomputerized, self-contained power units were quickly utilized, and it became the hub in cross-state Market operations, a mighty storehouse-headquarters, humming with activity. After more than a century of obsolescence, it was now the only living structure in a dead city.

Logan came to the Giant for R-11.

Jonath had told him that he would have no trouble with Scavengers in New York. This was one city they did not control. "The Marketers are in charge there," Jonath had said.

"Who are they exactly?"

"Mostly ex-DS. A few key merchantmen. They keep the Scavengers in line. The city's wide open."

Flying over it at night, Logan got the impression of a vast, lightless range of man-made mountains, upthrusting peaks of steel and glass. Dominating the interior of the city, with flamebright gaudiness, standing two thousand feet above street level, light flooding out from its metal pores, stood the Green Giant.

As he swept over the shining structure, pinlights found his craft. Two Market patrolships soared up from the roof of the building to circle Logan, guiding him to a setdown on the Giant's illumined skyport.

Logan cut power, exited to the roof.

"No weapons allowed," a tall man in gray said to him. The Market guard carried a belted Fuser. His eyes were humorless.

Logan nodded, placed his holstered Gun inside the paravane, sealed the magnetic lock. "How long can I leave my ship here?" he asked.

"As long as you have business inside," said the guard. "We'll keep an eye on it."

"Thanks," said Logan.

Another gray-clad guard walked up to him as he neared the entrance shaft. "Name?"

"Logan 3."

"Seeing who?"

"Lacy 14."

"You'll need a contact pass."

Logan handed him the foilslip he'd obtained from Rawls. The guard studied it for a moment, notched one corner with a foilpunch, handed it back.

"Go ahead," he said, activating the shaft release.

Logan stepped inside.

The interior corridors shimmered with light; this intensity of artificial illumination stunned Logan. He'd seen nothing like it since the days of Arcade. Because the Giant was able to generate its own electricity, and had never depended on the Thinker for power, the death of the great computer had not affected it. Restoration had been relatively simple – and now this city-within-a-city was functioning at peak efficiency after long years of darkness. Indeed, a sleeping Giant had awakened to serve new masters.

Although the outer surface of the building glowed beacon-bright, the majority of its two hundred floors were dark; the Market occupied only the Penthouse area and the three floors just beneath for storage. The Giant was private, off-limits, except to those who ran the Market, and to the few special customers allowed to deal inside for highgrade goods. Such as R-11.

At the end of the corridor another guard stopped Logan. Same gray uniform. Same eyes. The hard look of the Sandman. Ex-DS, fitting their new roles as skin fits muscle.

"Pass," said the guard.

Logan produced the notched foilslip.

The guard pressed a section of wall. A door oiled back.

"Keep moving," said the guard.

Another corridor. Much shorter.

Logan faced a heavy flexcurtain, woven entirely from gold mesh. The curtain stirred, folded back.

"Come in, Logan 3."

A woman's voice. Sensual. Low-pitched.

Logan entered a chamber draped in silks and lit by firebirds. The small, feathered creatures, whose metallic bodies pulsed with inner light, swooped in glowing arcs around the large center room, settling, strutting, ruffling their multicolored plumage . . .

Logan hesitated, scanning the room. He saw no one. Only the birds, like moving fire jewels.

Then the woman appeared, rising from one corner of the chamber. She had been lying on a fall of snowpillows and, in standing, seemed to materialize from the room itself, seemed made of silks and smoked ivory.

Her body was perfection – a rich orchestration of scented peaks and soft valleys, tautly accented by the white flow-gown she wore. A cat-emerald burned at her throat.

"I'm Lacy 14," she said.

"Since you know my name," said Logan. "I assume you also know what I came for."

A firebird fluttered to her shoulder and she stroked the glowing plumage, her large green-black eyes fixed on Logan.

"Why so abrupt?" she smiled. "I never conduct business without getting to know my buyers. Sit down, Logan."

Snowpillows. A soft peltrug of worked silver. No couch or chairs. Logan sat, adjusting one of the larger pillows at his back.

"Much better," said Lacy. "Drink?"

"No."

"I insist. I have a really excellent fruitwine from Spain which is impossible to duplicate," she told him.

Logan nodded. "Since you insist."

She brought him the wine, settled next to him. "Let us drink to the satisfactory conclusion of pleasure."

Logan was edgy, off-balance; he had expected a hard-faced Marketer who would waste no time, no words. He'd expected to deal quickly and be gone without ceremony. But, instead, here was Lacy . . .

Logan tasted the wine, allowing the smoked flavor to permeate his tongue. "You're right," he said. "This is excellent."

"I've heard about you, Logan."

"What have you heard?"

"That you sought out and destroyed the Borgias. Alone, at Steinbeck. One against twelve. Is it true?"

"It's true," said Logan. "But I'm not going to talk about it."

"That's not necessary," she smiled. "You're obviously a man of great passion. I've . . . been waiting for someone extraordinary."

Logan slipped a sack of Mooncoins from his belt.

"All I want here is what I came to get," he said. "A quantampac of R-11."

"That will be produced in due course. After you've earned it."

"I have these," he said, handing her the Mooncoins. "There's nothing like them on Earth."

She put the sack aside, unopened. "We'll deal with these later. *I* come first."

Logan was suddenly angry.

"Get a merchantman to penetrate you," he said. "Or one of your ex-DS. They all have fine bodies. They'll do a very satisfactory job."

She laughed, a throaty sound, deep and assured. "I don't want you – or any other male," she told him. "I never allow a man to touch me. Ever."

"Well, what *do* you want?"

"Follow me and find out." She stood, putting aside her wine.

Logan got up. "Can't we just – "

"This way," said Lacy. "If you want the pac, you do as I say."

Sighing, Logan followed her out of the chamber.

They moved together down a short hallway. Lacy opened a mirrored door, beckoned Logan forward.

The room he entered was a large bedchamber, draped in crimson and gold. Soft lights shone through the draperies, and at least half of the floor area was occupied by two deep, expansive flowbeds.

"Recline," said Lacy. "On the farther bed. I'll take this one."

Logan did as she asked. What did she have planned for him?

Lacy kept her eyes on Logan as she touched a magclasp at her neck; the gown fell away from her body in a soft spill of white. "Am I not beautiful?" she asked him.

"You are," he said.

Her breasts were coned and delicate, tapering to a waist which swelled to perfect hips and long, superbly-muscled legs. "Many men have desired me. Do you desire me, Logan?"

"At another time, in another place . . ."

She draped herself across the bed, facing his, cat-smiled at him. "I am not your concern here," she said. "You shall provide a show . . . for my stimulation."

"I don't understand."

She clapped her hands sharply.

The drapes parted at the rear of the chamber.

There were three of them. All nude. All beautiful. All black-skinned and full-figured and arousing. Perfect females, who would have been the pride of any glasshouse from Moscow to Paris.

"They're for you, Logan," said Lacy. "And you are for them."

"You expect me to – "

"Pleasure them. That's what you shall do if you want to please me. And if you do *not* please me, you will not get the thing you came for."

She turned to the girls. Her eyes were bright and hot. "Undress him," she said. "Caress him. Erect him."

They swayed toward Logan like dusky flowers.

So *this* is how she obtains her satisfaction? All right, Logan told himself, I'll do as she asks. I'll give her a show. And I'll enjoy what I'm doing. I'll steep myself in warm flesh . . . lose myself in sexuality.

Indeed, why not?

And Logan took them into his arms.

Logan followed Lacy 14 down the short hallway. As they entered her living quarters a firebird settled on Logan's shoulder, splashing his face with vivid colors. He shook the bird off, and the creature wing whispered away.

"I did what you asked," he said to Lacy.

"A splendid performance," she agreed. She was wearing the white gown once again, and it billowed as she turned.

"Do I get the pac now?"

"Let me see what you've brought." She picked up the sack of Mooncoins, spilled them into her hand. They were round, bright, stamped with Moon symbols.

"I brought them down from Darkside," said Logan. "You won't find any others. Anywhere."

"They're . . . attractive," she said. "I can use them. But they won't pay for a full dex. Not of R-11."

Logan flushed with anger. "I did what you asked with the females . . ."

"And enjoyed yourself handsomely in the process," she said.

"Wasn't that what you wanted – to watch me pleasuring them to pleasure yourself?" He tightened his jaw. "I've given you all I have. Everything."

"Not everything," she said.

"What's left?"

"Your paravane. It should fetch a good price. I'll take the coins, *and* your ship." She smiled. "You know, I'm really being generous about this. You're here alone, unarmed. Normally, I would just have my men *take* your ship and give you nothing in return. But . . . since you've . . . amused me, I'm willing to turn over the drug."

"I can't get back to camp without my ship," said Logan. "And I *need* Jonath. It's impossible to take R-11 without someone to – "

"Take it here," said Lacy. "I'll provide a liftroom for you, and see to your needs."

Logan considered it. There was nothing left for him in Old Washington. Why *not* stay here in the New York Complex? One city was no better or worse than another now, without Jess.

"I accept," said Logan.

"There's risk in a full dex," said Lacy. "It could kill you."

Logan said nothing.

"There's no body or mind control with such a high dosage," she said. "You're at the mercy of the drug."

"I want maximum lift," said Logan. "A *full* re-live. And only a dex will give me that."

"Your decision," shrugged Lacy. "Get whatever personal belongings you have in the ship, then come back here. I'll have the R-11."

He hated losing the paravane. It was a high price to pay. Still, Lacy could have simply taken it, as she said. In dealing with the Market there were no guarantees. You took what they gave you.

Logan had the Gun when the guard said, "You can't go back inside with that." His name was Stile, and he captained Lacy's men. Huge. Slab-bodied. Cruel-faced.

"Lacy made the deal," said Logan. "She gets the ship and I get my personal belongings. This is mine. It goes with me."

Stile looked sullen. "All right . . . I'll make an exception this time," he said. "But keep it holstered."

"Couple of Fusers in there you can have," said Logan. "They were never mine to begin with."

He fixed the Gun holster to his belt.

There was nothing else. The ship was theirs now.

As the R-11 would soon be his.

The small liftroom was stark and empty, dun-colored, without ornament or decoration. Four walls, a floor and a ceiling. No windows or vents.

"You'll need this," Lacy said, and gestured. A gray-clad

142

guard dumped a bodymat, quickly unrolled it. The mat covered the floor, wall to wall.

"What about oxygen?"

"Enough. The room's not sealed."

"I'll need water."

"At necessary intervals. Pelletgun . . . directly into your system."

"I don't want to be observed," said Logan.

"You won't be," said Lacy. "But if you convulse . . ."

"*No* observation. Just the injections . . . water when I require it. Agreed?"

"Agreed."

"The drug?" asked Logan.

From her belt, Lacy withdrew a small silver disc. She pressed its center and the disc released a single milky-white pearl. It rolled, catching the light, in the palm of her hand.

"Hard to believe that's a full dex," said Logan.

She smiled. "You've never used R-11?"

"No," he admitted.

"A normal dosage is almost microscopic," she told him. "This is a quantam, full-dex strength. Usually this much R-11 is broken into powder, administered in several stages. I've never seen anyone take a pearl."

"The Re-Live drawers died with the cities," said Logan. "This is the only way left to go back."

"Is going back *that* important?"

"Yes," said Logan. "It's that important."

She looked at him for a long moment, then handed him the pearl.

"Just place it in the middle of your tongue," she said. "Let it dissolve directly into the tissue. It's effective immediately after ingestion."

And she left him.

Logan brought up the pearl, holding it between the thumb and index finger of his right hand; he studied it in the subdued light of the room. Harmless looking. Beautiful in its simple perfection.

But potent. Very, very potent.

The surface-distortion drug he'd been given by the Scavengers was Candee next to R-11, which was designed to penetrate to the deepest levels of stored life-experience. Science had long since proven, beyond any doubt, that every experience, however trivial, is permanently retained: every sight, sound, odor, every sensory moment of touch, every spoken word . . . all there, all three-dimensionally alive in the depths of the human brain.

The Re-Live parlors were built on this principle. In their metal wombs it had been possible to re-experience, at choice, any hour, or day, or moment of one's past.

That was the key word: *choice*. The Re-Live drawers gave you selective control, provided you wished to exercise it. And there were built-in shutoffs if the emotional surge threatened body-health. A Re-Live drawer was safe.

Not so with R-11. At maximum dosage, there was no control; it prowled the vaults of memory at will, and all choice was removed. However, short of maximum, Logan was not certain he could reach his full experiences with Jaq and Jessica. Under a light dosage he might never find them again.

R-11 had one basic advantage over any other minddrug. It gave back *truth*, not fantasy; experiences, not hallucinations. It did not distort as Lysergic Foam did. What Logan re-lived would be *real* events from his past.

And, buried in that past, his wife and son waited for him.

Logan sat down on the mat which gave softly under his weight.

Now.

Pearl into mouth. On the tongue. Dissolving . . .

Logan was fighting for balance. The wind whipped at his tunic, fisting him with short, savage gusts. He wasn't sure he could maintain his footing – and a fall was death.

He was sixteen, and new to DS. A raw Sandman, just out of Deep Sleep Training, hunting his first female, nervous, and over-anxious to prove himself.

Logan's runner, Brandith 2, had glass-danced the Arcades before her flower blacked; she was extremely agile, with an incredible sense of body-control. She had lured her nervous pursuer onto a narrow outside repair-ramp, dipping and weaving her way along the thin ridge of metal ahead of him. Luring him forward.

You should have fired the homer; the homer would have finished her!

In his excitement, Logan had set the Gun at ripper, and to be effective a ripper must be fired at fairly close range. He could re-set for homer, but to do so would require taking both hands off the ledgerail, and that was impossible. He'd lose his balance for sure.

"What's the matter, Sandman?" her voice mocked him. "Can't you catch me?"

She had passed an angle-beam, and was no longer in direct sight. Logan moved faster along the ramp, reached the beam. She was waiting for him.

"You're dead, Sandman!" And, braced on the beam, Brandith 2 delivered a smashing blow to his chest with her left foot.

Logan swayed, pitched forward to his knees. The Gun slipped from his clawing fingers. He twisted, hooking his right arm into a strut-support, and slashed up with the heel of his left hand.

The surprise blow took Brandith 2 at throat level, and crushed her windpipe. She clutched at her neck, gasped blood, and fell over the edge in a long, screaming death drop.

Logan felt relief, and instant shame. He'd failed to homer her, and worse yet – much worse – he'd lost the Gun. A Sandman must *never* relinquish his weapon: the first rule of DS. And now he had allowed a female runner to disarm him, and almost kill him.

On the ramp, alone in the crying wind, Logan could not move. He was locked into his misery. "Failure!" he said aloud. "Failure!"

Would he *ever* deserve to wear the uniform of a Sandman?

Egypt was a bore.

Logan was eight, and had taken a robocamel to the Pyramids with his best friend, Evans 9. They'd been to Japan earlier that morning, and found Kyoto dull with its restored temples and fat, bronze deities. But, in Tokyo, a sumo wrestler had taught them how to immobilize an opponent by a theatrical display of aggression, without actual body contact. Fascinating.

But Egypt was all heat and endless sand and ugly-snouted robot camels. The Pyramids were a disappointment – smaller than Logan expected, and badly in need of repair. The surface was pitted and crumbling, with many large stones near the top missing entirely.

"They ought to fix them," said Logan. "Smooth them out."

"No, tear them down," said Evans. "Put up new ones, *better* ones. Old things aren't worth saving."

"Old things are ugly," said Logan.

And that night they took a mazecar to Uganda.

"I can leave here, go with you," she told him.

"No, that's not possible."

"Why isn't it?"

"Because it isn't."

"But you find me exciting? You enjoy my body?"

"Yes."

"Then we'll pair-bond. Until it goes bad. When it goes bad, I'll leave. What's wrong with that?"

"A lot," he said. "I live alone."

"Why?"

"Because of what I am."

This silenced her.

The lovelights of the glasshouse played over their bodies. Gold . . .

Silver . . .

Red . . .

Yellow . . .

Blue . . .

And still she did not speak.

When Logan left the glasshouse he was angry. Why *couldn't* he form an alliance? Why *must* he live alone, finding sexual satisfaction on this fragmented, impulse basis?

Because of what I am.

A DS man cannot function effectively if he is pair-bonded. All emotional ties must be severed. Commitments must not be made. Nothing must interfere with duty.

Duty.

Duty.

"Show me your hand, Logan," said the psyc doctor.

Logan obeyed.

"Do you know why you have this?" he said, tapping the palmflower with an index finger.

"To tell my age," Logan said.

"And how old are you?"

"I'm six."

"And what happens when you're seven?"

Logan looked down at his palm. "It goes to blue. And I . . . leave Nursery."

The doctor nodded. He had kind eyes. "And you are afraid?"

"Yes," said Logan.

"Why? Why are you afraid, Logan?"

The words spilled out in a rush: "Because I love my talk puppet and because I don't want to leave Nursery and because . . ."

"Go on, tell me."

"Because the world is so big and I'm so little."

"But every boy and girl feels that way, and *they're* not afraid."

"I'll bet *some* of them are," said Logan. "Or they wouldn't use a machine like you."

"I deal with many problems at Nursery," said the doctor. He whirred to a medcab, took out a packet of Candees.

"I don't want a Candee," said Logan.

"But they taste good and they make you feel good," said the doctor.

"They make me sleepy."

"Take a Candee, Logan."

"No."

"*Do as I say!* Take one."

"No."

Logan backed away, but the square machine whirred after him. The doctor's kind eyes were no longer kind. They glittered with determination.

"I'll report this to Autogoverness," he threatened. "You'll be punished."

"I don't care," said Logan defiantly.

"Very well," said the doctor. And he pushed a button on his desk. An Autogoverness rolled into the office.

"Logan 3 is to be punished. After punishment, he will be given a Candee."

"Yes, doctor," said the round, many-armed robot. She took Logan's hand in one of hers.

"You see, Logan," said the doctor as the boy was being led out. "You *can't* win."

"How long has he been under?" asked Lacy.

"Two days, six hours," said Stile.

"Convulsions?"

"Minor so far."

148

"Heartbeat?"

"Erratic, but holding."

"Skincount?"

"One over fifteen. The chemical balance is distorted, but not critical. Of course, he's going in deeper. It could get worse. No way of telling."

"If he dies, notify me immediately."

"Of course," said Stile.

The blow caught Logan at the upper part of the shoulder, a deltoid chop, delivered with force and precision. He felt his left arm go numb, angled his body sharply to keep Francis in the direct line of attack.

He lashed out with a reverse savate kick, catching Francis at rib-level, causing him to lurch back, gasping for breath.

"You're good, Logan," said the tall, mantis-thin man, slowly circling his opponent.

"You're better, damn you!" Logan said. "But I'm learning."

"More each day," agreed Francis. "Shall we end this?"

Logan nodded, rubbing his shoulder. "I've had enough."

They hit the needleshower, standing together silently in the cutting spray. Francis had paid for his reputation; his body, in contrast to Logan's unmarked one, bore the scars of a hundred near-death encounters with fanatic runners, cubs, gypsies . . . Of the crack DS men at Angeles Complex, Francis was the fastest, the most dangerous, the best. Logan was still his pupil, but soon he might be his equal – with natural talent, good fortune, supreme dedication.

Francis had all these.

They walked back into the combat room, got into fresh grays.

"There's a lift party tonight at Stanhope's," said Logan. "Why not unbend, take it in?"

Francis smiled thinly. The smile was bloodless. "I don't party," he said.

149

"But we're off-duty until – "

"A Sandman's never off-duty," said Francis coldly. "We could be called in for backup."

"That's never happened to me yet," declared Logan.

"It might," said Francis.

Logan looked at him. "What *do* you do with your free time?"

"Use it properly. I don't waste it on witless females and lift parties."

"I give up," sighed Logan. He grinned. "You know, Francis, I wouldn't be surprised to find little wires and cogs and springs under your skin . . . You're not *quite* human."

"I get my job done," said Francis stiffly.

"Sure. Sure you do," said Logan. "Forget what I said."

But, as he watched Francis walk out, Logan wondered: what the hell *does* he do with his free time?

"This one's dangerous," said Evans. "He's stolen a para-vane and he's got a Fuser with him. I think we need backup."

Logan agreed. "Get on it, while I see if I can run him down."

"With a stick? Can you handle one?"

"I've ridden them before," said Logan. "They're much faster than a paravane."

"Take care," said Evans, sprinting for a callbox.

Logan checked his ammopac. Full load. He could use a nitro on the runner's ship if he had to. He kicked the hoverstick into life, soaring up at a dizzy angle. Too much thrust. He throttled down a bit, gained full control, gra-dually increasing his airspeed.

The runner's paravane had been tracked at dead center on the Kansas Missouri line – which meant if he cut through Greater KC, Logan should intercept near the Jefferson Complex.

The Missouri River rolled below him, brown and sluggish. A few speedtugs, a private sailjet or two, otherwise the river was undisturbed. It didn't worry about runners or callboxes or backups or devilsticks or Sleep. Old Man River . . . just keeps rolling along.

Logan had been correct in his calculations. He spotted the stolen paravane just past Jefferson. Moving at full bladepower.

The runner saw Logan bearing in, swung his ship to face the new threat.

He's bringing up the Fuser! Time to show him what you can do with a stick.

The runner fired.

And missed.

And fired again.

Logan was a sun-dazzled dragonfly – darting, dipping, swooping erratically. An impossible target.

He unholstered the Gun.

The paravane rushed at him.

Logan had the charge set at nitro. *Now!*

The runner and his ship erupted into gouting, blue-white flame. The stricken craft tipped over and down, diving into Missouri earth with a roar.

Logan brought the stick in, dismounted, checked the runner. Nothing left of him but his right arm and hand, jutting grotesquely out of the flame-charred control pod.

Centered in his palm: a black flower.

"Any change?" asked Lacy.

"He's worse," said Stile. "Into severe muscle convulsions. Skincount's up. And his heart is taking a beating."

"He can't go on, then?"

"He's a hard man," Stile said. "He might surprise you."

They were waiting at Darkside, where their rocket was being readied for the jump to Argos – and Logan held

151

Jessica close, telling her how much he loved her, telling her he'd never known that it was possible to experience such intense emotion, such care-bonding.

"We're free now," she told him. "We can live without fear, build a life together, raise children, be thirty, forty, fifty . . ."

He smiled, touched at her hair. God, but she was lovely!

"I want a son," he told her.

"We'll have him," she said squeezing Logan's hand.

"And he'll have children of *his* own . . . and we'll be . . . what did they call them?"

"Grandparents," she said. "Grandma and Grandpa."

Logan chuckled, shaking his head. "That's hard to believe, to accept. No dreams. No fantasies. A *real* life ahead of us on Argos."

"Ballard said it wouldn't be easy there," she reminded him. Her eyes clouded. "I wish – "

"What?"

"– that Ballard could have come with us. We *need* a man like that on Argos."

"He's needed more on Earth," said Logan. "To handle the Sanctuary Line. To help more runners."

"I know," she nodded. "We owe him our lives."

"Everybody here owes him the same debt," said Logan.

And, touching, they stared out beyond the port, at the chalked, lifeless horizon of the Moon.

When Jaq was five Logan and Jess gave him a special party. Only the spaceborn were invited – those who had been conceived on Argos and who, like Jaq, had never known their mother planet.

Logan told the children about Earthgames he'd played in Nursery, about vibroballs and teeter-swings and talk puppets. It seemed they could never hear enough about Earth.

"Were there really Sandmen who chased you?" asked a girl of six.

Logan nodded.

"And were the Sandmen really bad?" asked the little girl.

"Yes," said Logan. "But they were taught to be. Some of them changed . . . They didn't all stay bad."

"You were one, weren't you?" asked a ten-year-old, eyes alight.

"I was one," admitted Logan.

"And were you bad?"

"For a while."

"No!" screamed little Jaq, running across the chamber to his father, hugging him fiercely. "Logan was *never* bad!"

The boy was sobbing.

Jessica came to them, held them both. She kissed Logan's cheek.

In the sudden, strained silence a six-year-old tugged at Logan's wrist.

"Can we play now? *Can we?*"

"He's calmer," said Stile. "Relaxed. Almost tranquil. His mind seems to have found what it was looking for. He's in very deep."

Lacy looked pensive. "What do you think a Sandman's Gun would bring on the Market?"

"A great deal. But it would have to be de-fused, the pore-pattern detonation device neutralized."

"Can that be done?"

"It can be. It's a very delicate procedure."

She paced the room, thinking.

"He'll never trade or sell the Gun," said Stile.

"I know," she said. "It won't be possible to negotiate with him." She stopped, looked directly at Stile. "We'll have to kill him."

Sprawled face-down across the mat, deep in his mental dreamworld with Jessica and Jaq, Logan was not aware that the room had changed, that something was being *added*

153

to the atmosphere. From a small opening under the door a colorless substance was being piped into the chamber.

Tetrahyde. Toxic and totally effective on human body-tissue. Once absorbed into the lungs, it destroyed them with deadly efficiency.

Logan breathed in . . . breathed out . . . breathed in . . .

He had exactly ten more minutes of life.

Logan, Logan, do you hear me?

I . . . hear you.

You are in great danger. You must come out!

No. Here with Jessica . . . with Jaq.

Listen to me, Logan. It's Dia.

How? How did you find me?

Jonath. When you didn't return to the camp he sent word to me. He knew no one else could reach you.

Where – are you now?

Close to you. Close to the Giant. I knew they'd never let me see you – so I'm sending my mind to you, my thoughts . . . You must come out to me!

No. Won't come out.

They're killing you, Logan.

Not true. They help me, give me water . . .

All that's over. The woman, Lacy, she has made up her mind to take the Gun. I know her thoughts . . . she wills you dead. Poison is in the air. You must come out, now! I'll help you . . . our two minds, together . . . Only minutes remain!

Logan willed his body to fight the drug – and Dia linked her mind to his; the images inside Logan's head began to mix, break up . . .

. . . and Jessica was . . .

    the Loveroom, and "Mother loves you," said Ballard . . .

    who was Francis, who was . . . Jaq, only five,

      but already he . . .

        kissed her deeply, knowing they were

never going to . . .

Harder! Try harder, Logan!
Trying. Can't. No use.
Fight! Break free!

. . . because Box was . . . in the cave . . .

falling . . .
    and love was . . .
                fa
               l
                    ling . . .
everything w
           a
              s
                fa
               l
                 l
                   i
                     n
                       g
                        .
                         .
                          .

No. Too deep . . . too far in . . .
But you're doing it . . . we're doing it together . . . you're
almost . . .
. . . out!

Logan blinked stupidly; his head pounded – as if a thousand
hot needles had been driven into his skull.

Only a few seconds left! Use the Gun, Logan! Use it!

Logan fumbled dizzily at his belt holster, his nostrils filled with the acid odor of Tetrahyde . . . The gas was upon him. He held his breath, pulled the Gun free . . .

Fired.

The nitro charge exploded the door from its hingelocks, flooding the liftroom with fresh air.

Logan staggered to his feet, plowed across the mat toward the gaping exit.

Where are you, Dia?

Outside. On the street just below the Giant. You'll see me. I'll be there. Soon.

Stile was in the corridor, running toward Logan, a weapon in his hand.

Gun on ripper.

Logan fired, tearing him apart. He scooped up Stile's Fuser.

Lacy saw this, darted back into her chambers. The firebirds cawed and fluttered.

Gaining strength by the second, Logan swept past her, reached the outside door, raced for the roofport.

Behind him, Lacy was screaming: "Stop him! Stop him!"

Three guards tried to – without success. Logan chopped them aside with blows from Gun and body.

Lacy appeared in the roof door, Fuser in hand, firing as Logan reached his paravane. Her first beamblast sheared away a section of alum sheeting next to Logan's head.

He swung bitterly toward her, triggered the Gun, on tangler.

The swift whirl of steelmesh filament engulfed her – and she fell back, clawing at the choking, constricting coils of metal.

Dia was not alone when Logan reached her. The man from the Wilderness camp who had flown her to New York was there.

"How did you find another paravane?" Logan asked him.

"There are still a few around," the man told him. "Found this one in West Virginia. She needed a new gyrounit, but she's fine now."

"Tell Jonath how grateful I am," said Logan.

"He'll be glad to hear you're all right."

Thanks to you, Logan thought, looking at Dia.

And she smiled at him.

"Will you be going back?" the man asked Logan.

No. We're going west. Together.

"No," said Logan. "We'll be going west."

The two men shook hands.

Where now? asked Logan. *How far west?*

All the way to the Coast, she told him, sitting beside him in the humming paravane. The New York Territory unrolled below them, nightblack and massive.

I want to take you home, Logan. She smiled, her hands touching gently at the planes of his face. *West, to my home.*

As heat is felt on skin, Logan felt the passion radiating from her mind.

He owed her his life, but could he give her something more than gratitude? Was he capable, now, of a greater commitment to her?

Logan wasn't sure.

He would know when the time for knowing was at hand.

STAR TREK: THE MOTION PICTURE

> (Paramount, 1979)
> Starring: William Shatner, Leonard Nimoy
> & DeForest Kelley
> Directed by Robert Wise
> Television story "The Unreal McCoy" by James Blish

Ten years after it had been an NBC television series which lasted for just three seasons, *Star Trek* graduated to the cinema screen and there became a huge box office winner which has helped turn the adventures of the Starship *Enterprise* and her crew into an unparalleled phenomenon. Expansively directed by Robert Wise with impressive-looking hardware special effects by Douglas Trumbull (again), John Dykstra and Dave Stewart, the picture's success has led to five sequels (at the present count) and two further television series: all of which have made *Star Trek* into a world-wide cult and multi-million-dollar merchandising industry. This is all, though, a far cry from the original low-budget TV concept devised by Gene Roddenberry, a former Second World War bomber pilot, who had begun his career in television writing for shows such as *Dragnet* and *Highway Patrol*, before being asked by NBC for an idea for a series and coming up with *Star Trek* inspired, he claimed, by his admiration for C. S. Forester's historical maritime novels featuring Captain Horatio Hornblower! Gene's stories about Captain James Kirk, Science Officer Spock, Doctor McCoy and the other members of the Enterprise who "boldly go where no man has gone before" – to quote one of the series' well-known catch-phrases – not only took viewers into the far reaches of space, but also made some important statements about racial and sexual equality, humanity and optimism. These elements have con-

The Unreal McCoy

tinued in the subsequent movies as well as in the TV series, helping to enhance the legend still further . . .

Interestingly, the plot of *Star Trek: The Motion Picture* was not very different from one of the earliest episodes in the original TV series. In the movie, Kirk, Spock and McCoy found themselves in conflict with an alien who had taken on the form of one of the crew members. Earlier, in "The Unreal McCoy", the same trio faced a similar threat, but one more intent on enslaving the doctor. This adaptation of the television script is by James Blish (1921–1975), a Science Fiction fan who studied microbiology and zoology before becoming one of the leading writers of "intellectual" SF with books like *A Case of Conscience* (1959), one of the first serious attempts to deal with religion in SF. In complete contrast to these works, Jim wrote a number of the earliest novels to be based on *Star Trek* during the years its popularity was developing and first editions of these are now eagerly collected. Other writers have since followed James Blish in expanding the legend of *Star Trek*, but in the following pages he retells one of the stories of how it all began . . .

The crater campsite – or the Bierce campsite, as the records called it – on Regulus VIII was the crumbling remains of what might once have been a nested temple, surrounded now by archeological digs, several sheds, and a tumble of tools, tarpaulins, and battered artifacts. Outside the crater proper, the planet was largely barren except for patches of low, thorny vegetation, all the way in any direction to wherever the next crater might be – there were plenty of those, but there'd been no time to investigate them, beyond noting that they had all been inhabited once, unknown millennia ago. There was nothing uncommon about that, the galaxy was strewn with ruins about which nobody knew anything, there were a hundred such planets for every archeologist who could even dream of scratching such a surface. Bierce had just been lucky – fantastically lucky.

All the same, Regulus VIII made Kirk – Capt. James Kirk of the starship *Enterprise*, who had seen more planets than most men knew existed – feel faintly edgy. The *Enterprise* had landed here in conformity to the book; to be specific, to that part of the book which said that research personnel on alien planets must have their health certified by a starship's surgeon at one-year intervals. The *Enterprise* had been in Bierce's vicinity at the statutory time, and Ship's Surgeon McCoy had come down by transporter from the orbiting *Enterprise* to do the job. Utterly, completely routine, except for the fact that McCoy had mentioned that Bierce's wife Nancy had been a serious interest of McCoy's pre-Bierce, well over ten years ago. And after all, what could be more commonplace than that?

Then Nancy came out of the temple – if that is what it was – to meet them.

There were only three of them: McCoy and a crewman, Darnell, out of duty, and Kirk, out of curiosity. She came forward with outstretched hands, and after a moment's hesitation, McCoy took them. "Leonard!" she said. "Let me look at you."

"Nancy," McCoy said. "You . . . haven't aged a year."

Kirk restrained himself from smiling. Nancy Bierce was handsome, but nothing extraordinary: a strongly built woman of about forty, moderately graceful, her hair tinged with gray. It wasn't easy to believe that the hard-bitten medico could have been so smitten, even at thirty or less, as to be unable to see the signs of aging now. Still she did have a sweet smile.

"This is the Captain of the *Enterprise*, Jim Kirk," McCoy said. "And this is Crewman Darnell."

Nancy turned her smile on the Captain, and then on the crewman. Darnell's reaction was astonishing. His jaw swung open; he was frankly staring. Kirk would have kicked him had he been within reach.

"Come in, come in," she was saying. "We may have to wait a little for Bob; once he starts digging, he forgets time. We've made up some quarters in what seems to have been an old altar chamber – not luxurious, but lots of room. Come on in, Plum."

She ducked inside the low, crumbling stone door.

"Plum?" Kirk said.

"An old pet name," McCoy said, embarrassed. He followed her. Embarrassed himself at his own gaucherie, Kirk swung on the crewman.

"Just what are you goggling at, Mister?"

"Sorry, sir," Darnell said stiffly. "She reminds me of somebody is all. A girl I knew once on Wrigley's Planet. That is – "

"That's enough," Kirk said drily. "The next thought of that kind you have will probably be in solitary. Maybe you'd better wait outside."

"Yessir. Thanks." Darnell seemed genuinely grateful. "I'll explore a little, if that suits you, Captain."

"Do that. Just stay within call."

Commonplace; Darnell hadn't seen a strange woman since his last landfall. But most peculiar, too.

Bierce did not arrive, and after apologies, Nancy left again to look for him, leaving Kirk and McCoy to examine the stone room, trying not to speak to each other. Kirk could not decide whether he would rather be back on board the *Enterprise*, or just plain dead; his diplomacy had not failed him this badly in he could not think how many years.

Luckily, Bierce showed up before Kirk had to decide whether to run or suicide. He was an unusually tall man, all knuckles, knees, and cheekbones, wearing faded coveralls. Slightly taller than McCoy, his face was as craggy as his body; the glint in the eyes, Kirk thought, was somehow both intelligent and rather bitter. But then, Kirk had never pretended to understand the academic type.

"Dr. Briece," he said, "I'm Captain Kirk, and this is Ship's Surgeon – "

"I know who you are," Bierce broke in, in a voice with the blaring rasp of a busy signal. "We don't need you here. If you'll just refill us on aspirin, salt tablets, and the like, you needn't trouble yourselves further."

"Sorry, but the law requires an annual checkup," Kirk said. "If you'll co-operate, I'm sure Dr. McCoy will be as quick as possible." McCoy, in fact, already had his instruments out.

"McCoy?" Bierce said. "I've heard that name . . . Ah, yes, Nancy used to talk about you."

"Hands out from your sides, please, and breathe evenly . . . Yes, didn't she mention I'd arrived?"

After the slightest of pauses, Bierce said, "You've . . . seen Nancy?"

"She was here when we arrived," Kirk said. "She went to look for you."

"Oh. Quite so. I'm pleased, of course, that she can meet an old friend, have a chance of some company. I enjoy solitude, but it's difficult for a woman sometimes."

"I understand," Kirk said, but he was none too sure he did. The sudden attempt at cordiality rang false, somehow, after the preceding hostility. At least *that* had sounded genuine.

McCoy had finished his checkup with the tricorder and produced a tongue depressor with a small flourish. "She hasn't changed a bit," he said. "Open your mouth, please."

Reluctantly, Bierce complied. At the same instant, the air was split by a full-throated shriek of horror. For an insane moment Kirk had the impression that the sound had issued from Bierce's mouth. Then another scream ripped the silence, and Kirk realized that it was, of course, a female voice.

They all three bolted out of the door. In the open, Kirk and McCoy outdistanced Bierce quickly; for all his outdoor life, he was not a good runner. But they hadn't far to go. Just beyond the rim of the crater, Nancy, both fists to her mouth, was standing over the body of Darnell.

As they came pounding up she moved toward McCoy, but he ignored her and dropped beside the body. It was lying on its face. After checking the pulse, McCoy gently turned the head to one side, grunted, and then turned the body over completely.

It was clear even to Kirk that the crewman was dead. His face was covered with small ringlike red blotches slowly fading. "What hit him?" Kirk said tensely.

"Don't know. Petachiae a little like vacuum mottling, or maybe some sort of immunological – hullo, what's this?"

Bierce came panting up as McCoy slowly forced open one of Darnell's fists. In it was a twisted, scabrous-looking object of no particular color, like a mummified parsnip. It looked also as though part of it had been bitten away. Now *that* was incredible. Kirk swung on Nancy.

"What happened?" he asked tersely.

"Don't snap at my wife, Captain," Bierce said in his busy-signal voice. "Plainly it's not her fault!"

"One of my men is dead. I accuse nobody, but Mrs. Bierce is the only witness."

McCoy rose and said to Nancy, gently: "Just tell us what you saw, Nancy. Take your time."

"I was just . . ." she said, and then had to stop and swallow, as if fighting for control. "I couldn't find Bob, and I'd . . . I'd just started back when I saw your crewman. He had that borgia root in his hand and he was smelling it. I was just going to call out to him when – he bit into it. I had no idea he was going to – and then his face twisted and he fell – "

She broke off and buried her face in her hands. McCoy took her gently by one shoulder. Kirk, feeling no obligation to add one bedside more, said evenly: "How'd you know what the root was if you'd just come within calling distance?"

163

"This cross-examination – " Bierce grated.

"Bob, please. I didn't know, of course. Not until I saw it now. But it's dangerous to handle any plant on a new world."

Certainly true. Equally certainly, it would have been no news to Darnell. His face impassive, Kirk told McCoy: "Pack up, Bones. We can resume the physicals tomorrow."

"I'm sure that won't be necessary," Bierce said. "If you'll just disembark our supplies, Captain – "

"It's not going to be that easy, Dr. Bierce," Kirk said. He snapped open his communicator. "Kirk to Transporter Room. Lock and beam: two transportees and a corpse."

The autopsied body of Darnell lay on a table in the sick bay, unrecognizable now even by his mother, if so veteran a spaceman had ever had one. Kirk, standing near a communicator panel, watched with a faint physical uneasiness as McCoy lowered Darnell's brain into a shallow bowl and then turned and washed his hands until they were paper-white. Kirk had seen corpses in every conceivable state of distortion and age in one battle and another, but this clinical bloodiness was not within his experience.

"I can't rule poison out entirely," McCoy said, in a matter-of-fact voice. "Some of the best known act just as fast and leave just as little trace: botulinus, for example. But there's no trace of any woody substance in his stomach or even between his teeth. All I can say for sure is that he's got massive capillary damage – which could be due to almost anything, even shock – and those marks on his face."

McCoy covered the ruined body. "I'll be running some blood chemistry tests, but I'd like to know what I'm testing for. I'd also like to know what symptoms that 'borgia root' is *supposed* to produce. Until then, Jim, I'm really rather in the dark."

"Spock's running a library search on the plant," Kirk said. "It shouldn't take him long. But I must confess that what you've said thus far doesn't completely surprise me.

164

Darnell was too old a hand to bite into any old thing he happened to pick up."

"Then what's left? Nancy? Jim, I'm not quite trusting my own eyes lately, but Nancy didn't use to be capable of murder – certainly not of an utter stranger, to boot!"

"It's not only people who kill – hold it, here's the report. Go ahead, Mr. Spock."

"We have nothing on the borgia root but what the Bierces themselves reported in their project request six years ago," Spock's precise voice said. "There they call it an aconite resembling the *Lilium* family. Said to contain some twenty to fifty different alkaloids, none then identifiable specifically with the equipment to hand. The raw root is poisonous to mice. No mention of any human symptoms. Except . . ."

"Except what?" McCoy snapped.

"Well, Dr. McCoy, this isn't a symptom. The report adds that the root has a pleasant perfume, bland but edible-smelling, rather like tapioca. And that's all there is."

"Thanks." Kirk switched off. "Bones, I can't see Darnell having been driven irresistibly to bite into an unknown plant because it smelled like tapioca. He wouldn't have bitten into something that smelled like a brandied peach unless he'd known its pedigree. He was a seasoned hand."

McCoy spread his hands expressively. "You knew your man, Jim – but where does that leave us? The symptoms do vaguely resemble aconite poisoning. Beyond that, we're nowhere."

"Not quite," Kirk said. "We still have to check on the Bierces, I'm afraid, Bones. And for that I'm still going to need your help."

McCoy turned his back and resumed washing his hands. "You'll get it," he said; but his voice was very cold.

Kirk's method of checking on the Bierces was simple but drastic: he ordered them both on board the ship. Bierce raged.

"If you think you can beam down here, bully us, interfere with my work – considering the inescapable fact that you are a trespasser on my planet – "

"Your complaint is noted," Kirk said. "I apologize for the inconvenience. But it's also an inescapable fact that something we don't understand killed one of our men. It could very well be a danger to you, too."

"We've been here almost five years. If there was something hostile here we'd know about it by now, wouldn't we?"

"Not necessarily," Kirk said. "Two people can't know all the ins and outs of a whole planet, not even in five years – or a lifetime. In any event, one of the missions of the *Enterprise* is to protect human life in places like this. Under the circumstances, I'm going to have to be arbitrary and declare the argument closed."

It was shortly after they came aboard that McCoy forwarded his reports on the analyses of Darnell's body. "It was shock, all right," he told Kirk grimly by vid-screen. "But shock of a most peculiar sort. His blood electrolytes were completely deranged: massive salt depletion, hell – there isn't a microgram of salt in his whole body. Not in the blood, the tears, the organs, not anywhere. I can't even begin to guess how that could have happened at all, let alone all at once."

"What about the mottling on his face?"

"Broken capillaries. There are such marks all over the body. They're normal under the circumstances – except that I can't explain why they should be most marked on the face, or why the mottling should be ring-shaped. Clearly, though, he wasn't poisoned."

"Then the bitten plant," Kirk said equally grimly, "was a plant – in the criminal, not the botanical sense. A blind. That implies intelligence. I can't say I like that any better."

"Nor I," McCoy said. His eyes were averted.

"All right. That means we'll have to waste no time grilling the Bierces. I'll take it on. Bones, this has been a tremendous strain on you. I know, and you've been without sleep for two days. Better take a couple of tranquilizers and doss down."

"I'm all right."

"Orders," Kirk said. He turned off the screen and set off for the quarters he had assigned the Bierces.

But there was only one Bierce there. Nancy was missing.

"I expect she's gone below," Bierce said indifferently. "I'd go myself if I could get access to your Transporter for ten seconds. We didn't ask to be imprisoned up here."

"Darnell didn't ask to be killed, either. Your wife may be in serious danger. I must say, you seem singularly unworried."

"She's in no danger. This menace is all in your imagination."

"I suppose the body is imaginary, too?"

Bierce shrugged. "Nobody know what could have killed him. For all I know, you brought your own menace with you."

There was nothing further to be got out of him. Exasperated, Kirk went back to the bridge and ordered a general search. The results were all negative – including the report from the Transporter Room, which insisted that nobody had used its facilities since the party had returned to the ship from the camp.

But the search, though it did not find Nancy, found something else: Crewman Barnhart, dead on Deck Twelve. The marks on his body were the same as those on Darnell's.

Baffled and furious, Kirk called McCoy. "I'm sorry to bust in on your sleep, Bones, but this has gone far enough. I want Bierce checked out under pentathol."

"Um," McCoy said. His voice sounded fuzzy, as though he had still not quite recovered from his tranquilizer dose.

"Pentathol. Truth dope. Narcosynthesis. Um. Takes time. What about the patient's civil rights?"

"He can file a complaint if he wants. Go and get him ready."

An hour later, Bierce was lying on his bunk in half-trance. Kirk bent over him tensely; McCoy and Spock hovered in the background.

"Where's your wife?"

"Don't know . . . Poor Nancy, I loved her . . . The last of its kind . . ."

"Explain, please."

"The passenger pigeon . . . the buffalo . . ." Bierce groaned. "I feel strange."

Kirk beckoned to McCoy, who checked Bierce's pulse and looked under his eyelids. "He's all right," he said. "The transfer of questioner, from me to you, upset him. He's recovering."

"What about buffalo?" Kirk said, feeling absurd.

"Millions of them . . . prairies black with them. One single herd that covered three states. When they moved . . . like thunder. All gone now. Like the creatures here."

"Here? You mean down on the planet?"

"On the planet. Their temples . . . great poetry . . . Millions of them once, and now only one left. Nancy understood."

"Always the past tense," Spock's voice murmured. "Where is Nancy? Where is she *now*?"

"Dead. Buried up on the hill. It killed her."

"Buried! But – how long ago was this, anyhow?"

"A year . . ." Bierce said. "Or was it two? I don't know. So confusing, Nancy and not Nancy. They needed salt, you see. When it ran out, they died . . . all but one."

The implication stunned Kirk. It was Spock who put the question.

"Is the creature masquerading as your wife?"

"Not a masquerade," Bierce droned. "It can *be* Nancy."

"Or anybody else?"

"Anybody. When it killed Nancy, I almost destroyed it. But I couldn't. It was the last."

The repetition was becoming more irritating every minute. Kirk said stonily: "Is that the only reason, Bierce? Tell me this: When it's with you, is it always Nancy?"

Bierce writhed. There was no answer. McCoy came forward again.

"I wouldn't press that one if I were you, Jim," he said. "You can get the answer if you need it, but not without endangering the patient."

"I don't need any better answer," Kirk said. "So we've intruded here into a little private heaven. This thing can be wife, lover, best friend, idol, slave, wise man, fool – anybody. A great life, having everyone in the universe at your beck and call – and you win all the arguments."

"A one-way road to paranoia," Spock said. Kirk swung back to the drugged man.

"Then you can recognize the creature – no matter what form it takes?"

"Will you help us?"

"No."

Kirk had expected no more. He gestured to McCoy. "I've got to go organize a search. Break down that resistance, Bones, I don't care how you do it or how much you endanger Bierce. In his present state of mind he's as big a danger to us as his 'wife'. Spock, back him up, and be ready to shoot if he should turn violent."

He stalked out. On the bridge, he called a General Quarters Three; that would put pairs of armed men in every corridor, on every deck. "Every man inspect his mate closely," he told the intercom. "There's one extra person aboard, masquerading as one of us. Lieutenant Uhura, make television rounds of all posts and stations. If you see any person twice in different places, sound the alarm. Got it?"

A sound behind him made him swing around. It was Spock. His clothes were torn, and he was breathing heavily.

"Spock! I thought I told you – what happened?"

"It was McCoy," Spock said shakily. "Or rather, it wasn't McCoy. You were barely out of the cabin when it grabbed me. I got away, but it's got my sidearm. No telling where it's off to now."

"McCoy! I *thought* he seemed a little reluctant about the pentathol. Reluctant, and sort of searching his memory, too. No wonder. Well, there's only one place it can have gone to now; right back where it came from."

"The planet? It can't."

"No. McCoy's cabin." He started to get up, but Spock lifted a hand sharply.

"Better look first, Captain. It may not have killed him yet, and if we alarm it – "

"You're right." Quickly, Kirk dialed in the intercom to McCoy's cabin, and after only a slight hesitation, punched the override button which would give him vision without sounding the buzzer on the other end.

McCoy was there. He was there twice: a sleeping McCoy on the bunk, and another one standing just inside the closed doorway, looking across the room. The standing form moved, passing in front of the hidden camera and momentarily blocking the view. Then it came back into the frame – but no longer as McCoy. It was Nancy.

She sat down on the bed and shook the sleeping doctor. He muttered, but refused to wake.

"Leonard," Nancy's voice said. "It's me. Nancy. Wake up. Please wake up. Help me."

Kirk had to admire the performance. What he was seeing was no doubt an alien creature, but its terror was completely convincing. Quite possibly it *was* in terror; in any event, the human form conveyed it as directly as a blow.

She shook McCoy again. He blinked his eyes groggily, and then sat up.

"Nancy! What's this? How long have I been sleeping?"

"Help me, Leonard."

"What's wrong? You're frightened."

"I am, I am," she said. "Please help me. They want to kill me!"

"Who?" McCoy said. "Easy. Nobody's going to hurt you."

"That's enough," Kirk said, unconsciously lowering his voice, though the couple on the screen could not hear him. "Luckily, the thing's trying to persuade him of something instead of killing him. Let's get down there fast, before it changes its mind."

Moments later, they burst into McCoy's cabin. The surgeon and the girl swung towards them. "Nancy" cried out.

"Get away from her, Bones," Kirk said, holding his gun rock steady.

"What? What's going on here, Jim?"

"That isn't Nancy, Bones."

"It isn't? Of course it is. Are you off your rocker?"

"It killed two crewmen."

"Bierce, too," Spock put in, his own gun leveled.

"*It?*"

"It," Kirk said. "Let me show you."

Kirk held out his free hand, unclenching it slowly. In the palm was a little heap of white crystals, diminishing at the edges from perspiration. "Look, Nancy," he said. "Salt. Free for the taking. Pure, concentrated salt."

Nancy took a hesitant step toward him, then stopped.

"Leonard," she said in a low voice. "Send him away. If you love me, make him go away."

"By all means," McCoy said harshly. "This is crazy behavior, Jim. You're frightening her."

"Not fright," Kirk said. "Hunger. Look at her!"

The creature, as if hypnotized, took another step forward. Then, without the slightest warning, there was a hurricane of motion. Kirk had a brief impression of a blocky body, man-sized but not the least like a man, and of suction-cup tentacles reaching for his face. Then there was a blast of sound and he fell.

It took a while for both Kirk and McCoy to recover – the captain from the nimbus of Spock's close-range phaser bolt, McCoy from emotional shock. By the time they were all back on the bridge, Bierce's planet was receding.

"The salt was an inspiration," Spock said. "Evidently the creature only hunted when it couldn't get the pure stuff; that's how Bierce kept it in control."

"I don't think the salt supply was the only reason why the race died out, though," Kirk said. "It wasn't really very intelligent – didn't use its advantages nearly as well as it might have."

"They could well have been residual," Spock suggested. "We still have teeth and nails, but we don't bite and claw much these days."

"That could well be. There's one thing I don't understand, though. How did it get into your cabin in the first place, Bones? Or don't you want to talk about it?"

"I don't mind," McCoy said. "Though I do feel like six kinds of a fool. It was simple. She came in just after I'd taken the tranquilizer and was feeling a little afloat. She said she didn't love her husband any more – wanted me to take her back to Earth. Well . . . it was a real thing I had with Nancy, long ago. I wasn't hard to tempt, especially with the drug already in my system. And later on, while I was asleep, she must have given me another dose – otherwise I couldn't have slept through all the excitement, the general quarters call and so on. It just goes to prove all over again – never mess with civilians."

"A good principle," Kirk agreed. "Unfortunately, an impossible one to live by."

"There's something *I* don't understand, though," McCoy

added. "The creature and Bierce had Spock all alone in Bierce's cabin – and from what I've found during the dissection, it was twice as strong as a man anyhow. How did you get out, Mr. Spock, without losing anything but your gun?"

Spock smiled. "Fortunately, my ancestors spawned in quite another ocean than yours, Dr. McCoy," he said. "My blood salts are quite different from yours. Evidently, I wasn't appetizing enough."

"Of course," McCoy said. He looked over at Kirk. "You still look a little pensive, Jim. Is there still something else wrong?"

"Mmm?" Kirk said. "Wrong? No, not exactly. I was just thinking about the buffalo."

TOTAL RECALL

(Tristar Pictures, 1990)
Starring: Arnold Schwarzenegger, Rachel Ticotin
& Sharon Stone
Directed by Paul Verhoeven
Based on "We Can Remember It For You Wholesale"
by Philip K. Dick

Total Recall is in my opinion the best of the recent spate of "megabuck" spectaculars in which hardcore SF has been combined with nightmarish fantasy to provided vehicles for the monosyllabic acting styles of Sylvester Stallone, Jean-Claude Van Damme and the former Mr Universe, Arnold Schwarzenegger. Directed by Paul Verhoeven and awash with blood, gore and violence, *Total Recall* is said to have cost $70 million – a very large proportion of which was spent on the special effects. Indeed, it is these truly amazing effects created by Thomas Fisher and Eric Revig which remain longest in the memory about the story of Doug Quail, a construction worker in the year 2084, who has nightmares of living on Mars and suspects that his mind may have been tampered with. But by whom? The truth finally begins to dawn on him when he visits a simulated holiday agency that uses artificial memory implanting to give its clients the sensation of travel and encounters an android killer, "Michael Ironsides". The mayhem which follows certainly contributed to making *Total Recall* a huge box office success and the forerunner of a whole series of similar violent, SF-orientated movies. The film originated from a short story by the American Philip K. Dick (1928–1982) who many regard as one of the greatest of contemporary SF writers. British novelist Fay Weldon has gone even further in an essay on Dick's wildly imaginative and often halucinatory writing

174

by calling him, "California's own William Blake, a visionary and prophet". Certainly he was a man of contradictions and obsessions, and although largely self-educated, subsequently wrote a number of Science Fiction novels and short stories that are admired by fans and critics all over the world. Sadly, the adaptation of Philip Dick's work for the screen only began in the year of his death when Ridley Scott directed *Blade Runner*, starring Harrison Ford. This multi-layered story of a sinister Los Angeles of the future (circa 2019) was based on his novel, *Do Androids Dream of Electric Sheep?* (1968). *Total Recall*, in its turn, was derived from Dick's short story "We Can Remember It For You Wholesale" which had first appeared in the *Magazine of Fantasy & Science Fiction* in 1966. It was adapted for the screen by Ronald Shusett, Dan O'Bannon and Gary Goldman and provided another landmark in the history of Space Movies as well as bringing something of the genius of Philip K. Dick to an ever wider audience.

He awoke – and wanted Mars. The valleys, he thought. What would it be like to trudge among them? Great and greater yet: the dream grew as he became fully conscious, the dream and the yearning. He could almost feel the enveloping presence of the other world, which only Government agents and high officials had seen. A clerk like himself? Not likely.

"Are you getting up or not?" his wife Kirsten asked drowsily, with her usual hint of fierce crossness. "If you are, push the hot coffee button on the darn stove."

"Okay," Douglas Quail said, and made his way barefoot from the bedroom of their conapt to the kitchen. There, having dutifully pressed the hot coffee button, he seated himself at the kitchen table, brought out a yellow, small tin of fine Dean Swift snuff. He inhaled briskly, and the Beau Nash mixture stung his nose, burned the roof of his mouth. But still he inhaled; it woke him up and allowed his dreams, his nocturnal desires and random wishes, to condense into a semblance of rationality.

I will go, he said to himself. Before I die I'll see Mars.

It was, of course, impossible, and he knew this even as he dreamed. But the daylight, the mundane noise of his wife now brushing her hair before the bedroom mirror – everything conspired to remind him of what he was. A miserable little salaried employee, he said to himself with bitterness. Kirsten reminded him of this at least once a day and he did not blame her; it was a wife's job to bring her husband down to Earth. Down to Earth, he thought, and laughed. The figure of speech in this was literally apt.

"What are you sniggering about?" his wife asked as she swept into the kitchen, her long busy-pink robe wagging after her. "A dream, I bet. You're always full of them."

"Yes," he said, and gazed out the kitchen window at the hovercars and traffic runnels, and all the little energetic people hurrying to work. In a little while he would be among them. As always.

"I'll bet it has to do with some woman," Kirsten said witheringly.

"No," he said. "A god. The god of war. He has wonderful craters with every kind of plant-life growing deep down in them."

"Listen." Kirsten crouched down beside him and spoke earnestly, the harsh quality momentarily gone from her voice, "The bottom of the ocean – *our* ocean is much more, an infinity of times more beautiful. You know that; everyone knows that. Rent an artificial gill-outfit for both of us, take a week off from work, and we can descend and live down there at one of those year-round aquatic resorts. And in addition – " She broke off. "You're not listening. You should be. Here is something a lot better than that compulsion, that obsession you have about Mars, and you don't even listen!" Her voice rose piercingly. "God in heaven, you're doomed, Doug! What's going to become of you?"

"I'm going to work," he said, rising to his feet, his breakfast forgotten. "That's what's going to become of me."

She eyed him. "You're getting worse. More fanatical every day. Where's it going to lead?"

"To Mars," he said, and opened the door to the closet to get down a fresh shirt to wear to work.

Having descended from the taxi Douglas Quail slowly walked across three densely-populated foot runnels and to the modern, attractively inviting doorway. There he halted, impeding mid-morning traffic, and with caution read the shifting-color neon sign. He had, in the past, scrutinized this sign before . . . but never had he come so close. This was very different; what he did now was something else. Something which eventually had to happen.

REKAL, INCORPORATED

Was this the answer? After all, an illusion, no matter how convincing, remained nothing more than an illusion. At least objectively. But subjectively – quite the opposite entirely.

And anyhow he had an appointment. Within the next five minutes.

Taking a deep breath of mildly smog-infested Chicago air, he walked through the dazzling polychromatic shimmer of the doorway and up to the receptionist's counter.

The nicely-articulated blonde at the counter, bare-bosomed and tidy, said pleasantly, "Good morning, Mr Quail."

"Yes," he said. "I'm here to see about a Rekal course. As I guess you know."

"Not 'rekal' but recall," the receptionist corrected him. She picked up the receiver of the vidphone by her smooth elbow and said into it, "Mr Douglas Quail is here, Mr McClane. May he come inside, now? Or is it too soon?"

"Giz wetwa wum-wum wamp," the phone mumbled.

"Yes, Mr Quail," she said. "You may go on in; Mr McClane is expecting you." As he started off uncertainly she called after him, "Room D, Mr Quail. To your right."

After a frustrating but brief moment of being lost he found the proper room. The door hung open and inside, at a big genuine walnut desk, sat a genial-looking man, middle-aged, wearing the latest Martian frog-pelt gray suit; his attire alone would have told Quail that he had come to the right person.

"Sit down, Douglas," McClane said, waving his plump hand toward a chair which faced the desk. "So you want to have gone to Mars. Very good."

Quail seated himself, feeling tense. "I'm not so sure this is worth the fee," he said. "It costs a lot and as far as I can see I really get nothing." Costs almost as much as going, he thought.

"You get tangible proof of your trip," McClane disagreed emphatically. "All the proof you'll need. Here; I'll show you." He dug within a drawer of his impressive desk. "Ticket stub." Reaching into a manila folder he produced a small square of embossed cardboard. "It proves you went – and returned. Postcards." He laid out four franked picture 3-D full-color postcards in a neatly-arranged row on the desk for Quail to see. "Film. Shots you took of local sights on Mars with a rented movie camera." To Quail he displayed those, too. "Plus the names of people you met, two hundred poscreds worth of souvenirs, which will arrive – from Mars – within the following month. And passport, certificates listing the shots you received. And more." He glanced up keenly at Quail. "You'll know you went, all right," he said. "You won't remember us, won't remember me or ever having been here. It'll be a real trip in your mind; we guarantee that. A full two weeks of recall; every last piddling detail. Remember this: if at any time you doubt that you really took an extensive trip to Mars you can return here and get a full refund. You see?"

"But I didn't go," Quail said. "I won't have gone, no matter what proofs you provide me with." He took a deep, unsteady breath. "And I never was a secret agent with Interplan." It seemed impossible to him that Rekal, Incorporated's extra-factual memory implant would do its job – despite what he had heard people say.

"Mr Quail," McClane said patiently. "As you explained in your letter to us, you have no chance, no possibility in the slightest, of ever actually getting to Mars; you can't afford it, and what is much more important, you could never qualify as an undercover agent for Interplan or anybody else. This is the only way you can achieve your, ahem, life-long dream; am I not correct, sir? You can't be this; you can't actually do this." He chuckled. "But you can *have been* and *have done*. We see to that. And our fee is reasonable; no hidden charges." He smiled encouragingly.

"Is an extra-factual memory that convincing?" Quail asked.

"More than the real thing, sir. Had you really gone to Mars as an Interplan agent, you would by now have forgotten a great deal; our analysis of truemem systems – authentic recollections of major events in a person's life – shows that a variety of details are very quickly lost to the person. Forever. Part of the package we offer you is such deep implantation of recall that nothing is forgotten. The packet which is fed to you while you're comatose is the creation of trained experts, men who have spent years on Mars; in every case we verify details down to the last iota. And you've picked a rather easy extra-factual system; had you picked Pluto or wanted to be Emperor of the Inner Planet Alliance we'd have much more difficulty . . . and the charges would be considerably greater."

Reaching into his coat for his wallet, Quail said, "Okay. It's been my life-long ambition and I can see I'll never really do it. So I guess I'll have to settle for this."

"Don't think of it that way," McClane said severely. "You're not accepting second-best. The actual memory, with all its vagueness, omissions and ellipses, not to say distortions – that's second-best." He accepted the money and pressed a button on his desk. "All right, Mr Quail," he said, as the door of his office opened and two burly men swiftly entered. "You're on your way to Mars as a secret agent." He rose, came over to shake Quail's nervous, moist hand. "Or rather, you have been on your way. This afternoon at four-thirty you will, um, arrive back here on Terra; a cab will leave you off at your conapt and as I say you will never remember seeing me or coming here; you won't, in fact, even remember having heard of our existence."

His mouth dry with nervousness, Quail followed the two technicians from the office; what happened next depended on them.

Will I actually believe I've been on Mars? he wondered. That I managed to fulfill my lifetime ambition? He had a strange, lingering intuition that something would go wrong. But just what – he did not know.

He would have to wait to find out.

The intercom on McClane's desk, which connected him with the work-area of the firm, buzzed and a voice said, "Mr Quail is under sedation now, sir. Do you want to supervise this one, or shall we go ahead?"

"It's routine," McClane observed. "You may go ahead, Lowe; I don't think you'll run into any trouble." Programming an artificial memory of a trip to another planet – with or without the added fillip of being a secret agent – showed up on the firm's work-schedule with monotonous regularity. In one month, he calculated wryly, we must do twenty of these . . . ersatz interplanetary travel has become our bread and butter.

"Whatever you say, Mr McClane," Lowe's voice came, and thereupon the intercom shut off.

Going to the vault section in the chamber behind his office, McClane searched about for a Three packet – trip to Mars – and a Sixty-two packet: secret Interplan spy. Finding the two packets, he returned with them to his desk, seated himself comfortably, poured out the contents – merchandise which would be planted in Quail's conapt while the lab technicians busied themselves installing the false memory.

A one-poscred sneaky-pete side arm, McClane reflected; that's the largest item. Sets us back financially the most. Then a pellet-sized transmitter, which could be swallowed if the agent were caught. Code book that astonishingly resembled the real thing . . . the firm's models were highly accurate: based, whenever possible, on actual U.S. military issue. Odd bits which made no intrinsic sense but which would be woven into the warp and woof of Quail's imaginary trip, would coincide with his memory: half an ancient silver fifty cent piece, several quotations from John Donne's sermons written incorrectly, each on a separate piece of transparent tissue-thin paper, several match folders from bars on Mars, a stainless steel spoon engraved PROPER-TY OF DOME-MARKS NATIONAL KIBBUZIM, a wire tapping coil which –

The intercom buzzed. "Mr McClane, I'm sorry to bother you but something rather ominous has come up. Maybe it would be better if you were in here after all. Quail is already under sedation; he reacted well to the narkidrine; he's completely unconscious and receptive. But – "

"I'll be in." Sensing trouble, McClane left his office; a moment later he emerged in the work area.

On a hygienic bed lay Douglas Quail, breathing slowly and regularly, his eyes virtually shut; he seemed dimly – but only dimly – aware of the two technicians and now McClane himself.

"There's no space to insert false memory-patterns?" McClane felt irritation. "Merely drop out two work weeks; he's employed as a clerk at the West Coast Emigration Bureau, which is a government agency, so he undoubtedly has or had two weeks vacation within the last year. That ought to do it." Petty details annoyed him. And always would.

"Our problem," Lowe said sharply, "is something quite different." He bent over the bed, said to Quail, "Tell Mr McClane what you told us." To McClane he said, "Listen closely."

The gray-green eyes of the man lying in the bed focused on McClane's face. The eyes, he observed uneasily, had become hard; they had a polished, inorganic quality, like semi-precious tumbled stones. He was not sure that he liked what he saw; the brilliance was too cold. "What do you want now?" Quail said harshly. "You've broken my cover. Get out of here before I take you all apart." He studied McClane, "Especially you, you're in charge of this counter-operation."

Lowe said, "How long were you on Mars?"

"One month," Quail said gratingly.

"And your purpose there?" Lowe demanded.

The meager lips twisted; Quail eyed him and did not speak. At last, drawling the words out so that they dripped with hostility, he said, "Agent for Interplan. As I already told you. Don't you record everything that's said? Play your vid-aud tape back for your boss and leave me alone." He shut his eyes, then; the hard brilliance ceased. McClane felt, instantly, a rushing splurge of relief.

Lowe said quietly, "This is a tough man, Mr McClane."

"He won't be," McClane said. "After we arrange for him to lose his memory-chain again. He'll be as meek as before." To Quail he said, "So *this* is why you wanted to go to Mars so terribly badly."

Without opening his eyes Quail said, "I never wanted to go to Mars. I was assigned it – they handed it to me and there I was: stuck. Oh yeah, I admit I was curious about it;

who wouldn't be?" Again he opened his eyes and surveyed the three of them, McClane in particular. "Quite a truth drug you've got here; it brought up things I had absolutely no memory of." He pondered. "I wonder about Kirsten," he said, half to himself. "Could she be in on it? An Interplan contact keeping an eye on me . . . to be certain I didn't regain my memory? No wonder she's been so derisive about my wanting to go there." Faintly, he smiled; the smile – one of understanding – disappeared almost at once.

McClane said, "Please believe me, Mr Quail; we stumbled onto this entirely by accident. In the work we do – "

"I believe you," Quail said. He seemed tired, now; the drug was continuing to pull him under, deeper and deeper. "Where did I say I'd been?" he murmured. "Mars? Hard to remember – I know I'd like to see it; so would everybody else. But me – " His voice trailed off. "Just a clerk, a nothing clerk."

Straightening up, Lowe said to his superior. "He wants a false memory implanted that corresponds to a trip he actually took. And a false reason which is the real reason. He's telling the truth; he's a long way down in the narkidrine. The trip is very vivid in his mind – at least under sedation. But apparently he doesn't recall it otherwise. Someone, probably at a government military-sciences lab, erased his conscious memories; all he knew was that going to Mars meant something special to him, and so did being a secret agent. They couldn't erase that; it's not a memory but a desire, undoubtedly the same one that motivated him to volunteer for the assignment in the first place."

The other technician, Keeler, said to McClane, "What do we do? Graft a false memory-pattern over the real memory? There's no telling what the results would be; he might remember some of the genuine trip, and the confusion might bring on a psychotic interlude. He'd have to hold two opposite premises in his mind simultaneously: that he went to Mars and that he didn't. That he's a genuine agent for Interplan and he's not, that it's spurious. I think we ought to revive him without any false memory implantation and send him out of here; this is hot."

"Agreed," McClane said. A thought came to him. "Can you predict what he'll remember when he comes out of sedation?"

"Impossible to tell," Lowe said. "He probably will have some dim, diffuse memory of his actual trip, now. And he'd probably be in grave doubt as to its validity; he'd probably decide our programming slipped a gear-tooth. And he'd remember coming here – unless you want it erased."

"The less we mess with this man," McClane said, "the better I like it. This is nothing for us to fool around with; we've been foolish enough to – or unlucky enough to – uncover a genuine Interplan spy who has a cover so perfect that up to now even he didn't know what he was – or rather is." The sooner they washed their hands of the man calling himself Douglas Quail the better.

"Are you going to plant packets Three and Sixty-two in his conapt?" Lowe said.

"No," McClane said. "And we're going to return half his fee."

"Half! Why half?"

McClane said lamely, "It seems to be a good compromise."

As the cab carried him back to his conapt at the residential end of Chicago, Douglas Quail said to himself, It's sure good to be back on Terra.

Already the month-long period on Mars had begun to waver in his memory; he had only an image of profound gaping craters, an ever present ancient erosion of hills, of vitality, of motion itself. A world of dust where little happened, where a good part of the day was spent checking and rechecking one's portable oxygen source. And then the life forms, the unassuming and modest gray-brown cacti and maw-worms.

As a matter of fact he had brought back several moribund examples of Martian fauna; he had smuggled them through customs. After all, they posed no menace; they couldn't survive in Earth's heavy atmosphere.

Reaching into his coat pocket he rummaged for the container of Martian maw-worms –

And found an envelope instead.

Lifting it out, he discovered, to his perplexity, that it contained five hundred and seventy poscreds, in cred bills of low denomination. Where'd I get this? he asked himself. Didn't I spend every 'cred I had on my trip?

With the money came a slip of paper marked: *one-half fee ret'd. By McClane*. And then the date. Today's date.

"Recall," he said aloud.

"Recall what, sir or madam?" the robot driver of the cab inquired respectfully.

"Do you have a phone book?" Quail demanded.

"Certainly, sir or madam." A slot opened: from it slid a microtape phone book for Cook County.

"It's spelled oddly," Quail said as he leafed through the pages of the yellow section. He felt fear, then; abiding fear. "Here it is," he said. "Take me there, to Rekal, Incorporated. I've changed my mind; I don't want to go home."

"Yes, sir, or madam, as the case may be," the driver said. A moment later the cab was zipping back in the opposite direction.

"May I make use of your phone?" he asked.

"Be my guest," the robot driver said. And presented a shiny new emperor 3-D color phone to him.

He dialed his own conapt. And after a pause found himself confronted by a miniature but chillingly realistic image of Kirsten on the small screen. "I've been to Mars," he said to her.

"You're drunk." Her lips writhed scornfully. "Or worse."

"'S god's truth."

"When?" she demanded.

"I don't know." He felt confused. "A simulated trip, I think. By means of one of those artificial or extra-factual or whatever it is memory places. It didn't take."

Kirsten said witheringly, "You *are* drunk." And broke the connection at her end. He hung up, then, feeling his face flush. Always the same tone, he said hotly to himself. Always the retort, as if she knows everything and I know nothing. What a marriage. Keerist, he thought dismally.

A moment later the cab stopped at the curb before a modern, very attractive little pink building, over which a shifting, poly-chromatic neon sign read: REKAL, INCORPORATED.

The receptionist, chic and bare from the waist up, stared in surprise, then gained masterful control of herself. "Oh hello Mr Quail," she said nervously. "H-how are you? Did you forget something?"

"The rest of my fee back," he said.

More composed now, the receptionist said, "Fee? I think you are mistaken, Mr Quail. You were here discussing the feasibility of an extrafactual trip for you, but – " She shrugged her smooth pale shoulders. "As I understand it, no trip was taken."

Quail said, "I remember everything, miss. My letter to Rekal, Incorporated, which started this whole business off. I remember my arrival here, my visit with Mr McClane. Then the two lab technicians taking me in tow and administering a drug to put me out." No wonder the firm had returned half his fee. The false memory of his "trip to Mars" hadn't taken – at least not entirely, not as he had been assured.

"Mr Quail," the girl said, "although you are a minor clerk you are a good-looking man and it spoils your features

186

to become angry. If it would make you feel any better, I might, ahem, let you take me out . . ."

He felt furious, then. "I remember you," he said savagely. "For instance the fact that your breasts are sprayed blue; that stuck in my mind. And I remember Mr McClane's promise that if I remembered my visit to Rekal, Incorporated I'd receive my money back in full. Where is Mr McClane?"

After a delay – probably as long as they could manage – he found himself once more seated facing the imposing walnut desk, exactly as he had been an hour or so earlier in the day.

"Some technique you have," Quail said sardonically. His disappointment – and resentment – were enormous, by now. "My so-called 'memory' of a trip to Mars as an undercover agent for Interplan is hazy and vague and shot full of contradictions. And I clearly remember my dealings here with you people. I ought to take this to the Better Business Bureau." He was burning angry, at this point; his sense of being cheated had overwhelmed him, had destroyed his customary aversion to participating in a public squabble.

Looking morose, as well as cautious, McClane said, "We capitulate, Quail. We'll refund the balance of your fee. I fully concede the fact that we did absolutely nothing for you." His tone was resigned.

Quail said accusingly, "You didn't even provide me with the various artifacts that you claimed would 'prove' to me I had been on Mars. All that song-and-dance you went into – it hasn't materialized into a damn thing. Not even a ticket stub. Nor postcards. Nor passport. Nor proof of immunization shots. Nor – "

"Listen, Quail," McClane said. "Suppose I told you – " He broke off. "Let it go." He pressed a button on his intercom. "Shirley, will you disburse five hundred and seventy more creds in the form of a cashier's check made

Philip K. Dick

out to Douglas Quail? Thank you." He released the button, then glared at Quail.

Presently the check appeared; the receptionist placed it before McClane and once more vanished out of sight, leaving the two men alone, still facing each other across the desk.

"Let me give you a word of advice," McClane said as he signed the check and passed it over. "Don't discuss your, ahem, recent trip to Mars with anyone."

"What trip?"

"Well, that's the thing." Doggedly, McClane said, "The trip you partially remember. Act as if you don't remember; pretend it never took place. Don't ask me why; just take my advice: it'll be better for all of us." He had begun to perspire. Freely. "Now, Mr Quail, I have other business, other clients to see." He rose, showed Quail to the door.

Quail said, as he opened the door, "A firm that turns out such bad work shouldn't have any clients at all." He shut the door behind him.

On the way home in the cab Quail pondered the wording of his letter of complaint to the Better Business Bureau, Terra Division. As soon as he could get to his typewriter he'd get started; it was clearly his duty to warn other people away from Rekal, Incorporated.

When he got back to his conapt he seated himself before his Hermes Rocket portable, opened the drawers and rummaged for carbon paper – and noticed a small, familiar box. A box which he had carefully filled on Mars with Martian fauna and later smuggled through customs.

Opening the box, he saw, to his disbelief, six dead maw-worms and several varieties of the unicellular life on which the Martian worms fed. The protozoa were dried-up, dusty, but he recognized them; it had taken him an entire day picking among the vast dark alien boulders to find them. A wonderful, illuminated journey of discovery.

But I didn't go to Mars, he realized.

Yet on the other hand –

Kirsten appeared at the doorway to the room, an arm-load of pale brown groceries gripped. "Why are you home in the middle of the day?" Her voice, in an eternity of sameness, was accusing.

"*Did I go to Mars?*" he asked her. "You would know."

"No, of course you didn't go to Mars; *you* would know that, I would think. Aren't you always bleating about going?"

He said, "By God, I think I went." After a pause he added, "And simultaneously I think I didn't go."

"Make up your mind."

"How can I?" He gestured. "I have both memory-tracks grafted inside my head; one is real and one isn't but I can't tell which is which. Why can't I rely on you? They haven't tinkered with you." She could do this much for him at least – even if she never did anything else.

Kirsten said in a level, controlled voice, "Doug, if you don't pull yourself together, we're through. I'm going to leave you."

"I'm in trouble." His voice came out husky and coarse. And shaking. "Probably I'm heading into a psychotic episode; I hope not, but – maybe that's it. It would explain everything, anyhow."

Setting down the bag of groceries, Kirsten stalked to the closet. "I was not kidding," she said to him quietly. She brought out a coat, got it on, walked back to the door of the conapt. "I'll phone you one of these days soon," she said tonelessly. "This is goodbye, Doug. I hope you pull out of this eventually; I really pray you do. For your sake."

"Wait," he said desperately. "Just tell me and make it absolute; I did go or I didn't – tell me which one." But they may have altered your memory-track also, he realized.

The door closed. His wife had left. Finally!

A voice behind him said, "Well, that's that. Now put up your hands, Quail. And also please turn around and face this way."

189

He turned, instinctively, without raising his hands.

The man who faced him wore the plum uniform of the Interplan Police Agency, and his gun appeared to be UN issue. And, for some odd reason, he seemed familiar to Quail; familiar in a blurred, distorted fashion which he could not pin down. So, jerkily, he raised his hands.

"You remember," the policeman said, "your trip to Mars. We know all your actions today and all your thoughts – in particular your very important thoughts on the trip home from Rekal, Incorporated." He explained, "We have a teleptransmitter wired within your skull; it keeps us constantly informed."

A telepathic transmitter; use of a living plasma that had been discovered on Luna. He shuddered with self-aversion. The thing lived inside him, within his own brain, feeding, listening, feeding. But the Interplan police used them; that had come out even in the homeopapers. So this was probably true, dismal as it was.

"Why me?" Quail said huskily. What had he done – or thought? And what did this have to do with Rekal, Incorporated?

"Fundamentally," the Interplan cop said, "this has nothing to do with Rekal; it's between you and us." He tapped his right ear. "I'm still picking up your mentational processes by way of your cephalic transmitter." In the man's ear Quail saw a small white-plastic plug. "So I have to warn you: anything you think may be held against you." He smiled. "Not that it matters now; you've already thought and spoken yourself into oblivion. What's annoying is the fact that under narkidrine at Rekal, Incorporated you told them, their technicians and the owner, Mr McClane, about your trip; where you went, for whom, some of what you did. They're very frightened. They wish they had never laid eyes on you." He added reflectively, "They're right."

Quail said, "I never made any trip. It's a false memory-chain improperly planted in me by McClane's technicians."

But then he thought of the box, in his desk drawer, containing the Martian life forms. And the trouble and hardship he had had gathering them. The memory seemed real. And the box of life forms; that certainly was real. Unless McClane had planted it. Perhaps this was one of the "proofs" which McClane had talked glibly about.

The memory of my trip to Mars, he thought, doesn't convince me – but unfortunately it has convinced the Interplan Police Agency. They think I really went to Mars and they think I at least partially realize it.

"We not only know you went to Mars," the Interplan cop agreed, in answer to his thoughts, "but we know that you now remember enough to be difficult for us. And there's no use expunging your conscious memory of all this, because if we do you'll simply show up at Rekal, Incorporated again and start all over. And we can't do anything about McClane and his operation because we have no jurisdiction over anyone except our own people. Anyhow, McClane hasn't committed any crime." He eyed Quail. "Nor, technically, have you. You didn't go to Rekal, Incorporated with the idea of regaining your memory; you went, as we realize, for the usual reason people go there – a love by plain, dull people for adventure." He added, "Unfortunately you're not plain, not dull, and you've already had too much excitement; the last thing in the universe you needed was a course from Rekal, Incorporated. Nothing could have been more lethal for you or for us. And, for that matter, for McClane."

Quail said, "Why is it 'difficult' for you if I remember my trip – my alleged trip – and what I did there?"

"Because," the Interplan harness bull said, "what you did is not in accord with our great white all-protecting father public image. You did, for us, what we never do. As you'll presently remember – thanks to narkidrine. That box of dead worms and algae has been sitting in your desk drawer for six months, ever since you got back. And at no time have

you shown the slightest curiosity about it. We didn't even
know you had it until you remembered it on your way home
from Rekal; then we came here on the double to look for
it." He added, unnecessarily, "Without any luck; there
wasn't enough time."

A second Interplan cop joined the first one; the two briefly
conferred. Meanwhile, Quail thought rapidly. He did remember more, now; the cop had been right about narkidrine.
They – Interplan – probably used it themselves. Probably?
He knew darn well they did; he had seen them putting a
prisoner on it. Where would *that* be? Somewhere on Terra?
More likely Luna, he decided, viewing the image rising from
his highly defective – but rapidly less so – memory.

And he remembered something else. Their reason for
sending him to Mars; the job he had done.

No wonder they had expunged his memory.

"Oh God," the first of the two Interplan cops said,
breaking off his conversation with his companion. Obviously, he had picked up Quail's thoughts. "Well, this is
a far worse problem, now; as bad as it can get." He walked
toward Quail, again covering him with his gun. "We've got
to kill you," he said. "And right away."

Nervously, his fellow officer said, "Why right away?
Can't we simply cart him off to Interplan New York and
let them – "

"*He* knows why it has to be right away," the first cop
said; he too looked nervous, now, but Quail realized that it
was for an entirely different reason. His memory had been
brought back almost entirely, now. And he fully understood the officer's tension.

"On Mars," Quail said hoarsely, "I killed a man. After
getting past fifteen bodyguards. Some armed with sneakypete
guns, the way you are." He had been trained, by Interplan,
over a five year period to be an assassin. A professional killer.
He knew ways to take out armed adversaries . . . such as these
two officers; and the one with the earreceiver knew it, too.

If he moved swiftly enough –

The gun fired. But he had already moved to one side, and at the same time he chopped down the gun-carrying officer. In an instant he had possession of the gun and was covering the other, confused, officer.

"Picked my thoughts up," Quail said, panting for breath. "He knew what I was going to do, but I did it anyhow."

Half sitting up, the injured officer grated, "He won't use that gun on you, Sam; I pick that up, too. He knows he's finished, and he knows we know it, too. Come on, Quail." Laboriously, grunting with pain, he got shakily to his feet. He held out his hand. "The gun," he said to Quail. "You can't use it, and if you turn it over to me I'll guarantee not to kill you; you'll be given a hearing, and someone higher up in Interplan will decide, not me. Maybe they can erase your memory once more; I don't know. But you know the thing I was going to kill you for; I couldn't keep you from remembering it. So my reason for wanting to kill you is in a sense past."

Quail, clutching the gun, bolted from the conapt, sprinted for the elevator. If you follow me, he thought, I'll kill you. So don't. He jabbed at the elevator button and, a moment later, the doors slid back.

The police hadn't followed him. Obviously they had picked up his terse, tense thoughts and had decided not to take the chance.

With him inside the elevator descended. He had gotten away – for a time. But what next? Where could he go?

The elevator reached the ground floor, a moment later Quail had joined the mob of peds hurrying along the runnels. His head ached and he felt sick. But at least he had evaded death; they had come very close to shooting him on the spot, back in his own conapt.

And they probably will again, he decided. When they find me. And with this transmitter inside me, that won't take too long.

Ironically, he had gotten exactly what he had asked Rekal, Incorporated for. Adventure, peril, Interplan police at work, a secret and dangerous trip to Mars in which his life was at stake – everything he had wanted as a false memory.

The advantages of it being a memory – and nothing more – could now be appreciated.

On a park bench, alone, he sat dully watching a flock of perts: a semibird imported from Mars' two moons, capable of soaring flight, even against Earth's huge gravity.

Maybe I can find my way back to Mars, he pondered. But then what? It would be worse on Mars; the political organization whose leader he had assassinated would spot him the moment he stepped from the ship; he would have Interplan and *them* after him, there.

Can you hear me thinking? he wondered. Easy avenue to paranoia; sitting here along he felt them tuning in on him, monitoring, recording, discussing . . . he shivered, rose to his feet, walked aimlessly, his hands deep in his pockets. No matter where I go, he realized. You'll always be with me. As long as I have this device inside my head.

I'll make a deal with you, he thought to himself – and to them. Can't you imprint a false-memory template on me again, as you did before, that I lived an average, routine life, never went to Mars? Never saw an Interplan uniform up close and never handled a gun?

A voice inside his brain answered, "As has been carefully explained to you: that would not be enough."

Astonished, he halted.

"We formerly communicated with you in this manner," the voice continued. "When you were operating in the field, on Mars. It's been months since we've done it; we assumed, in fact, that we'd never have to do so again. Where are you?"

"Walking," Quail said, "to my death." By your officers' guns, he added as an afterthought. "How can you be sure it wouldn't be enough?" he demanded. "Don't the Rekal techniques work?"

"As we said. If you're given a set of standard, average memories you get – restless. You'd inevitably seek out Rekal or one of its competitors again. We can't go through this a second time."

"Suppose," Quail said, "once my authentic memories have been cancelled, something more vital than standard memories are implanted. Something which would act to satisfy my craving," he said. "That's been proved; that's probably why you initially hired me. But you ought to be able to come up with something else – something equal. I was the richest man on Terra but I finally gave all my money to educational foundations. Or I was a famous deep-space explorer. Anything of that sort; wouldn't one of those do?"

Silence.

"Try it," he said desperately. "Get some of your top-notch military psychiatrists; explore my mind. Find out what my most expansive daydream is." He tried to think. "Women," he said. "Thousands of them, like Don Juan had. An interplanetary playboy – a mistress in every city on Earth, Luna and Mars. Only I gave that up, out of exhaustion. Please," he begged. "Try it."

"You'd voluntarily surrender, then?" the voice inside his head asked. "If we agreed to arrange such a solution? *If* it's possible?"

After an interval of hesitation he said, "Yes." I'll take the risk, he said to himself. That you don't simply kill me.

"You make the first move," the voice said presently. "Turn yourself over to us. And we'll investigate that line of possibility. If we can't do it, however, if your authentic memories begin to crop up again as they've done at this time, then – " There was silence and then the voice finished, "We'll have to destroy you. As you must understand. Well, Quail, you still want to try?"

Philip K. Dick

"Yes," he said. Because the alternative was death row – and for certain. At least this way he had a chance, slim as it was.

"You present yourself at our main barracks in New York," the voice of the Interplan cop resumed. "At 580 Fifth Avenue, floor twelve. Once you've surrendered yourself we'll have our psychiatrists begin on you; we'll have personality-profile tests made. We'll attempt to determine your absolute, ultimate fantasy wish – and then we'll bring you back to Rekal, Incorporated, here; get them in on it, fulfilling that wish in vicarious surrogate retrospection. And – good luck. We do owe you something; you acted as a capable instrument for us." The voice lacked malice; if anything, they – the organization – felt sympathy toward him.

"Thanks," Quail said. And began searching for a robot cab.

"Mr Quail," the stern-faced, elderly Interplan psychiatrist said, "you possess a most interesting wish-fulfillment dream fantasy. Probably nothing such as you consciously entertain or suppose. This is commonly the way; I hope it won't upset you too much to hear about it."

The senior ranking Interplan officer present said briskly, "He better not be too much upset to hear about it, not if he expects not to get shot."

"Unlike the fantasy of wanting to be an Interplan undercover agent," the psychiatrist continued, "which, being relatively speaking a product of maturity, had a certain plausibility to it, this production is a grotesque dream of your childhood; it is no wonder you fail to recall it. Your fantasy is this: you are nine years old, walking alone down a rustic lane. An unfamiliar variety of space vessel from another star system lands directly in front of you. No one on Earth but you, Mr Quail, sees it. The creatures within are very small and helpless, somewhat on the order of field mice, although they are attempting to invade Earth; ships will soon be on their way, when this advance party gives the go-ahead signal."

"And I suppose I stop them," Quail said, experiencing a mixture of amusement and disgust. "Single-handed I wipe them out. Probably by stepping on them with my foot."

"No," the psychiatrist said patiently. "You halt the invasion, but not by destroying them. Instead, you show them kindness and mercy, even though by telepathy – their mode of communication – you know why they have come. They have never seen such humane traits exhibited by any sentient organism, and to show their appreciation they make a covenant with you."

Quail said, "They won't invade Earth as long as I'm alive."

"Exactly." To the Interplan officer the psychiatrist said, "You can see it does fit his personality, despite his feigned scorn."

"So by merely existing," Quail said, feeling a growing pleasure, "by simply being alive, I keep Earth safe from alien rule. I'm in effect, then, the most important person on Terra. Without lifting a finger."

"Yes indeed, sir," the psychiatrist said. "And this is bedrock in your psyche; this is a life-long childhood fantasy. Which, without depth and drug therapy, you never would have recalled. But it has always existed in you; it went underneath, but never ceased."

To McClane, who sat intently listening, the senior police official said, "Can you implant an extrafactual memory pattern that extreme in him?"

"We get handed every possible type of wish-fantasy there is," McClane said. "Frankly, I've heard a lot worse than this. Certainly we can handle it. Twenty-four hours from now he won't just *wish* he'd saved Earth; he'll devoutly believe it really happened."

The senior police official said, "You can start the job, then. In preparation we've already once again erased the memory in him of his trip to Mars."

Quail said, "What trip to Mars?"

Philip K. Dick

No one answered him, so, reluctantly, he shelved the question. And anyhow a police vehicle had now put in its appearance; he, McClane and the senior police officer crowded into it, and presently they were on their way to Chicago and Rekal, Incorporated.

"You had better make no errors this time," the police officer said to heavy-set, nervous-looking McClane.

"I can't see what could go wrong," McClane mumbled, perspiring. "This has nothing to do with Mars or Interplan. Single-handedly stopping an invasion of Earth from another star-system." He shook his head at that. "Wow, what a kid dreams up. And by pious virtue, too; not by force. It's sort of quaint." He dabbed at his forehead with a large linen pocket handkerchief.

Nobody said anything.

"In fact," McClane said, "it's touching."

"But arrogant," the police officer said starkly. "Inasmuch as when he dies the invasion will resume. No wonder he doesn't recall it; it's the most grandiose fantasy I ever ran across." He eyed Quail with disapproval. "And to think we put this man on our payroll."

When they reached Rekal, Incorporated, the receptionist, Shirley, met them breathlessly in the outer office. "Welcome back, Mr Quail," she fluttered, her melon-shaped breasts – today painted an incandescent orange – bobbing with agitation. "I'm sorry everything worked out so badly before; I'm sure this time it'll go better."

Still repeatedly dabbling at his shiny forehead with his neatly-folded Irish linen handkerchief, McClane said, "It better." Moving with rapidity he rounded up Lowe and Keeler, escorted them and Douglas Quail to the work area, and then, with Shirley and the senior police officer, returned to his familiar office. To wait.

"Do we have a packet made up for this, Mr McClane?" Shirley asked, bumping against him in her agitation, then coloring modestly.

"I think we do." He tried to recall; then gave up and consulted the formal chart. "A combination," he decided aloud, "of packages Eighty-one, Twenty, and Six." From the vault section of the chamber behind his desk he fished out the appropriate packets, carried them to his desk for inspection. "From Eighty-one," he explained, "a magic healing rod given him – the client in question, this time Mr Quail – by the race of beings from another system. A token of their gratitude."

"Does it work?" the police officer asked curiously.

"It did once," McClane explained. "But he, ahem, you see, used it up years ago, healing right and left. Now it's only a memento. But he remembers it working spectacularly." He chuckled, then opened packet Twenty. "Document from the UN Secretary General thanking him for saving Earth; this isn't precisely appropriate, because part of Quail's fantasy is that no one knows of the invasion except himself, but for the sake of verisimilitude we'll throw it in." He inspected packet Six, then. What came from this? He couldn't recall; frowning, he dug into the plastic bag as Shirley and the Interplan police officer watched intently.

"Writing," Shirley said. "In a funny language."

"This tells who they were," McClane said, "and where they came from. Including a detailed star map logging their flight here and the system of origin. Of course it's in *their* script, so he can't read it. But he remembers them reading it to him in his own tongue." He placed the three artifacts in the center of the desk. "These should be taken to Quail's conapt," he said to the police officer. "So that when he gets home he'll find them. And it'll confirm his fantasy. SOP – standard operating procedure." He chuckled apprehensively, wondering how matters were going with Lowe and Keeler.

The intercom buzzed. "Mr McClane, I'm sorry to bother you." It was Lowe's voice; he froze as he recognized it, froze and became mute. "But something's come up. Maybe it would be better if you came in here and supervised. Like before, Quail reacted well to the narkidrine; he's unconscious, relaxed and receptive. But – "

McClane sprinted for the work area.

On a hygienic bed Douglas Quail lay breathing slowly and regularly, eyes half-shut, dimly conscious of those around him.

"We started interrogating him," Lower said, white-faced. "To find out exactly when to place the fantasy memory of him single-handedly having saved Earth. And strangely enough – "

"They told me not to tell," Douglas Quail mumbled in a dull drug-saturated voice. "That was the agreement. I wasn't even supposed to remember. But how could I forget an event like that?"

I guess it would be hard, McClane reflected. But you did – until now.

"They even gave me a scroll," Quail mumbled. "of gratitude. I have it hidden in my conapt; I'll show it to you."

To the Interplan officer who had followed after him, McClane said, "Well, I offer the suggestion that you better not kill him. If you do they'll return."

"They also gave me a magic invisible destroying rod," Quail mumbled, eyes totally shut, now. "That's how I killed that man on Mars you sent me to take out. It's in my drawer along with the box of Martian maw-worms and dried-up plant life."

Wordlessly, the Interplan officer turned and stalked from the work area.

I might as well put those packets of proof-artifacts away, McClane said to himself resignedly. He walked, step by step, back to his office. Including the citation from the UN Secretary General. After all –

The real one probably would not be long in coming.

THE LAWNMOWER MAN

(Allied Vision, 1992)
Starring: Pierce Brosnan, Jeff Fahey & Jeremy Slate
Directed by Brett Leonard
Based on "The Lawnmower Man" by Stephen King

Special effects were not just a feature of *The Lawnmower Man*, but the subject of the movie itself. Indeed, its makers claimed when it was released that the picture "pioneered the concept of Virtual Reality in the cinema" – although there have been some dissenting voices to this claim, arguing that *The Lawnmower Man* is actually derivative of Ralph Nelson's *Charly* made in 1968 and Steven Lisberger's *Tron* (1982). But there can still be no denying that the movie represents another important landmark in the continuing story of Space Movies. Virtual Reality is, in fact, a set of 3-D environments, created by computors, which the person experiencing can touch, feel and even smell. In the movie, however, the world of Virtual Reality which is created in the confines of a laboratory is allowed to spread and soon threatens to transform reality itself. It tells the story of Dr Lawrence Angelo, played by Pierce Brosnan (the new James Bond), who is intent upon turning a dimwitted "lawnmower man" Jobe Smith (Jeff Fahey) into a genius. But when his work is tampered with at Cybertech, a top-secret science complex which experiments on chimpanzees, the unfortunate gardener turns aggressive and power hungry, wants to control everyone and everything, and then wreaks a terrible revenge on all those who have made him suffer in the past. The brilliant computer animation for the film was created by the specialist technicians at Angel Studios in Hollywood – a group who had previously worked with NASA and the U.S. Air Force. Yet despite all the praise heaped on the movie for these special effects and its popu-

larity with cinemagoers, author Stephen King (1946–), the world's leading writer of horror and fantasy fiction, complained that the film had strayed a long way from his original tale – in particular turning his obese, middle-aged villain into a handsome young man. **Notwithstanding this, *The Lawnmower Man* is certainly one of the most visually exciting versions of King's stories to have been brought to the screen – a list which includes adaptations of *Carrie* by Brian DePalma (1976); Stanley Kubrick's *The Shining* (1980); *Christine* directed by John Carpenter (1983); and *Pet Sematary* which Stephen King himself scripted in 1989. King's short story originally appeared in *Cavalier* magazine in August 1974, and it was the idea of producer Milton Subotsky, one of the veterans of the British horror film industry who ran Amicus Films for many years, to add the element of Virtual Reality and create what one critic has described as "a futuristic Frankensteinian tale with brilliant computer animation".**

In previous years, Harold Parkette had always taken pride in his lawn. He had owned a large silver Lawnboy and paid the boy down the block five dollars per cutting to push it. In those days Harold Parkette had followed the Boston Red Sox on the radio with a beer in his hand and the knowledge that God was in his heaven and all was right with the world, including his lawn. But last year, in mid-October, fate had played Harold Parkette a nasty trick. While the boy was mowing the grass for the last time of the season, the Castonmeyers' dog had chased the Smiths' cat under the mower.

Harold's daughter had thrown up half a quart of cherry Kool-Aid into the lap of her new jumper, and his wife had nightmares for a week afterward. Although she had arrived after the fact, she *had* arrived in time to see Harold and the green-faced boy cleaning the blades. Their daughter and Mrs Smith stood over them, weeping, although Alicia had taken time enough to change her jumper for a pair of blue jeans and one of those disgusting skimpy sweaters. She had a crush on the boy who mowed the lawn.

After a week of listening to his wife moan and gobble in the next bed, Harold decided to get rid of the mower. He didn't really *need* a mower anyway, he supposed. He had hired a boy this year; next year he would just hire a boy *and* a mower. And maybe Carla would stop moaning in her sleep. He might even get laid again.

So he took the silver Lawnboy down to Phil's Sunoco, and he and Phil dickered over it. Harold came away with a brand-new Kelly blackwall tire and a tankful of hi-test, and Phil put the silver Lawnboy out on one of the pump islands with a hand-lettered FOR SALE sign on it.

And this year, Harold just kept putting off the necessary hiring. When he finally got around to calling last year's boy, his mother told him Frank had gone to the state university. Harold shook his head in wonder and went to the refrigerator to get a beer. Time certainly flew, didn't it? My God, yes.

He put off hiring a new boy as first May and then June slipped past him and the Red Sox continued to wallow in fourth place. He sat on the back porch on the weekends and watched glumly as a never ending progression of young boys he had never seen before popped out to mutter a quick hello before taking his buxom daughter off to the local passion pit. And the grass thrived and grew in a marvelous way. It was a good summer for grass; three days of shine followed by one of gentle rain, almost like clockwork.

By mid-July, the lawn looked more like a meadow than a suburbanite's backyard, and Jack Castonmeyer had begun to make all sorts of extremely unfunny jokes, most of which concerned the price of hay and alfalfa. And Don Smith's four-year-old daughter Jenny had taken to hiding in it when there was oatmeal for breakfast or spinach for supper.

One day in late July, Harold went out on the patio during the seventh-inning stretch and saw a woodchuck sitting perkily on the overgrown back walk. The time had come, he decided. He flicked off the radio, picked up the paper, and turned to the classifieds. And half way down the Part Time column, he found this: *Lawns mowed. Reasonable. 776–2390.*

Harold called the number, expecting a vacuuming house-wife who would yell outside for her son. Instead, a briskly professional voice said, "Pastoral Greenery and Outdoor Services . . . how may we help you?"

Cautiously, Harold told the voice how Pastoral Greenery could help him. Had it come to this, then? Were lawncutters starting their own businesses and hiring office help? He asked the voice about rates, and the voice quoted him a reasonable figure.

Harold hung up with a lingering feeling of unease and went back to the porch. He sat down, turned on the radio, and stared out over his glandular lawn at the Saturday clouds moving slowly across the Saturday sky. Carla and Alicia were at his mother-in-law's and the house was his. It would be a pleasant surprise for them if the boy who was coming to cut the lawn finished before they came back.

He cracked a beer and sighed as Dick Drago was touched for a double and then hit a batter. A little breeze shuffled across the screened-in porch. Crickets hummed softly in the long grass. Harold grunted something unkind about Dick Drago and then dozed off.

He was jarred awake a half hour later by the doorbell. He knocked over his beer getting up to answer it.

A man in grass-stained denim overalls stood on the front stoop, chewing a toothpick. He was fat. The curve of his belly pushed his faded blue overall out to a point where Harold half suspected he had swallowed a basketball.

"Yes?" Harold Parkette asked, still half asleep.

The man grinned, rolled his toothpick from one corner of his mouth to the other, tugged at the seat of his overalls, and then pushed his green baseball cap up a notch on his forehead. There was a smear of fresh engine oil on the bill of his cap. And there he was, smelling of grass, earth, and oil, grinning at Harold Parkett.

"Pastoral sent me, buddy," he said jovially, scratching his crotch. "You called, right? Right, buddy?" He grinned on endlessly.

"Oh. The lawn. You?" Harold stared stupidly.

"Yep, me." The lawnmower man bellowed fresh laughter into Harold's sleep-puffy face.

Harold stood helplessly aside and the lawnmower man tromped ahead of him down the hall, through the living room and kitchen, and onto the back porch. Now Harold had placed the man and everything was all right. He had seen the type before, working for the sanitation department and the highway repair crews out on the turnpike. Always with a spare minute to lean on their shovels and smoke Lucky Strikes or Camels, looking at you as if they were the salt of the earth, able to hit you for five or sleep with your wife anytime they wanted to. Harold had always been slightly afraid of men like this; they were always tanned dark brown, there were always nets of wrinkles around their eyes, and they always knew what to do.

"The back lawn's the real chore," he told the man, unconsciously deepening his voice. "It's square and there are no obstructions, but it's pretty well grown up." His voice faltered back into its normal register and he found himself apologizing: "I'm afraid I've let it go."

"No sweat, buddy. No strain. Great-great-great." The lawnmower man grinned at him with a thousand traveling-salesman jokes in his eyes. "The taller, the better. Healthy soil, that's what you got there, by Circe. That's what I always say."

By Circe?

The lawnmower man cocked his head at the radio. Yastrzemski had just struck out. "Red Sox fan? I'm a Yankees man, myself." He clumped back into the house and down the front hall. Harold watched him bitterly.

205

He sat back down and looked accusingly for a moment at the puddle of beer under the table with the overturned Coors can in the middle of it. He thought of getting the mop from the kitchen and decided it would keep.

No sweat. No strain.

He opened his paper to the financial section and cast a judicious eye at the closing stock quotations. As a good Republican, he considered the Wall Street executives behind the columned type to be at least minor demigods –

(*By Circe??*)

– and he had wished many times that he could better understand the Word, as handed down from the mount not on stone tablets but in such enigmatic abbreviations as pct. and Kdk and 3.28 up 23. He had once bought a judicious three shares in a company called Midwest Bisonburgers, Inc., that had gone broke in 1968. He had lost his entire seventy-five-dollar investment. Now, he understood, bisonburgers were quite the coming thing. The wave of the future. He had discussed this often with Sonny, the bartender down at the Goldfish Bowl. Sonny told Harold his trouble was that he was five years ahead of his time, and he should . . .

A sudden racketing roar startled him out of the new doze he had just been slipping into.

Harold jumped to his feet, knocking his chair over and staring around wildly.

"That's a lawnmower?" Harold Parkette asked the kitchen. "My God, *that's* a lawnmower?"

He rushed through the house and stared out the front door. There was nothing out there but a battered green van with the words PASTORAL GREENERY, INC. painted on the side. The roaring sound was in back now. Harold rushed through his house again, burst onto the back proch, and stood frozen.

It was obscene.

It was a travesty.

The Lawnmower Man

The aged red power mower the fat man had brought in his van was running on its own. No one was pushing it; in fact, no one was within five feet of it. It was running at a fever pitch, tearing through the unfortunate grass of Harold Parkette's back lawn like an avenging red devil straight from hell. It screamed and bellowed and farted oily blue smoke in a crazed kind of mechanical madness that made Harold feel ill with terror. The overripe smell of cut grass hung in the air like sour wine.

But the lawnmower man was the true obscenity.

The lawnmower man had removed his clothes – every stitch. They were folded neatly in the empty birdbath that was at the center of the back lawn. Naked and grass-stained, he was crawling along about five feet behind the mower, eating the cut grass. Green juice ran down his chin and dripped onto his pendulous belly. And every time the lawnmower whirled around a corner, he rose and did an odd, skipping jump before prostrating himself again.

"*Stop!*" Harold Parkette screamed. "*Stop that!*"

But the lawnmower man took no notice, and his screaming scarlet familiar never slowed. If anything, it seemed to speed up. Its nicked steel grill seemed to grin sweatily at Harold as it raved by.

Then Harold saw the mole. It must have been hiding in stunned terror just ahead of the mower, in the swath of grass about to be slaughtered. It bolted across the cut band of lawn toward safety under the porch, a panicky brown streak.

The lawnmower swerved.

Blatting and howling, it roared over the mole and spat it out in a string of fur and entrails that reminded Harold of the Smiths' cat. The mole destroyed, the lawnmower rushed back to the main job.

The lawnmower man crawled rapidly by, eating grass. Harold stood paralyzed with horror, stocks, bonds, and bisonburgers completely forgotten. He could actually see that huge, pendulous belly expanding. *The lawnmower man swerved and ate the mole.*

That was when Harold Parkette leaned out the screen door and vomited into the zinnias. The world went gray, and suddenly he realized he was fainting, *had* fainted. He collapsed backward onto the porch and closed his eyes . . .

Someone was shaking him. Carla was shaking him. He hadn't done the dishes or emptied the garbage and Carla was going to be very angry but that was all right. As long as she was waking him up, taking him out of the horrible dream he had been having, back into the normal world, nice normal Carla with her Playtex Living Girdle and her buck teeth –

Buck teeth, yes. But not Carla's buck teeth. Carla had weak-looking chipmunk buck teeth. But these teeth were –

Hairy.

Green hair was growing on these buck teeth. It almost looked like –

Grass?

"Oh my God," Harold said.

"You fainted, buddy, right, huh?" The lawnmower man was bending over him, grinning with his hairy teeth. His lips and chin were hairy, too. Everything was hairy. And green. The yard stank of grass and gas and too sudden silence.

Harold bolted up to a sitting position and stared at the dead mower. All the grass had been neatly cut. And there would be no need to rake this job, Harold observed sickly. If the lawnmower man had missed a single cut blade, he couldn't see it. He squinted obliquely at the lawnmower man and winced. He was still naked, still fat, still terrifying. Green trickles ran from the corners of his mouth.

"What is this?" Harold begged.

The man waved an arm benignly at the lawn. "This? Well, it's a new thing the boss has been trying. It works out real good. Real good, buddy. We're killing two birds with one stone. We keep getting along toward the final stage, and we're making money to support our other operations to boot. See what I mean? Of course every now and then we run into a customer who doesn't understand – some people got no respect for efficiency, right? – but the boss is always agreeable to a sacrifice. Sort of keeps the wheels greased, if you catch me."

Harold said nothing. One word knelled over and over in his mind, and that word was "sacrifice". In his mind's eye he saw the mole spewing out from under the battered red mower.

He got up slowly, like a palsied old man. "Of course," he said, and could only come up with a line from one of Alicia's folk-rock records. "God bless the grass."

The lawnmower man slapped one summer-apple-colored thigh. "That's pretty good, buddy. In fact, that's damned good. I can see you got the right spirit. Okay if I write that down when I get back to the office? Might mean a promotion."

"Certainly," Harold said, retreating toward the back door and striving to keep his melting smile in place. "You go right ahead and finish. I think I'll take a little nap – "

"Sure, buddy," the lawnmower man said, getting ponderously to his feet. Harold noticed the unusually deep split between the first and second toes, almost as if the feet were . . . well, cloven.

"It hits everybody kinda hard at first," the lawnmower man said. "You'll get used to it." He eyed Harold's portly figure shrewdly. "In fact, you might even want to give it a whirl yourself. The boss has always got an eye out for new talent."

"The boss," Harold repeated faintly.

The lawnmower man paused at the bottom of the steps and gazed tolerantly up at Harold Parkette. "Well, say, buddy. I figured you must have guessed . . . God bless the grass and all."

Harold shook his head carefully and the lawnmower man laughed.

"Pan. Pan's the boss." And he did a half hop, half shuffle in the newly cut grass and the lawnmower screamed into life and began to trundle around the house.

"The neighbors – " Harold began, but the lawnmower man only waved cheerily and disappeared.

Out front the lawnmower blatted and howled. Harold Parkette refused to look, as if by refusing he could deny the grotesque spectacle that the Castonmeyers and Smiths – wretched Democrats both – were probably drinking in with horrified but no doubt righteously I-told-you-so eyes.

Instead of looking, Harold went to the telephone, snatched it up, and dialed police headquarters from the emergency decal pasted on the phone's handset.

"Sergeant Hall," the voice at the other end said.

Harold stuck a finger in his free ear and said, "My name is Harold Parkette. My address is 1421 East Endicott Street. I'd like to report . . ." What? What would he like to report? A man is in the process of raping and murdering my lawn and he works for a fellow named Pan and has cloven feet?

"Yes, Mr Parkette?"

Inspiration struck. "I'd like to report a case of indecent exposure."

"Indecent exposure," Sergeant Hall repeated.

"Yes. There's a man mowing my lawn. He's in the, uh, altogether."

"You mean he's naked?" Sergeant Hall asked, politely incredulous.

"Naked!" Harold agreed, holding tightly to the frayed ends of his sanity. "Nude. Unclothed. Bare-assed. On my front lawn. Now will you get somebody the hell over here?"

"That address was 1421 West Endicott?" Sergeant Hall asked bemusedly.

"East!" Harold yelled. "For God's sake – "

210

The Lawnmower Man

"And you say he's definitely naked? You are able to observe his, uh, genitals and so on?"

Harold tried to speak and could only gargle. The sound of the insane lawnmower seemed to be growing louder and louder, drowning out everything in the universe. He felt his gorge rise.

"Can you speak up?" Sergeant Hall buzzed. "There's an awfully noisy connection there at your end – "

The front door crashed open.

Harold looked around and saw the lawnmower man's mechanized familiar advancing through the door. Behind it came the lawnmower man himself, still quite naked. With something approaching true insanity, Harold saw the man's pubic hair was a rich fertile green. He was twirling his basball cap on one finger.

"That was a mistake, buddy," the lawnmower man said reproachfully. "You shoulda stuck with God bless the grass."

"Hello? Hello, Mr Parkette – "

The telephone dropped from Harold's nerveless fingers as the lawnmower began to advance on him, cutting through the nap of Carla's new Mohawk rug and spitting out brown hunks of fiber as it came.

Harold stared at it with a kind of bird-and-snake fascination until it reached the coffee table. When the mower shunted it aside, shearing one leg into sawdust and splinters as it did so, he climbed over the back of his chair and began to retreat toward the kitchen, dragging the chair in front of him.

"That won't do any good, buddy," the lawnmower man said kindly. "Apt to be messy, too. Now if you was just to show me where you keep your sharpest butcher knife, we could get this sacrifice business out of the way real painless . . . I think the bird-bath would do . . . and then – "

Harold shoved the chair at the lawnmower, which had been craftily flanking him while the naked man drew his

211

attention, and bolted through the doorway. The lawnmower roared around the chair, jetting out exhaust, and as Harold smashed open the porch screen door and leaped down the steps, he heard it – smelled it, felt it – right at his heels.

The lawnmower roared off the top step like a skier going off a jump. Harold sprinted across his newly cut back lawn, but there had been too many beers, too many afternoon naps. He could sense it nearing him, then on his heels, and then he looked over his shoulder and tripped over his own feet.

The last thing Harold Parkette saw was the grinning grill of the charging lawnmower, rocking back to reveal its flashing, greenstained blades, and above it the fat face of the lawnmower man, shaking his head in good-natured reproof.

"Hell of a thing," Lieutenant Goodwin said as the last of the photographs were taken. He nodded to the two men in white, and they trundled their basket across the lawn. "He reported some naked guy on his lawn not two hours ago."

"Is that so?" Patrolman Cooley asked.

"Yeah. One of the neighbors called in, too. Guy named Castonmeyer. He thought it was Parkette himself. Maybe it was, Cooley. Maybe it was."

"Sir?"

"Crazy with the heat," Lieutenant Goodwin said gravely, and tapped his temple. "Schizo-fucking-phrenia."

"Yes sir," Cooley said respectfully.

"Where's the rest of him?" one of the white-coats asked.

"The birdbath," Goodwin said. He looked profoundly up at the sky.

"Did you say the birdbath?" the white-coat asked.

"Indeed I did," Lieutenant Goodwin agreed. Patrolman Cooley looked at the birdbath and suddenly lost most of his tan.

"Sex maniac," Lieutenant Goodwin said. "Must have been."

"Prints?" Cooley asked thickly.

"You might as well ask for footprints," Goodwin said. He gestured at the the newly cut grass.

Patrolman Cooley made a strangled noise in his throat.

Lieutenant Goodwin stuffed his hands into his pockets and rocked back on his heels. "The world," he said gravely, "is full of nuts. Never forget that, Cooley. Schizos. Lab boys say somebody chased Parkette through his own living room with a lawnmower. Can you imagine that?"

"No sir," Cooley said.

Goodwin looked out over Harold Parkette's neatly manicured lawn. "Well, like the man said when he saw the black-haired Swede, it surely is a Norse of a different color."

Goodwin strolled around the house and Cooley followed him. Behind them, the scent of newly mown grass hung pleasantly in the air.

CANDYMAN

> (Tristar Pictures, 1993)
> Starring: Virginia Madsen, Tony Todd
> & Xander Berkeley
> Directed by Bernard Rose
> Based on "The Forbidden" by Clive Barker

Few of today's film makers are more fascinated by special effects and working harder to extend the boundaries of what is possible on the screen than the English writer-turned-director Clive Barker (1952–). Barker's books have put him in the same category as Stephen King and he admits to being a great admirer of Hollywood's leading exponents of movie wizardry, George Lucas and Steven Spielberg. Like King, too, a number of Clive's stories have been filmed with varying degrees of success – in particular the Hellraiser series with their grotesque and terrifying character Pinhead (played by Doug Bradley). The first of these Barker directed himself at a cost of $1million and the picture has subsequently taken over $30 million at the box office and inspired two sequels – all of which are notable for their spellbinding special effects. The same is also true of the most recent of Barker's stories to be filmed, *Candyman*, the success of which has already generated a follow-up and shows every sign of becoming a series, too. It takes for its theme an "urban myth" – one of those stories of supernatural creatures or contact with aliens which have been around for some years in magazines and books but now seem destined to become one of the latest developments in the SF genre. This particular tale concerns a folklorist (Virginia Madsen) who is researching a legend about the Candyman (Tony Todd), a hook-handed, supernatural black killer accompanied by a swarm of deadly bees, who she quickly discovers is no myth and by merely speaking his name five times finds herself plunged into a living hell. The special effects for the movie were created by Jane Stewart, one of the hottest new talents in Hollywood, who came to attention in 1991 for masterminding the ingenious wizardry in *Beetlejuice* starring Michael Keaton. Although *Candyman* was filmed amidst the run-down project buildings of Chicago, the original story was actually located in Clive Barker's native Liverpool – but other than that, Bernard Rose's screenplay remained faithful to Barker's short tale "The Forbidden". The story had originally been written for the fifth volume of Clive's ambitious *Books of Blood* series, launched in 1984, which has subsequently captured the reading public's imagination and led him to Hollywood where he now lives and plays a leading role in the making of fantasy movies. It has been a remarkable achievement for a young man who started out writing plays such as *The History of the Devil* and *Frankenstein in Love* for small theatre productions in London, and can now command millions of dollars for his scripts or directorial assignments. When *Candyman* was released in March 1993, *Time Out* magazine hailed it as "setting the standard for the 90's". There seems little doubt that Clive Barker is destined to become one of the film makers who will ensure the SF picture continues to flourish into the Twenty-First Century. And that the special effects which have been such an integral part of the genre since its inception at the start of this century will also reach even greater heights.

Like a flawless tragedy, the elegance of which structure is lost upon those suffering in it, the perfect geometry of the Spector Street Estate was only visible from the air. Walking in its drear canyons, passing through its grimy corridors from one grey concrete rectangle to the next, there was little to seduce the eye or stimulate the imagination. What few saplings had been planted in the quadrangles had long since been mutilated or uprooted; the grass, though tall, resolutely refused a healthy green.

No doubt the estate and its two companion developments had once been an architect's dream. No doubt the city-planners had wept with pleasure at a design which housed three and thirty-six persons per hectare, and still boasted space for a children's playground. Doubtless fortunes and reputations had been built upon Spector Street, and at its opening fine words had been spoken of it being a yardstick by which all future developments would be measured. But the planners – tears wept, words spoken – had left the estate to its own devices; the architects occupied restored Georgian houses at the other end of the city, and probably never set foot here.

They would not have been shamed by the deterioration of the estate even if they had. Their brain-child (they would doubtless argue) was as brilliant as ever: Its geometries as precise, its ratios as calculated; it was *people* who had spoiled Spector Street. Nor would they have been wrong in such an accusation. Helen had seldom seen an inner city environment so comprehensively vandalized. Lamps had been shattered and back-yard fences overthrown; cars, whose wheels and engines had been removed and chassis then burned, blocked garage facilities. In one courtyard three or four ground-floor maisonettes had been entirely gutted by fire, their windows and doors boarded up with planks and corrugated iron.

More startling still was the graffiti. That was what she had come here to see, encouraged by Archie's talk of the place, and she was not disappointed. It was difficult to believe, staring at the multiple layers of designs, names, obscenities, and dogmas that were scrawled and sprayed on every available brick, that Spector Street was barely three and a half years old. The walls, so recently virgin, were now so profoundly defaced that the Council Cleaning Department could never hope to return them to their former condition. A layer of whitewash to cancel this visual cacophony would only offer the scribes a fresh and yet more tempting surface on which to make their mark.

Helen was in seventh heaven. Every corner she turned offered some fresh material for her thesis: *"Graffiti: the semiotics of urban despair"*. It was a subject which married her two favourite disciplines – sociology and aesthetics – and as she wandered around the estate she began to wonder if there wasn't a book, in addition to her thesis, in the subject. She walked from courtyard to courtyard, copying down a large number of the more interesting scrawlings, and noting their location. Then she went back to the car to collect her camera and tripod and returned to the most fertile of the areas, to make a thorough visual record of the walls.

It was a chilly business. She was not an expert photographer, and the late October sky was in full flight, shifting the light on the bricks from one moment to the next. As she adjusted and readjusted the exposure to compensate for the light changes her fingers steadily became clumsier, her temper correspondingly thinner. But she struggled on, the idle curiosity of passers-by notwithstanding. There were so many designs to document. She reminded herself that her present discomfort would be amply repaid when she showed the slides to Trevor, whose doubt of the project's validity had been perfectly apparent from the beginning.

"The writing on the wall?" he'd said, half smiling in that irritating fashion of his. "It's been done a hundred times."

This was true, of course; and yet not. There certainly were learned works on graffiti, chock-full of sociological jargon: *cultural disenfranchisement; urban alienation*. But she flattered herself that *she* might find something amongst this litter of scrawlings that previous analysts had not: Some unifying convention perhaps, that she could use as the lynchpin of her thesis. Only a vigorous cataloguing and cross-referencing of the phrases and images before her would reveal such a correspondence; hence the importance of the photographic study. So many hands had worked here; so many minds left their mark, however casually: If she could find some pattern, some predominant motive, or *motif*, the thesis would be guaranteed some serious attention, and so, in turn, would she.

"What are you doing?" a voice from behind her asked.

She turned from her calculations to see a young woman with a pushchair on the pavement behind her. She looked weary, Helen thought, and pinched by the cold. The child in the pushchair was mewling, his grimy fingers clutching an orange lollipop and the wrapping from a chocolate bar. The bulk of the chocolate, and the remains of previous jujubes, was displayed down the front of his coat.

Helen offered a thin smile to the woman; she looked in need of it.

"I'm photographing the walls," she said in answer to the initial enquiry, though surely this was perfectly apparent.

The woman – Helen judged she could barely be twenty – said: "You mean the filth?"

"The writing and the pictures," Helen said. Then: "Yes. The filth."

"You from the Council?"

"No, the University."

"It's bloody disgusting," the woman said. "The way they do that. It's not just kids, either."

"No?"

"Grown men. Grown men, too. They don't give a damn. Do it in broad daylight. You see 'em . . . broad daylight." She glanced down at the child, who was sharpening his lollipop on the ground. "Kerry!" she snapped, but the boy took no notice. "Are they going to wipe it off?" she asked Helen.

"I don't know," Helen said, and reiterated: "I'm from the University."

"Oh," the woman replied, as if this was new information, "so you're nothing to do with the Council?"

"No."

"Some of it's obscene, isn't it? Really dirty. Makes me embarrassed to see some of the things they draw."

Helen nodded, casting an eye at the boy in the pushchair. Kerry had decided to put his sweet in his ear for safe-keeping.

"Don't do that!" his mother told him, and leaned over to slap the child's hand. The blow, which was negligible, began the child bawling. Helen took the opportunity to return to her camera. But the woman still desired to talk. "It's not just on the outside, neither," she commented.

"I beg your pardon?" Helen said.

"They break into the flats when they go empty. The Council tried to board them up, but it does no good. They break in anyway. Use them as toilets, and write more filth on the walls. They light fires too. Then nobody can move back in."

The description piqued Helen's curiosity. Would the graffiti on the *inside* walls be substantially different from the public displays? It was certainly worth an investigation.

"Are there any places you know of around here like that?"

"Empty flats, you mean?"

"With graffiti."

"Just by us, there's one or two," the woman volunteered. "I'm in Butts' Court."

"Maybe you could show me?" Helen asked.

The woman shrugged.

"By the way, my name's Helen Buchanan."

"Anne-Marie," the mother replied.

"I'd be very grateful if you could point me to one of those empty flats."

Anne-Marie was baffled by Helen's enthusiasm, and made no attempt to disguise it, but she shrugged again and said: "There's nothing much to see. Only more of the same stuff."

Helen gathered up her equipment and they walked side by side through the intersecting corridors between one square and the next. Though the estate was lowrise, each court only five storeys high, the effect of each quadrangle was horribly claustrophobic. The walkways and staircases were a thief's dream, rife with blind corners and ill-lit tunnels. The rubbish-dumping facilities – chutes from the upper floors down which bags of refuse could be pitched – had long since been sealed up, thanks to their efficiency as fire-traps. Now plastic bags of refuse were piled high in the corridors, many torn open by roaming dogs, their contents strewn across the ground. The smell, even in the cold weather, was unpleasant. In high summer it must have been overpowering.

"I'm over the other side," Anne-Marie said, pointing across the quadrangle. "The one with the yellow door." She then pointed along the opposite side of the court. "Five or six maisonettes from the far end," she said. "There's two of them been emptied out. Few weeks now. One of the family's moved into Ruskin Court; the other did a bunk in the middle of the night."

With that, she turned her back on Helen and wheeled Kerry, who had taken to trailing spittle from the side of his pushchair, around the side of the square.

"Thank you," Helen called after her. Anne-Marie glanced over her shoulder briefly, but did not reply. Appetite whetted, Helen made her way along the row of ground floor maisonettes, many of which, though inhabited, showed little sign of being so. Their curtains were closely drawn; there were no milk-bottles on the doorsteps, nor children's toys left where they had been played with. Nothing, in fact, *of life* here. There *was* more graffiti however, sprayed, shockingly, on the doors of occupied houses. She granted the scrawlings only a casual perusal, in part because she feared one of the doors opening as she examined a choice obscenity sprayed upon it, but more

because she was eager to see what revelations the empty
flats ahead might offer.

The malign scent of urine, both fresh and stale, welcomed
her at the threshold of number 14, and beneath that the
smell of burnt paint and plastic. She hesitated for fully ten
seconds, wondering if stepping into the maisonette was a
wise move. The territory of the estate behind her was
indisputably foreign, sealed off in its own misery, but the
rooms in front of her were more intimidating still: A dark
maze which her eyes could barely penetrate. But when her
courage faltered she thought of Trevor, and how badly she
wanted to silence his condescension. So thinking, she
advanced into the place, deliberately kicking a piece of
charred timber aside as she did so, in the hope that she
would alert any tenant into showing himself.

There was no sound of occupancy however. Gaining
confidence, she began to explore the front room of the
maisonette which had been – to judge by the remains of a
disembowelled sofa in one corner and the sodden carpet
underfoot – a living room. The pale-green walls were, as
Anne-Marie had promised, extensively defaced, both by
minor scribblers – content to work in pen, or even more
crudely in sofa charcoal – and by those with aspirations to
public works, who had sprayed the walls in half a dozen
colours.

Some of the comments were of interest, though many she
had already seen on the walls outside. Familiar names and
couplings repeated themselves. Though she had never set
eyes on these individuals she knew how badly Fabian J.
(A.OK.) wanted to deflower Michelle; and that Michelle, in
her turn, had the hots for somebody called Mr Sheen. Here,
as elsewhere, a man called White Rat boasted of his
endowment, and the return of the Syllabub Brothers was
promised in red paint. One or two of the pictures accom-
panying, or at least adjacent to these phrases were of
particular interest. An almost emblematic simplicity in-

formed them. Beside the word *Christos* was a stick man with his hair radiating from his head like spines, and other heads impaled on each spine. Close by was an image of intercourse so brutally reduced that at first Helen took it to illustrate a knife plunging into a sightless eye. But fascinating as the images were, the room was too gloomy for her film, and she had neglected to bring a flash. If she wanted a reliable record of these discoveries she would have to come again, and for now be content with a simple exploration of the premises.

The maisonette wasn't that large, but the windows had been boarded up throughout, and as she moved further from the front door the dubious light petered out altogether. The smell of urine, which had been strong at the door, intensified too, until by the time she reached the back living room and stepped along a short corridor into another room beyond, it was as cloying as incense. This room, being furthest from the front door, was also the darkest, and she had to wait a few moments in the cluttered gloom to allow her eyes to become useful. This, she guessed, had been the bedroom. What little furniture the residents had left behind them had been smashed to smithereens. Only the mattress had been left relatively untouched, dumped in the corner of the room amongst a wretched litter of blankets, newspapers, and pieces of crockery.

Outside, the sun found its way between the clouds, and two or three shafts of sunlight slipped between the boards nailed across the bedroom window and pierced the room like annunciations, scoring the opposite wall with bright lines. Here, the graffitists had been busy once more: The usual clamour of love-letters and threats. She scanned the wall quickly, and as she did so her eye was led by the beams of light across the room to the wall which contained the door she had stepped through.

Here, the artists had also been at work, but had produced an image the like of which she had not seen anywhere else.

Using the door, which was centrally placed in the wall, as a mouth, the artists had sprayed a single, vast head on to the stripped plaster. The painting was more adroit than most she had seen, rife with detail that lent the image an unsettling veracity. The cheekbones jutting through skin the colour of buttermilk; the teeth – sharpened to irregular points – all converging on the door. The sitter's eyes were, owing to the room's low ceiling, set mere inches above the upper lip, but this physical adjustment only lent force to the image, giving the impression that he had thrown his head back. Knotted strands of his hair snaked from his scalp across the ceiling.

Was it a portrait? There was something naggingly *specific* in the details of the brows and the lines around the wide mouth; in the careful picturing of those vicious teeth. A nightmare certainly: A facsimile, perhaps, of something from a heroin fugue. Whatever its origins, it was potent. Even the illusion of door-as-mouth worked. The short passageway between living room and bedroom offered a passable throat, with a tattered lamp in lieu of tonsils. Beyond the gullet, the day burned white in the nightmare's belly. The whole effect brought to mind a ghost train painting. The same heroic deformity, the same unashamed intention to scare. And it worked. She stood in the bedroom almost stupified by the picture, its red-rimmed eyes fixing her mercilessly. Tomorrow, she determined, she would come here again, this time with high-speed film and a flash to illuminate the masterwork.

As she prepared to leave the sun went in, and the bands of light faded. She glanced over her shoulder at the boarded windows, and saw for the first time that one four-word slogan had been sprayed on the wall beneath them.

"*Sweets to the sweet*" it read. She was familiar with the quote, but not with its source. Was it a profession of love? If so, it was an odd location for such an avowal. Despite the mattress in the corner, and the relative privacy of this room,

223

she could not imagine the intended reader of such words ever stepping in here to receive her bouquet. No adolescent lovers, however heated, would lie down here to play at mothers and fathers; not under the gaze of the terror on the wall. She crossed to examine the writing. The paint looked to be the same shade of pink as had been used to colour the gums of the screaming man; perhaps the same hand?

Behind her, a noise. She turned so quickly she almost tripped over the blanket-strewn mattress.

"Who –?"

At the other end of the gullet, in the living room, was a scab-kneed boy of six or seven. He stared at Helen, eyes glittering in the half-light, as if waiting for a cue.

"Yes?" she said.

"Anne-Marie says do you want a cup of tea?" he declared without pause or intonation.

Her conversation with the woman seemed hours past. She was grateful for the invitation however. The damp maisonette had chilled her.

"Yes . . ." she said to the boy. "Yes please."

The child didn't move, but simply stared on at her.

"Are you going to lead the way?" she asked him.

"If you want," he replied, unable to raise a trace of enthusiasm.

"I'd like that."

"You taking photographs?" he asked.

"Yes. Yes, I am. But not in here."

"Why not?"

"It's too dark," she told him.

"Don't it work in the dark?" he wanted to know.

"No."

The boy nodded at this, as if the information somehow fitted well into his scheme of things, and about-turned without another word, clearly expecting Helen to follow.

If she had been taciturn in the street, Anne-Marie was

anything but in the privacy of her own kitchen. Gone was the guarded curiosity, to be replaced by a stream of lively chatter and a constant scurrying between half-a-dozen minor domestic tasks, like a juggler keeping several plates spinning simultaneously. Helen watched this balancing act with some admiration; her own domestic skills were negligible. At last, the meandering conversation turned back to the subject that had brought Helen here.

"Them photographs," Anne-Marie said, "why'd you want to take them?"

"I'm writing about graffiti. The photos will illustrate my thesis."

"It's not very pretty."

"No, you're right, it isn't. But I find it interesting."

Anne-Marie shook her head. "I hate the whole estate," she said. "It's not safe here. People getting robbed on their own doorsteps. Kids setting fire to the rubbish day in, day out. Last summer we had the fire brigade here two, three times a day, 'til they sealed them chutes off. Now people just dump the bags in the passageways, and that attracts rats."

"Do you live here alone?"

"Yes," she said, "since Davey walked out."

"That your husband?"

"He was Kerry's father, but we weren't never married. We lived together two years, you know. We had some good times. Then he just upped and went off one day when I was at me Mam's with Kerry." She peered into her tea-cup. "I'm better off without him," she said. "But you get scared sometimes. Want some more tea?"

"I don't think I've got time."

"Just a cup," Anne-Marie said, already up and unplugging the electric kettle to take it across for a re-fill. As she was about to turn on the tap she saw something on the draining board, and drove her thumb down, grinding it out. "Got you, you bugger," she said, then turned to Helen: "We got these bloody ants."

"Ants?"

"Whole estate's infected. From Egypt, they are: Pharoah ants, they're called. Little brown sods. They breed in the central heating ducts, you see; that way they get into all the flats. Place is plagued with them."

This unlikely exoticism (ants from Egypt?) struck Helen as comical, but she said nothing. Anne-Marie was staring out of the kitchen window and into the backyard.

"You should tell them – " she said, though Helen wasn't certain whom she was being instructed to tell, "tell them that ordinary people can't even walk the sreets any longer – "

"Is it really so bad?" Helen said, frankly tiring of this catalogue of misfortunes.

Anne-Marie turned from the sink and looked at her hard.

"We've had murders here," she said.

"Really?"

"We had one in the summer. An old man he was, from Ruskin. That's just next door. I didn't know him, but he was a friend of the sister of the woman next door. I forget his name."

"And he was murdered?"

"Cut to ribbons in his own front room. They didn't find him for almost a week."

"What about his neighbours? Didn't they notice his absence?"

Anne-Marie shrugged, as if the most important pieces of information – the murder and the man's isolation – had been exchanged, and any further enquiries into the problem were irrelevant. But Helen pressed the point.

"Seems strange to me," she said.

Anne-Marie plugged in the filled kettle. "Well, it happened," she replied, unmoved.

"I'm not saying it didn't, I just – "

"His eyes had been taken out," she said, before Helen could voice any further doubts.

Helen winced. "No," she said, under her breath.

"That's the truth," Anne-Marie said. "And that wasn't all'd been done to him." She paused, for effect, then went on: "You wonder what kind of person's capable of doing things like that, don't you? You wonder." Helen nodded. She was thinking precisely the same thing.

"Did they ever find the man responsible?"

Anne-Marie snorted her disparagement. "Police don't give a damn what happens here. They keep off the estate as much as possible. When they do patrol all they do is pick up kids for getting drunk and that. They're afraid, you see. That's why they keep clear."

"Of this killer?"

"Maybe," Anne-Marie replied. Then: "He had a hook."

"A hook?"

"The man what done it. He had a hook, like Jack the Ripper."

Helen was no expert on murder, but she felt certain that the Ripper hadn't boasted a hook. It seemed churlish to question the truth of Anne-Marie's story however; though she silently wondered how much of this – the eyes taken out, the body rotting in the flat, the hook – was elaboration. The most scrupulous of reporters was surely tempted to embellish a story once in a while.

Anne-Marie had poured herself another cup of tea, and was about to do the same for her guest.

"No thank you," Helen said, "I really should go."

"You married?" Anne-Marie asked, out of the blue.

"Yes. To a lecturer from the University."

"What's his name?"

"Trevor."

Anne-Marie put two heaped spoonfuls of sugar into her cup of tea. "Will you be coming back?" she asked.

"Yes, I hope to. Later in the week. I want to take some photographs of the pictures in the maisonette across the court."

"Well, call in."

"I shall. And thank you for your help."

"That's all right," Anne-Marie replied. "You've got to tell somebody, haven't you?"

"The man apparently had a hook instead of a hand."

Trevor looked up from his plate of *tagliatelle con prosciutto*.

"Beg your pardon?"

Helen had been at pains to keep her recounting of this story as uncoloured by her own response as she could. She was interested to know what Trevor would make of it, and she knew that if she once signalled her own stance he would instinctively take an opposing view out of plain bloody-mindedness.

"He had a hook," she repeated, without inflexion.

Trevor put down his fork, and plucked at his nose, sniffing. "I didn't read anything about this," he said.

"You don't look at the local press," Helen returned. "Neither of us do. Maybe it never made any of the nationals."

"'Geriatric Murdered By Hook-Handed Maniac'?" Trevor said, savouring the hyperbole. "I would have thought it very newsworthy. "When was all of this supposed to have happened?"

"Sometime last summer. Maybe we were in Ireland."

"Maybe," said Trevor, taking up his fork again. Bending to his food, the polished lens of his spectacles reflected only the plate of pasta and chopped ham in front of him, not his eyes.

"Why do you say *maybe*?" Helen prodded.

"It doesn't sound quite right," he said. "In fact it sounds bloody preposterous."

"You don't believe it?" Helen said.

Trevor looked up from his food, tongue rescuing a speck of *tagliatelle* from the corner of his mouth. His face had relaxed into that non-committal expression of his – the same face he wore, no doubt, when listening to his students.

"Do *you* believe it?" he asked Helen. It was a favourite time-gaining device of his, another seminar trick, to question the questioner.

"I'm not certain," Helen replied, too concerned to find some solid ground in this sea of doubts to waste energy scoring points.

"All right, forget the tale – " Trevor said, deserting his food for another glass of red wine. "– What about the teller? Did *you* trust her?"

Helen pictured Anne-Marie's earnest expression as she told the story of the old man's murder. "Yes," she said. "Yes; I think I would have known if she'd been lying to me."

"So why's it so important, anyhow? I mean, whether she's lying or not, what the fuck does it matter?"

It was a reasonable question, if irritatingly put. Why *did* it matter? Was it that she wanted to have her worst feelings about Spector Street proved false? That such an estate be filthy, be hopeless, be a dump where the undesirable and the disadvantaged were tucked out of public view – all that was a liberal commonplace, and she accepted it as an unpalatable social reality. But the story of the old man's murder and mutilation was something other. An image of violent death that, once with her, refused to part from her company.

She realized, to her chagrin, that this confusion was plain on her face, and that Trevor, watching her across the table, was not a little entertained by it.

"If it bothers you so much," he said, "why don't you go back there and ask around, instead of playing believe-in-it-or-not over dinner?"

She couldn't help but rise to his remark. "I thought you liked guessing games," she said.

He threw her a sullen look.

"Wrong again."

The suggestion that she investigate was not a bad one, though doubtless he had ulterior motives for offering it. She

229

viewed Trevor less charitably day by day. What she had once thought in him a fierce commitment to debate she now recognized as mere power-play. He argued, not for the thrill of dialectic, but because he was pathologically competitive. She had seen him, time and again, take up attitudes she knew he did not espouse, simply to spill blood. Nor, more's the pity, was he alone in this sport. Academe was one of the last strongholds of the professional time-waster. On occasion their circle seemed entirely dominated by educated fools, lost in a wasteland of stale rhetoric and hollow commitment.

From one wasteland to another. She returned to Spector Street the following day, armed with a flashgun in addition to her tripod and high-sensitive film. The wind was up today, and it was Arctic, more furious still for being trapped in the maze of passageways and courts. She made her way to number 14, and spent the next hour in its befouled confines, meticulously photographing both the bedroom and living-room walls. She had half expected the impact of the head in the bedroom to be dulled by re-acquaintance; it was not. Though she struggled to capture its scale and detail as best she could, she knew the photographs would be at best a dim echo of its perpetual howl.

Much of its power lay in its context, of course. That such an image might be stumbled upon in surroundings so drab, so conspicuously lacking in mystery, was akin to finding an icon on a rubbish-heap: A gleaming symbol of transcendence from a world of toil and decay into some darker but more tremendous realm. She was painfully aware that the intensity of her response probably defied her articulation. Her vocabulary was analytic, replete with buzz-words and academic terminology, but woefully impoverished when it came to evocation. The photographs, pale as they would be, would, she hoped, at least hint at the potency of this picture, even if they couldn't conjure the way it froze the bowels.

The Forbidden

When she emerged from the maisonette the wind was as uncharitable as ever, but the boy was waiting outside – the same child as had attended upon her yesterday – dressed as if for spring weather. He grimaced in his effort to keep the shudders at bay.

"Hello," Helen said.

"I waited," the child announced.

"Waited?"

"Anne-Marie said you'd come back.

"I wasn't planning to come until later in the week," Helen said. "You might have waited a long time."

The boy's grimace relaxed a notch. "It's all right," he said, "I've got nothing to do."

"What about school?"

"Don't like it," the boy replied, as if unobliged to be educated if it wasn't to his taste.

"I see," said Helen, and began to walk down the side of the quadrangle. The boy followed. On the patch of grass at the centre of the quadrangle several chairs and two or three dead saplings had been piled.

"What's this?" she said, half to herself.

"Bonfire Night," the boy informed her. "Next week."

"Of course."

"You going to see Anne-Marie?" he asked.

"Yes."

"She's not in."

"Oh. Are you sure?"

"Yeah."

"Well, perhaps *you* can help me . . ." She stopped and turned to face the child; smooth sacs of fatigue hung beneath his eyes. "I heard about an old man who was murdered near here," she said to him. "In the summer. Do you know anything about that?"

"No."

"Nothing at all? You don't remember anybody getting killed?"

231

"No," the boy said again, with impressive finality. "I don't remember."

"Well; thank you anyway."

This time, when she retraced her steps back to the car, the boy didn't follow. But as she turned the corner out of the quadrangle she glanced back to see him standing on the spot where she'd left him, staring after her as if she were a madwoman.

By the time she had reached the car and packed the photographic equipment into the boot there were specks of rain in the wind, and she was sorely tempted to forget she'd ever heard Anne-Marie's story and make her way home, where the coffee would be warm even if the welcome wasn't. But she needed an answer to the question Trevor had put the previous night. Do *you* believe it?, he'd asked when she'd told him the story. She hadn't known how to answer then, and she still didn't. Perhaps (why did she sense this?) the terminology of verifiable truth was redundant here; perhaps the final answer to his question was not an answer at all, only another question. If so; so. She had to find out.

Ruskin Court was as forlorn as its fellows, if not more so. It didn't even boast a bonfire. On the third floor balcony a woman was taking washing in before the rain broke; on the grass in the centre of the quadrangle two dogs were absent-mindedly rutting, the fuckee staring up at the blank sky. As she walked along the empty pavement she set her face determinedly; a purposeful look, Bernadette had once said, deterred attack. When she caught sight of the two women talking at the far end of the court she crossed over to them hurriedly, grateful for their presence.

"Excuse me?"

The women, both in middle-age, ceased their animated exchange and looked her over.

"I wonder if you can help me?"

She could feel their appraisal, and their distrust; they

went undisguised. One of the pair, her face florid, said plainly: "What do you want?"

Helen suddenly felt bereft of the least power to charm. What was she to say to these two that wouldn't make her motives appear ghoulish? "I was told . . ." she began, and then stumbled, aware that she would get no assistance from either woman. ". . . I was told there'd been a murder near here. Is that right?"

The florid woman raised eyebrows so plucked they were barely visible. "Murder?" she said.

"Are you from the press?" the other woman enquired. The years had soured her features beyond sweetening. Her small mouth was deeply lined; her hair, which had been dyed brunette, showed a half-inch of grey at the roots.

"No, I'm not from the press," Helen said, "I'm a friend of Anne-Marie's in Butts' Court." This claim of *friend* stretched the truth, but it seemed to mellow the women somewhat.

"Visiting are you?" the florid woman asked.

"In a manner of speaking – "

"You missed the warm spell – "

"Anne-Marie was telling me about somebody who'd been murdered here, during the summer. I was curious about it."

"Is that right?"

"– do you know anything about it?"

"Lots of things go on around here," said the second woman. "You don't know the half of it."

"So it's true," Helen said.

"They had to close the toilets," the first woman put in.

"That's right. They did," the other said.

"The toilets?" Helen said. What had this to do with the old man's death?

"It was terrible," the first said. "Was it your Frank, Josie, who told you about it?"

"No, not Frank," Josie replied. "Frank was still at sea. It was Mrs Tyzack."

The witness established, Josie relinquished the story to her companion, and turned her gaze back upon Helen. The suspicion had not yet died from her eyes.

"This was only the month before last," Josie said. "Just about the end of August. It was August, wasn't it?" She looked to the other woman for verification. "You've got the head for dates, Maureen."

Maureen looked uncomfortable. "I forget, she said, clearly unwilling to offer testimony.

"I'd like to know," Helen said. Josie, despite her companion's reluctance, was eager to oblige.

"There's some lavatories," she said, "outside the shops – you know, public lavatories. I'm not quite sure how it all happened exactly, but there used to be a boy . . . well, he wasn't a boy really, I mean he was a man of twenty or more, but he was . . ." she fished for the words, ". . . mentally subnormal, I suppose you'd say. His mother used to have to take him around like he was a four-year-old. Anyhow, she let him go into the lavatories while she went to that little supermarket, what's it called?" she turned to Maureen for a prompt, but the other woman just looked back, her disapproval plain. Josie was ungovernable, however. "Broad daylight, this was," she said to Helen. "Middle of the day. Anyhow, the boy went to the toilet, and the mother was in the shop. And after a while, you know how you do, she's busy shopping, she forgets about him, and then she thinks he's been gone a long time . . ."

At this juncture Maureen couldn't prevent herself from butting in: The accuracy of the story apparently took precedence over her wariness.

"– She got into an argument," she corrected Josie, "with the manager. About some bad bacon she'd had from him. That was why she was such a time . . ."

"I see," said Helen.

"– anyway," said Josie, picking up the tale, "she finished her shopping and when she came out he still wasn't there – "

"So she asked someone from the supermarket – " Maureen began, but Josie wasn't about to have her narrative snatched back at this vital juncture.

"She asked one of the men from the supermarket – " she repeated over Maureen's interjection, "to go down into the lavatory and find him."

"It was terrible," said Maureen, clearly picturing the atrocity in her mind's eye.

"He was lying on the floor, in a pool of blood."

"Murdered?"

Josie shook her head. "He'd have been better off dead. He'd been attacked with a razor – " she let this piece of information sink in before delivering the *coup de grâce*, "– and they'd cut off his private parts. Just cut them off and flushed them down a toilet. No reason on earth to do it."

"Oh my God."

"Better off dead," Josie repeated. "I mean, they can't mend something like that, can they?"

The appalling tale was rendered worse still by the *sang-froid* of the teller, and by the casual repetition of "Better off dead".

"The boy," Helen said, "Was he able to describe his attackers?"

"No," said Josie, "he's pratically an imbecile. He can't string more than two words together."

"And nobody saw anyone go into the lavatory? Or leaving it?"

"People come and go all the time – " Maureen said. This, though it sounded like an adequate explanation, had not been Helen's experience. There was not a great bustle in the quadrangle and passageways; far from it. Perhaps the shopping mall was busier, she reasoned, and might offer adequate cover for such a crime.

"So they haven't found the culprit," she said.

"No," Josie replied, her eyes losing their fervour. The crime and its immediate consequences were the nub of this story; she had little or no interest in either the culprit or his capture.

"We're not safe in our own beds," Maureen observed. "You ask anyone."

"Anne-Marie said the same," Helen replied. "That's how she came to tell me about the old man. Said he was murdered during the summer, here in Ruskin Court."

"I do remember something," Josie said. "There *was* some talk I heard. An old man, and his dog. He was battered to death, and the dog ended up . . . I don't know. It certainly wasn't here. It must have been one of the other estates.

"Are you sure?"

The woman looked offended by this slur on her memory. "Oh yes," she said, "I mean if it had been here, we'd have known the story, wouldn't we?"

Helen thanked the pair for their help and decided to take a stroll around the quadrangle anyway, just to see how many more maisonettes were out of operation here. As in Butts' Court, many of the curtains were drawn and all the doors locked. But then if Spector Street *was* under siege from a maniac capable of the murder and mutilation such as she'd heard described, she was not surprised that the residents took to their homes and stayed there. There was nothing much to see around the court. All the unoccupied maisonettes and flats had been recently sealed, to judge by a litter of nails left on a doorstep by the council workmen. One sight *did* catch her attention, however. Scrawled on the paving stones she was walking over – and all but erased by rain and the passage of feet – the same phrase she'd seen in the bedroom of number 14: *Sweets to the sweet.* The words were so benign; why did she seem to sense menace in them? Was it in their excess, perhaps, in the sheer overabundance of sugar upon sugar, honey upon honey?

The Forbidden

She walked on, though the rain persisted, and her walk-about gradually led her away from the quadrangles and into a concrete no-man's-land through which she had not previously passed. This was – or had been – the site of the estate's amenities. Here was the children's playground, its metal-framed rides overturned, its sandpit fouled by dogs, its paddling pool empty. And here too were shops. Several had been boarded up now; those that hadn't were dingy and unattractive, their windows protected by heavy wire-mesh.

She walked along the row, and rounded a corner, and there in front of her was a squat brick building. The public lavatory, she guessed, though the signs designating it as such had gone. The iron gates were closed and padlocked. Standing in front of the charmless building, the wind gusting around her legs, she couldn't help but think of what had happened here. Of the man-child, bleeding on the floor, helpless to cry out. It made her queasy even to contemplate it. She turned her thoughts instead to the felon. What would he look like, she wondered, a man capable of such depravities? She tried to make an image of him, but no detail she could conjure carried sufficient force. But then monsters were seldom very terrible once hauled into the plain light of day. As long as this man was known only by his deeds he held untold power over the imagination; but the human truth beneath the terrors would, she knew, be bitterly disappointing. No monster he; just a whey-faced apology for a man more needful of pity than awe.

The next gust of wind brought the rain on more heavily. It was time, she decided, to be done with adventures for the day. Turning her back on the public lavatories she hurried back through the quadrangles to the refuge of the car, the icy rain needling her face to numbness.

The dinner guests looked gratifyingly appalled at the story, and Trevor, to judge by the expression on his face, was furious. It was done now, however; there was no taking it back. Nor could she deny the satisfaction she took in having silenced the interdepartmental babble about the table. It was Bernadette, Trevor's assistant in the History Department, who broke the agonizing hush.

"When was this?"

"During the summer," Helen told her.

"I don't recall reading about it," said Archie, much the better for two hours of drinking; it mellowed a tongue which was otherwise fulsome in its self-corruscation.

"Perhaps the police are suppressing it," Daniel commented.

"Conspiracy?" said Trevor, plainly cynical.

"It's happening all the time," Daniel shot back.

"Why should they suppress something like this?" Helen said. "It doesn't make sense."

"Since when has police procedure made sense?" Daniel replied.

Bernadette cut in before Helen could answer. "We don't even bother to read about these things any longer," she said.

"Speak for yourself," somebody piped up, but she ignored them and went on:

"We're punch-drunk with violence. We don't see it any longer, even when it's in front of our noses."

"On the screen every night," Archie put in, "Death and disaster in full colour."

"There's nothing very modern about that," Trevor said. "An Elizabethan would have seen death all the time. Public executions were a very popular form of entertainment."

The table broke up into a cacophony of opinions. After two hours of polite gossip the dinner-party had suddenly caught fire. Listening to the debate rage Helen was sorry she hadn't had time to have the photographs processed and printed; the graffiti would have added further fuel to this exhilarating row. It was Purcell, as usual, who was the last to weigh in with his point of view; and – again, as usual – it was devastating.

"Of course, Helen, my sweet – " he began, that affected weariness in his voice edged with the anticipation of controversy "– your witnesses could all be lying, couldn't they?"

The talking around the table dwindled, and all heads turned in Purcell's direction. Perversely, he ignored the attention he'd garnered, and turned to whisper in the ear of the boy he'd brought – a new passion who would, on past form, be discarded in a matter of weeks for another pretty urchin.

"Lying?" Helen said. She could feel herself bristling at the observation already, and Purcell had only spoken a dozen words.

"Why not?" the other replied, lifting his glass of wine to his lips. "Perhaps they're all weaving some elaborate fiction or other. The story of the spastic's mutilation in the public toilet. The murder of the old man. Even that hook. All quite familiar elements. You must be aware that there's something *traditional* about these atrocity stories. One used to exchange them all the time; there was a certain *frisson* in them. Something competitive maybe, in attempting to find a new detail to add to the collective fiction; a fresh twist that would render the tale that little bit more appalling when you passed it on."

"It may be familiar to you – " said Helen defensively. Purcell was always so *poised*; it irritated her. Even if there were validity in his argument – which she doubted – she was damned if she'd concede it. "– *I've* never heard this kind of story before."

"Have you not?" said Purcell, as though she were admitting to illiteracy. "What about the lovers and the escaped lunatic, have you heard that one?"

"I've heard that . . ." Daniel said.

"The lover is disembowelled – usually by a hook-handed man – and the body left on the top of the car, while the fiancée cowers inside. It's a cautionary tale, warning of the evils of rampant heterosexuality." The joke won a round of laughter from everyone but Helen. "These stories are very common."

"So you're saying that they're telling me lies – " she protested.

"Not lies, exactly – "

"You said *lies*."

"I was being provocative," Purcell returned, his placatory tone more enraging than ever. "I don't mean to imply there's any serious mischief in it. But you *must* concede that so far you haven't met a single *witness*. All these events have happened at some unspecified date to some unspecified person. They are reported at several removes. They occurred at best to the brothers of friends of distant relations. Please consider the possibility that perhaps these events do not exist in the real world at all, but are merely titillation for bored housewives – "

Helen didn't make an argument in return, for the simple reason that she lacked one. Purcell's point about the conspicuous absence of witnesses was perfectly sound; she herself had wondered about it. It was strange, too, the way the women in Ruskin Court had speedily consigned the old man's murder to another estate, as though these atrocities always occurred just out of sight – round the next corner, down the next passageway – but never *here*.

"So why?" said Bernadette.

"Why what?" Archie puzzled.

"The stories. Why tell these horrible stories if they're not true?"

"Yes," said Helen, throwing the controversy back into Purcell's ample lap. "*Why?*"

Purcell preened himself, aware that his entry into the debate had changed the basic assumption at a stroke. "I don't know," he said, happy to be done with the game now that he'd shown his arm. "You really mustn't take me too

240

seriously, Helen. *I* try not to." The boy at Purcell's side tittered.

"Maybe it's simply taboo material," Archie said.

"Suppressed – " Daniel prompted.

"Not the way you mean it," Archie retorted. "The whole world isn't politics, Daniel."

"Such naiveté."

"What's so *taboo* about death?" Trevor said. "Bernadette already pointed out: It's in front of us all the time. Television; newspapers."

"Maybe that's not close enough," Bernadette suggested.

"Does anyone mind if I smoke?" Purcell broke in. "Only dessert seems to have been indefinitely postponed – "

Helen ignored the remark, and asked Bernadette what she meant by "not close enough"?

Bernadette shrugged. "I don't know precisely," she confessed, "maybe just that death has to be *near*; we have to *know* it's just round the corner. The television's not intimate enough – "

Helen frowned. The observation made some sense to her, but in the clutter of the moment she couldn't root out its significance.

"Do you think they're stories too?" she asked.

"Andrew has a point – " Bernadette replied.

"Most kind," said Purcell. "Has somebody got a match? The boy's pawned my lighter."

"– about the absence of witnesses."

"All that proves is that I haven't met anybody who's actually *seen* anything," Helen countered, "not that witnesses don't exist."

"All right," said Purcell. "Find me one. If you can prove to me that your atrocity-monger actually lives and breathes, I'll stand everyone dinner at *Appollinaires*. How's that? Am I generous to a fault, or do I just know when I can't lose?" He laughed, knocking on the table with his knuckles by way of applause.

"Sounds good to me," said Trevor. "What do you say, Helen?"

She didn't go back to Spector Street until the following Monday, but all weekend she was there in thought: Standing outside the locked toilet, with the wind bringing rain or in the bedroom, the portrait looming. Thoughts of the estate claimed all her concern. When, late on Saturday afternoon, Trevor found some petty reason for an argument, she let the insults pass, watching him perform the familiar ritual of self-martyrdom without being touched by it in the least. Her indifference only enraged him further. He stormed out in high dudgeon, to visit whichever of his women was in favour this month. She was glad to see the back of him. When he failed to return that night she didn't even think of weeping about it. He was foolish and vacuous. She despaired of ever seeing a haunted look in his dull eyes; and what worth was a man who could not be haunted?

He did not return Sunday night either, and it crossed her mind the following morning, as she parked the car in the heart of the estate, that nobody even knew she had come, and that she might lose herself for days here and nobody be any the wiser. Like the old man Anne-Marie had told her about: Lying forgotten in his favourite armchair with his eyes hooked out, while the flies feasted and the butter went rancid on the table.

It was almost Bonfire Night, and over the weekend the small heap of combustibles in Butts' Court had grown to a substantial size. The construction looked unsound, but that didn't prevent a number of boys and young adolescents clambering over it and into it. Much of its bulk was made up of furniture, filched, no doubt, from boarded-up properties. She doubted if it could burn for any time: If it did, it would go chokingly. Four times, on her way across to Anne-Marie's house, she was waylaid by children begging for money to buy fireworks.

"Penny for the guy," they'd say, though none had a guy to display. She had emptied her pockets of change by the time she reached the front door.

Anne-Marie was in today, though there was no welcoming smile. She simply stared at her visitor as if mesmerised.

"I hope you don't mind me calling . . ."

Anne-Marie made no reply.

". . . I just wanted a word."

"I'm busy," the woman finally announced. There was no invitation inside, no offer of tea.

"Oh. Well . . . it won't take more than a moment."

The back door was open and the draught blew through the house. Papers were flying about in the back yard. Helen could see them lifting into the air like vast white moths.

"What do you want?" Anne-Marie asked.

"Just to ask you about the old man."

The woman frowned minutely. She looked as if she was sickening, Helen thought: Her face had the colour and texture of stale dough, her hair was lank and greasy.

"What old man?"

"Last time I was here, you told me about an old man who'd been murdered, do you remember?"

"No."

"You said he lived in the next court."

"I don't remember," Anne-Marie said.

"But you *distinctly* told me – "

Something fell to the floor in the kitchen, and smashed. Anne-Marie flinched, but did not move from the doorstep, her arm barring Helen's way into the house. The hallway was littered with the child's toys, gnawed and battered.

"Are you all right?"

Anne-Marie nodded. "I've got work to do," she said.

"And you don't remember telling me about the old man?"

"You must have misunderstood," Anne-Marie replied, and then, her voice hushed: "You shouldn't have come. Everybody *knows*."

"Knows what?"

The girl had begun to tremble. "You don't understand, do you? You think people aren't watching?"

"What does it matter? All I asked was – "

"I don't know *anything*," Anne-Marie reiterated. "Whatever I said to you, I lied about it."

"Well, thank you anyway," Helen said, too perplexed by the confusion of signals from Anne-Marie to press the point any further. Almost as soon as she had turned from the door she heard the lock snap closed behind her.

That conversation was only one of several disappointments that morning brought. She went back to the row of shops, and visited the supermarket that Josie had spoken of. There she inquired about the lavatories, and their recent history. The supermarket had only changed hands in the last month, and the new owner, a taciturn Pakistani, insisted that he knew nothing of when or why the lavatories had been closed. She was aware, as she made her enquiries, of being scrutinized by the other customers in the shop; she felt like a pariah. That feeling deepened when, after leaving the supermarket, she saw Josie emerging from the launderette, and called after her only to have the woman pick up her pace and duck away into the maze of corridors. Helen followed, but rapidly lost both her quarry and her way.

Frustrated to the verge of tears, she stood amongst the overturned rubbish bags, and felt a surge of contempt for her foolishness. She didn't belong here, did she? How many times had she criticized others for their presumption in claiming to understand societies they had merely viewed from afar? And here was she, committing the same crime, coming here with her camera and her questions, using the lives (and deaths) of these people as fodder for party conversation. She didn't blame Anne-Marie for turning her back; had she deserved better?

Tired and chilled, she decided it was time to concede Purcell's point. It *was* all fiction she had been told. They had

244

played with her – sensing her desire to be fed some horrors – and she, the perfect fool, had fallen for every ridiculous word. It was time to pack up her credulity and go home.

One call demanded to be made before she returned to the car however: She wanted to look a final time at the painted head. Not as an anthropologist amongst an alien tribe, but as a confessed ghost train rider: For the thrill of it. Arriving at number 14, however, she faced the last and most crushing disappointment. The maisonette had been sealed up by conscientious council workman. The door was locked; the front window boarded over.

She was determined not to be so easily defeated however. She made her way around the back of Butt's Court and located the yard of number 14 by simple mathematics. The gate was wedged closed from the inside, but she pushed hard upon it, and, with effort on both parts, it opened. A heap of rubbish – rotted carpets, a box of rain-sodden magazines, a denuded Christmas tree – had blocked it.

She crossed the yard to the boarded-up windows, and peered through the slats of wood. It wasn't bright outside, but it was darker still within; it was difficult to catch more than the vaguest hint of the painting on the bedroom wall. She pressed her face close to the wood, eager for a final glimpse.

A shadow moved across the room, momentarily blocking her view. She stepped back from the window, startled, not certain of what she'd seen. Perhaps merely her own shadow, cast through the window? But then *she* hadn't moved; it had.

She approached the window again, more cautiously. The air vibrated; she could hear a muted whine from some-where, though she couldn't be certain whether it came from inside or out. Again, she put her face to the rough boards, and suddenly, something leapt at the window. This time she let out a cry. There was a scrabbling sound from within, as nails raked the wood.

A dog! – And a big one to have jumped so high.

"Stupid," she told herself aloud. A sudden sweat bathed her.

The scrabbling had stopped almost as soon as it had started, but she couldn't bring herself to go back to the window. Clearly the workmen who had sealed up the maisonette had failed to check it properly, and incarcerated the animal by mistake. It was ravenous, to judge by the slavering she'd heard; she was grateful she hadn't attempted to break in. The dog – hungry, maybe half-mad in the stinking darkness – could have taken out her throat.

She stared at the boarded-up window. The slits between the boards were barely a half-inch wide, but she sensed that the animal was up on its hind legs on the other side, watching her through the gap. She could hear its panting now that her own breath was regularizing; she could hear its claws raking the sill.

"Bloody thing . . ." she said. "Damn well stay in there."

She backed off towards the gate. Hosts of wood-lice and spiders, disturbed from their nests by moving the carpets behind the gate, were scurrying underfoot, looking for a fresh darkness to call home.

She closed the gate behind her, and was making her way around the front of the block when she heard the sirens; two ugly spirals of sound that made the hair on the back of her neck tingle. They were approaching. She picked up her speed, and came round into Butts' Court in time to see several policemen crossing the grass behind the bonfire and an ambulance mounting the pavement and driving around to the other side of the quadrangle. People had emerged from their flats and were standing on their balconies, staring down. Others were walking around the court, nakedly curious, to join a gathering congregation. Helen's stomach seemed to drop to her bowels when she realized *where* the hub of interest lay: At Anne-Marie's doorstep. The police were clearing a path through the throng for the ambulance men. A second police-car had followed the route of the ambulance onto the pavement; two plain-clothes officers were getting out.

She walked to the periphery of the crowd. What little talk there was amongst the on-lookers was conducted in low voices; one or two of the older women were crying. Though she peered over the heads of the spectators she could see nothing. Turning to a bearded man, whose child was perched on his shoulders, she asked what was going on. He didn't know. Somebody dead, he'd heard, but he wasn't certain.

"Anne-Marie?" she asked.

A woman in front of her turned and said: "You know her?" almost awed, as if speaking of a loved one.

"A little," Helen replied hesitantly. "Can you tell me what's happened?"

The woman involuntarily put her hand to her mouth, as if to stop the words before they came. But here they were nevertheless: "The child – " she said.

"Kerry?"

"Somebody got into the house around the back. Slit his throat."

Helen felt the sweat come again. In her mind's eye the newspapers rose and fell in Anne-Marie's yard.

"No," she said.

"Just like that."

She looked at the tragedian who was trying to sell her this obscenity, and said, "No," again. It defied belief; yet her denials could not silence the horrid comprehension she felt.

She turned her back on the woman and paddled her way out of the crowd. There would be nothing to see, she knew, and even if there had been, she had no desire to look. These people – still emerging from their homes as the story spread – were exhibiting an appetite she was disgusted by. She was not of them; would never *be* of them. She wanted to slap every eager face into sense; wanted to say: "It's pain and grief you're going to spy on. Why? Why?" But she had no courage left. Revulsion had drained her of all but the energy to wander away, leaving the crowd to its sport.

Trevor had come home. He did not attempt an explanation of his absence, but waited for her to cross-question him. When she failed to do so he sank into an easy *bonhomie* that was worse than his expectant silence. She was dimly aware that her disinterest was probably more unsettling for him than the histrionics he had been anticipating. She couldn't have cared less.

She tuned the radio to the local station, and listened for news. It came surely enough, confirming what the woman in the crowd had told her. Kerry Latimer was dead. Person or persons unknown had gained access to the house via the back yard and murdered the child while he played on the kitchen floor. A police spokesman mouthed the usual platitudes, describing Kerry's death as an "unspeakable crime", and the miscreant as "a dangerous and deeply disturbed individual". For once, the rhetoric seemed justified, and the man's voice shook discernibly when he spoke of the scene that had confronted the officers in the kitchen of Anne-Marie's house.

"Why the radio?" Trevor casually inquired, when Helen had listened for news through three consecutive bulletins. She saw no point in withholding her experience at Spector Street from him; he would find out sooner or later. Coolly, she gave him a bald outline of what had happened at Butts' Court.

"This Anne-Marie is the woman you first met when you went to the estate; am I right?"

She nodded, hoping he wouldn't ask her too many questions. Tears were close, and she had no intention of breaking down in front of him.

"So you were right," he said.

"Right?"

"About the place having a maniac."

"No," she said. "No."

"But the kid – "

She got up and stood at the window, looking down two storeys into the darkened street below. Why did she feel the need to reject the conspiracy theory so urgently? Why was she now praying that Purcell had been right, and that all she'd been told had been lies? She went back and back to the way Anne-Marie had been when she'd visited her that morning: Pale, jittery; *expectant*. She had been like a woman anticipating some arrival, hadn't she? – eager to shoo unwanted visitors away so that she could turn back to the business of waiting. But waiting for what, or *whom*? Was it possible that Anne-Marie actually knew the murderer? Had perhaps invited him into the house?

"I hope they find the bastard," she said still watching the street."

"They will," Trevor replied. "A baby-murderer, for Christ's sake. They'll make it a high priority."

A man appeared at the corner of the street, turned, and whistled. A large Alsatian came to heel, and the two set off down towards the Cathedral.

"The dog," Helen murmured.

"What?"

She had forgotten the dog in all that had followed. Now the shock she'd felt as it had leapt at the window shook her again.

"What dog?" Trevor pressed.

"I went back to the flat today – where I took the pictures of the graffiti. There was a dog in there. Locked in."

"So?"

"It'll starve. Nobody knows it's there."

"How do you know it wasn't locked in to kennel it?"

"It was making such a noise – " she said.

"Dogs bark," Trevor replied. "That's all they're good for."

"No . . ." she said very quietly, remembering the noises through the boarded window. "It didn't bark . . ."

"Forget the dog," Trevor said. "And the child. There's nothing you can do about it. You were just passing through."

His words only echoed her own thoughts of earlier in the day, but somehow – for reasons that she could find no words to convey – that conviction had decayed in the last hours. She was not just passing through. Nobody ever just *passed through*; experience always left its mark. Sometimes it merely scratched; on occasion it took off limbs. She did not know the extent of her present wounding, but she knew it more profound than she yet understood, and it made her afraid.

"We're out of booze," she said, emptying the last dribble of whisky into her tumbler.

Trevor seemed pleased to have a reason to be accommodating. "I'll go out, shall I?" he said. "Get a bottle or two?"

"Sure," she replied. "If you like."

He was gone only half an hour; she would have liked him to have been longer. She didn't want to talk, only to sit and think through the unease in her belly. Though Trevor had dismissed her concern for the dog – and perhaps justifiably so – she couldn't help but go back to the locked maisonette in her mind's eye: To picture again the raging face on the bedroom wall, and hear the animal's muffled growl as it pawed the boards over the window. Whatever Trevor had said, she didn't believe the place was being used as a makeshift kennel. No, the dog was *imprisoned* in there, no doubt of it, running round and round, driven, in its desperation, to eat its own faeces, growing more insane with every hour that passed. She became afraid that somebody – kids maybe, looking for more tinder for their bonfire – would break into the place, ignorant of what it contained. It wasn't that she feared for the intruders' safety, but that the dog, once liberated, would come for her. It would know where she was (so her drunken head construed) and come sniffing her out.

Trevor returned with the whisky, and they drank together until the early hours, when her stomach revolted. She took refuge in the toilet – Trevor outside asking her if she needed anything, her telling him weakly to leave her alone. When, an hour later, she emerged, he had gone to bed. She did not join him, but lay down on the sofa and dozed through until dawn.

The murder was news. The next morning it made all the tabloids as a front page splash, and found prominent positions in the heavy-weights too. There were photo-graphs of the stricken mother being led from the house, and others, blurred but potent, taken over the back yard wall and through the open kitchen door. Was that blood on the floor, or shadow?

Helen did not bother to read the articles – her aching head rebelled at the thought – but Trevor, who had bought the newspapers in, was eager to talk. She couldn't work out if this was further peace-making on his part, or a genuine interest in the issue.

"The woman's in custody," he said, poring over the *Daily Telegraph*. It was a paper he was politically averse to, but its coverage of violent crime was notoriously detailed.

The observation demanded Helen's attention, unwilling or not. "Custody?" she said. "Anne-Marie?"

"Yes."

"Let me see."

He relinquished the paper, and she glanced over the page. "Third column," Trevor prompted.

She found the place, and there it was in black and white. Anne-Marie had been taken into custody for questioning to justify the time-lapse between the estimated hour of the child's death, and the time that it had been reported. Helen read the relevant sentences over again, to be certain that she'd understood properly. Yes, she had. The police pathologist estimated Kerry to have died between six and six-thirty that morning; the murder had not been reported until twelve.

She read the report over a third and fourth time, but repetition did not change the horrid facts. The child had been murdered before dawn. When she had gone to the house that morning Kerry had already been dead four hours. The body had been in the kitchen, a few yards down the hallway from where she had stood, and Anne-Marie had said *nothing*. That air of expectancy she had had about her – what had it signified? That she awaited some cue to lift the receiver and call the police?

"My Christ . . ." Helen said, and let the paper drop.

"What?"

"I have to go to the police."

"Why?"

"To tell them I went to the house," she replied. Trevor looked mystified. "The baby was dead, Trevor. When I saw Anne-Marie yesterday morning, Kerry was already dead."

She rang the number in the paper for any persons offering information, and half an hour later a police car came to pick her up. There was much that startled her in the two hours of interrogation that followed, not least the fact that nobody had reported her presence on the estate to the police, though she had surely been noticed.

"They don't want to know – " the detective told her. "You'd think a place like that would be swarming with witnesses. If it is, they're not coming forward. A crime like this . . ."

"Is it the first?" she said.

He looked at her across a chaotic desk. "First?"

"I was told some stories about the estate. Murders. This summer."

The detective shook his head. "Not to my knowledge.

There's been a spate of muggings; one woman was put in hospital for a week or so. But no; no murders."

She liked the detective. His eyes flattered her with their lingering, and his face with their frankness. Past caring whether she sounded foolish or not, she said: "Why do they tell lies like that? About people having their eyes cut out. Terrible things."

The detective scratched his long nose. "We get it too," he said. "People come in here, they confess to all kinds of crap. Talk all night, some of them, about things they've done, or *think* they've done. Give you it all in the minutest detail. And when you make a few calls, it's all invented. Out of their minds."

"Maybe if they didn't tell you those stories . . . they'd actually go out and do it."

The detective nodded. "Yes," he said. "God help us. You might be right at that."

And the stories *she'd* been told, were they confessions of uncommitted crimes? Accounts of the worst-imaginable, imagined to keep fiction from becoming fact? The thought chased its own tail: These terrible stories still needed a *first cause*, a well-spring from which they leapt. As she walked home through the busy streets she wondered how many of her fellow citizens knew such stories. Were these inventions common currency, as Purcell had claimed? Was there a place, however small, reserved in every heart for the monstrous?

"Purcell rang," Trevor told her when she got home. "To invite us out to dinner."

The invitation wasn't welcome, and she made a face.

"Appollinaires, remember?" he reminded her. "He said he'd take us all to dinner, if you proved him wrong."

The thought of getting a dinner out of the death of Anne-Marie's infant was grotesque, and she said so.

"He'll be offended if you turn him down."

"I don't give a damn. I don't want dinner with Purcell."

"Please," he said softly. "He can get difficult; and I want to keep him smiling just at the moment."

She glanced across at him. The look he'd put on made him resemble a drenched spaniel. Manipulative bastard, she thought; but said: "All right, I'll go. But don't expect any dancing on the tables."

"We'll leave that to Archie," he said. "I told Purcell we were free tomorrow night. Is that all right with you?"

"Whenever."

"He's booking a table for eight o'clock."

The evening papers had relegated The Tragedy of Baby Kerry to a few column inches on an inside page. In lieu of much fresh news they simply described the house-to-house enquiries that were now going on at Spector Street. Some of the later editions mentioned that Anne-Marie had been released from custody after an extended period of questioning, and was now residing with friends. They also mentioned, in passing, that the funeral was to be the following day.

Helen had not entertained any thoughts of going back to Spector Street for the funeral when she went to bed that night, but sleep seemed to change her mind, and she woke with the decision made for her.

Death had brought the estate to life. Walking through to Ruskin Court from the street she had never seen such numbers out and about. Many were already lining the kerb to watch the funeral cortège pass, and looked to have claimed their niche early, despite the wind and the ever-present threat of rain. Some were wearing items of black clothing – a coat, a scarf – but the overall impression, despite the lowered voices and the studied frowns, was one of celebration. Children running around, untouched by reverence; occasional laughter escaping from between gossiping adults – Helen could feel an air of anticipation which made her spirits, despite the occasion, almost buoyant.

Nor was it simply the presence of so many people that reassured her; she was, she conceded to herself, happy to be back here in Spector Street. The quadrangles, with their stunted saplings and their grey grass, were more real to her than the carpeted corridors she was used to walking; the anonymous faces on the balconies and streets meant more than her colleagues at the University. In a word, she felt *home*.

Finally, the cars appeared, moving at a snail's pace through the narrow streets. As the hearse came into view – its tiny white casket decked with flowers – a number of women in the crowd gave quiet voice to their grief. One on-looker fainted; a knot of anxious people gathered around her. Even the children were stilled now.

Helen watched, dry-eyed. Tears did not come very easily to her, especially in company. As the second car, containing Anne-Marie and two other women, drew level with her, Helen saw that the bereaved mother was also eschewing any public display of grief. She seemed, indeed, to be almost elevated by the proceedings, sitting upright in the back of the car, her pallid features the source of much admiration. It was a sour thought, but Helen felt as though she was seeing Anne-Marie's finest hour; the one day in an other-wise anonymous life in which she was the centre of atten-tion. Slowly, the cortège passed by and disappeared from view.

The crowd around Helen was already dispersing. She detached herself from the few mourners who still lingered at the kerb and wandered through from the street into Butts' Court. It was her intention to go back to the locked maisonette, to see if the dog was still there. If it was, she would put her mind at rest by finding one of the estate caretakers and informing him of the fact.

The quadrangle was, unlike the other courts, practically empty. Perhaps the residents, being neighbours of Anne-Marie's, had gone on to the Crematorium for the service.

Whatever the reason, the place was eerily deserted. Only children remained, playing around the pyramid bonfire, their voices echoing across the empty expanse of the square.

She reached the maisonette and was surprised to find the door open again, as it had been the first time she'd come here. The sight of the interior made her lightheaded. How often in the past several days had she imagined standing here, gazing into that darkness. There was no sound from inside. The dog had surely run off; either that, or died. There could be no harm, could there? in stepping into the place one final time, just to look at the face on the wall, and its attendant slogan.

Sweets to the sweet. She had never looked up the origins of that phrase. No matter, she thought. Whatever it had stood for once, it was transformed here, as everything was; herself included. She stood in the front room for a few moments, to allow herself time to savour the confrontation ahead. Far away behind her the children were screeching like mad birds.

She stepped over a clutter of furniture and towards the short corridor that joined living-room to bedroom, still delaying the moment. Her heart was quick in her: A smile played on her lips.

And there! At last! The portrait loomed, compelling as ever. She stepped back in the murky room to admire it more fully and her heel caught on the mattress that still lay in the corner. She glanced down. The squalid bedding had been turned over, to present its untorn face. Some blankets and and a rag-wrapped pillow had been tossed over it. Something glistened amongst the folds of the uppermost blanket. She bent down to look more closely and found there a handful of sweets – chocolate and caramels – wrapped in bright paper. And littered amongst them, neither so attractive nor so sweet, a dozen razor-blades. There was blood on several. She stood up again and backed away from the mattress, and as she did so a buzzing sound reached her ears from the next room. She turned, and the light in the bedroom diminished as a figure stepped into the gullet between her and the outside world. Silhouetted against the light, she could scarcely see the man in the doorway, but she smelt him He smelt like candy-floss; and the buzzing was with him or in him.

"I just came to look – " she said, "– at the picture."

The buzzing went on: The sound of a sleepy afternoon, far from here. The man in the doorway did not move.

"Well . . ." she said, "I've seen what I wanted to see." She hoped against hope that her words would prompt him to stand aside and let her pass, but he didn't move, and she couldn't find the courage to challenge him by stepping towards the door

"I have to go," she said, knowing that despite her best efforts fear seeped between every syllable. "I'm expected . . ."

That was not entirely untrue. Tonight they were all invited to Appollinaires for dinner. But that wasn't until eight, which was four hours away. She would not be missed for a long while yet.

"If you'll excuse me," she said.

The buzzing had quietened a little, and in the hush the man in the doorway spoke. His unaccented voice was almost as sweet as his scent.

"No need to leave yet," he breathed.

"I'm due . . . due . . ."

Though she couldn't see his eyes, she felt them on her, and they made her feel drowsy, like that summer that sang in her head.

"I came for you," he said.

She repeated the four words in her head. *I came for you.* If they were meant as a threat, they certainly weren't spoken as one.

"I don't . . . know you," she said.

"No," the man murmured. "But you doubted me."

"Doubted?"

"You weren't content with the stories, with what they wrote on the walls. So I was obliged to come."

The drowsiness slowed her mind to a crawl, but she grasped the essentials of what the man was saying. That he was legend, and she, in disbelieving him, had obliged him to show his hand. She looked, now, down at those hands. One of them was missing. In its place, a hook.

"There will be some blame," he told her. "They will say your doubts shed innocent blood. But I say – what's blood for, if not for shedding? And in time the scrutiny will pass. The police will leave, the cameras will be pointed at some fresh horror, and they will be left alone, to tell stories of the Candyman again."

"Candyman?" she said. Her tongue could barely shape that blameless word.

"I came for you," he murmured so softly that seduction might have been in the air. And so saying, he moved through the passageway and into the light.

She knew him, without doubt. She had known him all along, in that place kept for terrors. It was the man on the wall. His portrait painter had not been a fantasist: The picture that howled over her was matched in each extraordinary particular by the man she now set eyes upon. He was bright to the point of gaudiness: His flesh a waxy yellow, his thin lips pale blue, his wild eyes glittering as if their irises were set with rubies. His jacket was a patchwork, his trousers the same. He looked, she thought, almost ridiculous, with his blood-stained motley, and the hint of rouge on his jaundiced cheeks. But people were facile. They needed these shows and shams to keep their interest. Miracles; murders; demons driven out and stones rolled from tombs. The cheap glamour did not taint the sense beneath. It was only, in the natural history of the mind, the bright feathers that drew the species to mate with its secret self.

And she was almost enchanted. By his voice, by his colours, by the buzz from his body. She fought to resist the rapture, though. There was a *monster* here, beneath this fetching display; its nest of razors was at her feet, still drenched in blood. Would it hesitate to slit her own throat if it once laid hands on her?

As the Candyman reached for her she dropped down and snatched the blanket up, flinging it at him. A rain of razors and sweetmeats fell around his shoulders. The blanket followed, blinding him. But before she could snatch the moment to slip past him, the pillow which had lain on the blanket rolled in front of her.

It was not a pillow at all. Whatever the forlorn white casket she had seen in the hearse had contained, it was not the body of Baby Kerry. That was *here*, at her feet, its blood-drained face turned up to her. He was naked. His body showed everywhere signs of the fiend's attentions.

In the two heartbeats she took to register this last horror, the Candyman threw off the blanket. In his struggle to escape from its folds, his jacket had come unbuttoned, and she saw – though her senses protested – that the contents of his torso had rotted away, and the hollow was now occupied by a nest of bees. They swarmed in the vault of his chest, and encrusted in a seething mass the remnants of flesh that hung there. He smiled at her plain repugnance.

"Sweets to the sweet," he murmured, and stretched his hooked hand towards her face. She could no longer see light from the outside world, nor hear the children playing in Butts' Court. There was no escape into a saner world than this. The Candyman filled her sight; her drained limbs had no strength to hold him at bay.

"Don't kill me," she breathed.

"Do you believe in me?" he said.

She nodded minutely. "How can I not?" she said.

"Then why do you want to live?"

She didn't understand, and was afraid her ignorance would prove fatal, so she said nothing.

"If you would learn," the fiend said, "just a *little* from me . . . you would not beg to live." His voice had dropped to a whisper. "I am rumour," he sang in her ear. "It's a blessed condition, believe me. To live in people's dreams; to be whispered at street-corners; but not have to *be*. Do you understand?"

Her weary body understood. Her nerves, tired of jangling, understood. The sweetness he offered was life without living: Was to be dead, but remembered everywhere; immortal in gossip and graffiti.

"Be my victim," he said.

"No . . ." she murmured.

"I won't force it upon you," he replied, the perfect gentleman. "I won't oblige you to die. But think; *think*. If I kill you here – if I unhook you . . ." he traced the path of the promised wound with his hook. It ran from groin to neck. "Think how they would mark this place with their talk . . . point it out as they passed by and say: '*She* died there; the woman with the green eyes'. Your death would be a parable to frighten children with. Lovers would use it as an excuse to cling closer together . . ."

She had been right: This *was* a seduction.

"Was fame ever so easy?" he asked.

She shook her head. "I'd prefer to be forgotten," she replied, "than be remembered like that."

He made a tiny shrug. "What do they know?" he said. "Except what the bad teach them by their excesses?" He raised his hooked hand. "I said I would not oblige you to die and I'm true to my word. Allow me, though, a kiss at least . . ."

He moved towards her. She murmured some nonsensical threat, which he ignored. The buzzing in his body had risen in volume. The thought of touching his body, of the proximity of the insects, was horrid. She forced her lead-heavy arms up to keep him at bay.

His lurid face eclipsed the portrait on the wall. She couldn't bring herself to touch him, and instead stepped back. The sound of the bees rose; some, in their excitement, had crawled up his throat and were flying from his mouth. They climbed about his lips; in his hair.

She begged him over and over to leave her alone, but he would not be placated. At last she had nowhere left to retreat to, the wall was at her back. Steeling herself against the stings, she put her hands on his crawling chest and pushed. As she did so his hand shot out and around the back of her neck, the hook nicking the flushed skin of her throat. She felt blood come; felt certain he would open her jugular in one terrible slash. But he had given his word: And he was true to it.

Aroused by this sudden activity, the bees were everywhere. She felt them moving on her, searching for morsels of wax in her ears, and sugar at her lips. She made no attempt to swat them away. The hook was at her neck. If she so much as moved it would wound her. She was trapped, as in her childhood nightmares, with every chance of escape stymied. When sleep had brought her to such hopelessness – the demons on every side, waiting to tear her limb from limb – one trick remained. To let go; to give up all ambition to life, and leave her body to the dark. Now, as the Candyman's face pressed to hers, and the sound of bees blotted out even her own breath, she played that hidden hand. And, as surely as in dreams, the room and the fiend were painted out and gone.

She woke from brightness into dark. There were several panicked moments when she couldn't think of where she was, then several more when she remembered. But there was no pain about her body. She put her hand to her neck; it was, barring the nick of the hook, untouched. She was lying on the mattress she realized. Had she been assaulted as she lay in a faint? Gingerly, she investigated her body. She was

not bleeding; her clothes were not disturbed. The Candyman had, it seemed, simply claimed his kiss.

She sat up. There was precious little light through the
boarded window – and none from the front door. Perhaps it
was closed, she reasoned. But no; even now she heard
somebody whispering on the threshold. A woman's voice.

She didn't move. They were crazy, these people. They had
known all along what her presence in Butts' Court had
summoned, and they had *protected* him – this honeyed
psychopath; given him a bed and an offering of bon-
bons, hidden him away from prying eyes, and kept their
silence when he brought blood to their doorsteps. Even
Anne-Marie, dry-eyed in the hallway of her house, knowing
that her child was dead a few yards away.

The child! That was the evidence she needed. Somehow
they had conspired to get the body from the casket (what
had they substituted; a dead dog?) and brought it here – to
the Candyman's tabernacle – as a toy, or a lover. She would
take Baby Kerry with her – to the police – and tell the whole
story. Whatever they believed of it – and that would
probably be very little – the fact of the child's body was
incontestable. That way at least some of the crazies would
suffer for their conspiracy. Suffer for *her* suffering.

The whispering at the door had stopped. Now somebody
was moving towards the bedroom. They didn't bring a light
with them. Helen made herself small, hoping she might
escape attention.

A figure appeared in the doorway. The gloom was too
impenetrable for her to make out more than a slim figure,
who bent down and picked up a bundle on the floor. A fall
of blonde hair identified the newcomer as Anne-Marie: The
bundle she was picking up was undoubtedly Kerry's corpse.
Without looking in Helen's direction, the mother about-
turned and made her way out of the bedroom.

Helen listened as the footsteps receded across the living
room. Swiftly, she got to her feet, and crossed to the

passage-way. From there she could vaguely see Anne-Marie's outline in the doorway of the maisonette. No lights burned in the quadrangle beyond. The woman disappeared and Helen followed as speedily as she could, eyes fixed on the door ahead. She stumbled once, and once again, but reached the door in time to see Anne-Marie's vague form in the night ahead.

She stepped out of the maisonette and into the open air. It was chilly; there were no stars. All the lights on the balconies and corridors were out, nor did any burn in the flats; not even the glow of a television. Butts' Court was deserted.

She hesitated before going in pursuit of the girl. Why didn't she slip away now, cowardice coaxed her, and find her way back to the car? But if she did that the conspirators would have time to conceal the child's body. When she got back here with the police there would be sealed lips and shrugs, and she would be told she had imagined the corpse and the Candyman. All the terrors she had tasted would recede into rumour again. Into words on a wall. And every day she lived from now on she would loathe herself for not going in pursuit of sanity.

She followed. Anne-Marie was not making her way around the quadrangle, but moving towards the centre of the lawn in the middle of the court. To the bonfire! Yes; to the bonfire! It loomed in front of Helen now, blacker than the night-sky. She could just make out Anne-Marie's figure, moving to the edge of the piled timbers and furniture, and ducking to climb into its heart. *This* was how they planned to remove the evidence. To bury the child was not certain enough; but to cremate it, and pound the bones – who would ever know?

She stood a dozen yards from the pyramid and watched as Anne-Marie climbed out again and moved away, folding her figure into the darkness.

Quickly, Helen moved through the long grass and located the narrow space in amongst the piled timbers into which

Anne-Marie had put the body. She thought she could see the pale form; it had been laid in a hollow. She couldn't reach it however. Thanking God that she was as slim as the mother, she squeezed through the narrow aperture. Her dress snagged on a nail as she did so. She turned round to disengage it, fingers trembling. When she turned back she had lost sight of the corpse.

She fumbled blindly ahead of her, her hands finding wood and rags and what felt like the back of an old armchair, but not the cold skin of the child. She had hardened herself against contact with the body: She had endured worse in the last hours than picking up a dead baby. Determined not to be defeated, she advanced a little further, her shins scraped and her fingers spiked with splinters. Flashes of light were appearing at the corners of her aching eyes; her blood whined in her ears. But there! *there*! the body was no more a yard and a half ahead of her. She ducked down to reach beneath a beam of wood, but her fingers missed the forlorn bundle by millimetres. She stretched further, the whine in her head increasing, but still she could not reach the child. All she could do was bend double and squeeze into the hidey-hole the children had left in the centre of the bonfire.

It was difficult to get through. The space was so small she could barely crawl on hands and knees; but she made it. The child lay face down. She fought back the remnants of squeamishness and went to pick it up. As she did so, something landed on her arm. The shock startled her. She almost cried out, but swallowed the urge, and brushed the irritation away. It buzzed as it rose from her skin. The whine she had heard in her ears was not her blood, but the hive.

"I knew you'd come," the voice behind her said, and a wide hand covered her face. She fell backwards and the Candyman embraced her.

"We have to go," he said in her ear, as flickering light spilled between the stacked timbers. "Be on our way, you and I."

She fought to be free of him, to cry out for them not to light the bonfire, but he held her lovingly close. The light grew: Warmth came with it; and through the kindling and the first flames she could see figures approaching the pyre out of the darkness of Butts' Court. They had been there all along: Waiting, the lights turned out in their homes, and broken all along the corridors. Their final conspiracy.

The bonfire caught with a will, but by some trick of its construction the flames did not invade her hiding-place quickly; nor did the smoke creep through the furniture to choke her. She was able to watch how the children's faces gleamed; how the parents called them from going too close, and how they disobeyed; how the old women, their blood thin, warmed their hands and smiled into the flames. Presently the roar and the crackle became deafening, and the Candyman let her scream herself hoarse in the certain knowledge that nobody could hear her, and even if they had, would not have moved to claim her from the fire.

The bees vacated the fiend's belly as the air became hotter, and mazed the air with their panicked flight. Some, attempting escape, caught fire, and fell like tiny meteors to the ground. The body of Baby Kerry, which lay close to the creeping flames, began to cook. Its downy hair smoked, it back blistered.

Soon the heat crept down Helen's throat, and scorched her pleas away. She sank back, exhausted, into the Candyman's arms, resigned to his triumph. In moments they would be on their way, as he had promised, and there was no help for it.

Perhaps they would remember her, as he had said they might, finding her cracked skull in tomorrow's ashes. Perhaps she might become, in time, a story with which to frighten children. She had lied, saying she preferred death to such questionable fame; she did not. As to her seducer, he laughed as the conflagration sniffed them out. There was no permanence for him in this night's death. His deeds were on a hundred walls and ten thousand lips, and should he be doubted again his congregation could summon him with sweetness. He had reason to laugh. So, as the flames crept upon them, did she, as through the fire she caught sight of a familiar face moving between the on-lookers. It was Trevor. He had forsaken his meal at Appollinaires and come looking for her.

She watched him questioning this fire-watcher and that, but they shook their heads, all the while staring at the pyre with smiles buried in their eyes. Poor dupe, she thought, following his antics. She willed him to look past the flames in the hope he might see her burning. Not so that he could save her from death – she was long past hope of that – but because she pitied him in his bewilderment and wanted to give him, though he would not have thanked her for it, something to be haunted. That, and a story to tell.